Yahweh

Yahweh

Andrew Shepherd

authorHOUSE®

AuthorHouse™ UK
1663 Liberty Drive
Bloomington, IN 47403 USA
www.authorhouse.co.uk
Phone: 0800.197.4150

© 2015 Andrew Shepherd. All rights reserved.

No part of this book may be reproduced, stored in a retrieval system, or transmitted by any means without the written permission of the author.

Published by AuthorHouse 07/27/2015

ISBN: 978-1-5049-8765-3 (sc)
ISBN: 978-1-5049-8766-0 (e)

Print information available on the last page.

Any people depicted in stock imagery provided by Thinkstock are models, and such images are being used for illustrative purposes only.
Certain stock imagery © Thinkstock.

This book is printed on acid-free paper.

Because of the dynamic nature of the Internet, any web addresses or links contained in this book may have changed since publication and may no longer be valid. The views expressed in this work are solely those of the author and do not necessarily reflect the views of the publisher, and the publisher hereby disclaims any responsibility for them.

Conon woke up, the sun was shining through a small gap in the curtains like a spear into the dark room, he could smell bacon being cooked downstairs and the unmistakable sound of his grandfather chopping wood outside, even though it was early August Conon's Grandfather Tomas, chopped wood every morning for as long as it took his grandmother to make breakfast and hang out some washing. He leapt out of his bed knowing he and his grandfather were heading out to a fine trout loch, Loch Erogary for a day's fishing, he glanced at his watch and saw it was still only just after six a.m. Conon pulled the curtains apart and looked up over the railway line as he stretched and scratched his belly. He was still dressing as he clambered down the narrow stairs of the old cottage which sat on the hill above Morar. Conon loved staying with his grandparents, his grandmother was a language teacher, his grandfather was the ghillie and stalker on the estate, at the front of the cottage they had panoramic views out across the sands of Morar whilst at the back of the house there was the railway line, three or four times a day the trains would trundle past on their way to and from Fort William carrying loads of herring and bringing in supplies and in the summer tourists. His grandmother just pointed at the bathroom and with the smallest degree of reluctance, he made his way into the small but cosy bathroom where he quickly washed his face and brushed his teeth, as he walked into the kitchen his grandmother who was standing at the Aga cooking breakfast simply smiled at him and nodded her approval and he was gone in a flash. Conon ran out into the back yard where his grandfather who was in his early sixties but still a very fit man was swinging the huge axe, he split the beech logs with ease and shouted good morning at Conon. "Start piling the logs up Conon." His grandfather only spoke to him in Polish, he could speak perfect English but he wanted the boy to be able to speak fluently in his mother tongue. "Yes papa." Conon replied in perfect Polish and the two of them continued without saying another word, they worked well but more importantly, they adored each other, theirs was an exceptional bond and Conon soaked up every piece of wisdom his grandfather imparted on him. As Conon busied himself stacking the wood his grandfather had already chopped, he noticed that his grandfather's two black labs were sitting in their kennel watching every move they were making, they were well trained and extremely obedient dogs, Cruach and Liath. After twenty minutes of hard graft the back door of the cottage opened and Conon heard his grandmother shout that breakfast was ready, his grandfather waved to his wife and Conon quickly piled up the last of the remaining logs, his grandfather sharpened the edge of the axe, not too much just enough to keep the axe true, too sharp and it wouldn't chop so well, it gave Conon a moment to run to Cruach and Liath and pet them, he knew his grandfather disapproved but he loved the dogs and they returned his affection, eagerly licking his hands as he stroked and patted them before his grandfather shouted, "That's enough Conon, they'll have plenty of fun today."

"Yes Papa, just coming." Conon ran back towards his grandfather and the old man, towering above his grandson put his arm around his grandson's neck and mock wrestled with him. Quickly Conon at fourteen years old and seven and a half stones in weight, tried with all his might to grip the giant of a man behind his left knee and the boy dropped his weight, not that there was much of him and his grandfather pretended that Conon had overpowered him and he fell backwards onto his back on the grass at the back of the house as Conon rolled his head and pretended to punch his grandfather in the throat. "Ahhhh, you are too fast for an old man like me Conon." Cruach and Liath barked furiously in the background as their master was being attacked Conon and his grandfather laughed as they got up and dusted themselves down. Conon knew his grandfather was only playing but he loved practicing all the techniques he taught him in unarmed combat and hunting and stalking skills which he had learned at Meoble on the shores of Loch Morar during the war when he trained other Polish soldiers and resistance fighters for the S.O.E. The two of them washed at the outside water pump and dried themselves off in the early morning sun, they were both looking forward to a great day out.

Breakfast done, Conon without being told gathered the plates and went to the sink to wash them, his grandmother sipped on her cup of tea and told him to leave the dishes, she would get them, she knew young Conon was bursting with excitement at the prospect of spending a day out in the wilds with his grandfather, learning how to track, hunt, survive off the land and of course catch some fresh brown trout for dinner later.

It was the last week of his holidays and the sun shone brightly for the young boy and his grandfather as they pulled on their rucksacks and waved to his grandmother as they went out through the gate and onto the moor, Cruach and Liath ran and sniffed at every blade of grass and stock of heather, today they had the day off and they too knew it was going to be an easy day. Orphaned as a child, his adoptive grandparents lived at Morar, Lena and Artur, his mam and dad as he called them were brought up in the Mallaig area too but now lived and worked on a shooting estate near the town of Dingwall, he was content as a boy and later he would find out that the real parents he knew nothing about were junkies, his mother had killed herself after his father had overdosed on heroin and he'd been taken into care as a one year old baby, he didn't want to know anymore after finding that out when he was seventeen, he never really confided in anyone about his background, very few people knew anything about him. Once he'd left school he lost contact with most of his friends which didn't really bother him, they all just seemed to be interested in girls and drink and dope anyway. His adoptive parents were second generation Polish immigrants, his father was the head gamekeeper and his mother worked as the housekeeper and cook at Wyvis Lodge, on the shore of Loch Glass near Dingwall in the North Highlands, it was there he first saw men from the Special Air Service and the Special Boat Squadron training and he would practice sneaking up on them like his grandfather had taught him and on more than one occasion he'd stolen rifles from them for laughs,

Yahweh

many times they had chased him down off the hill having been caught out by the young terror. Many of the soldiers and Marines pleaded with their trainers to put a tracking device on him when they arrived but they regarded him even then as a useful asset, in fact several men had been returned to their units on the back of Conon and his so called pranks. Little did he know at the time but there were people in the wings watching him, people who had been made aware of his talents and they would one day try if needs be to coax him into a life of usefulness. His father's parents had come to Scotland during the war and stayed there and settled after the war ended. Conon's grandfather had been a Special Operations Operative and from an early age when Conon visited them on holidays, near Morar, his grandfather would teach him survival skills, how to live off the land, how to sneak up on people and listen, they would practice on badgers and otters and deer, they were easy. His Grandfather would only speak to him in Polish and German, rarely in English, his grandmother who was a translator during the war spoke fluent French, German, Russian and Cantonese as well as her mother tongue, Polish. They had taught him well as a child which had been easy as he seemed to relish the challenge of absorbing the different languages and by the time he went to school at Dingwall Academy he spoke, read and wrote more languages fluently than Mr Munro the Head languages teacher who would constantly and continually be challenged by Conon's sharp brain, there was nothing worse than being constantly proved wrong by a fourteen year old, at least he had the manners to speak to him in fluent Russian, Mr Munro would tell him, which none of the other students understood. A strange coincidence that Mr Munro and Lieutenant Munro had the same surname,

Conon didn't give it another thought. Conon knew his mother and father would be at his grandparents' house when he got home, they were staying for a few nights themselves before heading home to Wyvis.

After a walk of a hour and a half they arrived at Loch Erogary, the fish were rising to the flies settling on the water and the dogs sat near the stream running out of the loch and waited to be told to cool themselves down, one nod from Tomas and they jumped into the cold pool of water in the stream running out of the loch. Conon was rushing to beat his grandfather to cast the first fly on the water, his grandfather however was taking his time and smiled at the enthusiasm his grandson had for the outdoors, he hoped one day all that he would teach him would be of use to the boy. "Take your time Conon, never rush, good preparation will always win over haste." He smiled as he watched the boy visibly slow down his efforts and deliberately took his own time, he'd caught many fish over the years, this was his way of showing Conon taking your time can make you a winner. He didn't lift his head as he tightened the fly to the line and heard Conon's reel screech as he pulled out the line and cast the first fly on the still water. It was a fine morning, maybe a bit too bright but they'd enjoy the day nonetheless. Conon couldn't hide his glee and grinned broadly at his grandfather who winked at him and said, "I'll bet you the first pot of tea I'll catch the first fish!"

"Not a chance papa."

The pair began the day of casting and hopefully catching, high above Conon heard the sound of a jet, he could clearly see the three jets.

"What kind are they then?" his grandfather asked him.

"The first one is a Victor tanker and the other two behind it are Buccaneers probably from R.A.F. Lossiemouth."

Conon's grandfather knew exactly what they were but the young boy's knowledge of aircraft recognition amazed him, then as he looked up he felt his line tighten and instinctively he lifted the tip of his fly rod but he'd missed the strike and the fish turned with a huge swirl in the water and returned to the depths. Conon giggled at his grandfather and said cheekily, "So easily distracted, I hope there's lots of jets today!" He nodded towards the sky. The old man smiled and replied, "That'll be the only chance you have of catching more fish than me today Conon." The two fished on as high above the Buccaneers refuelled from the Victor tanker. About forty miles away the Ford Escort turned off the A82 and the driver and his passenger began the slow winding drive along the A830 towards Mallaig. At Mallaig pier the driver of the articulated lorry finished securing his load of fish and climbed into the cab to begin the long winding drive along the A830 towards Fort William on his way to Peterhead fish market, he fired up the massive Bedford lorry with the Detroit engine, the roar from the wagon was so impressive everyone on the harbour turned and watched as the driver rolled the lorry forwards and gave the lads who had been loading the fish a honk on the horn, everyone waved and Stan reached for his cigarettes and drew a deep breath in and filled his lungs with smoke and he settled down for the long drive. The radio was for its time state of the art, he was tuned into Radio 1 and listened to the radio and enjoyed the winding drive out of Mallaig and through Morar before stopping at Arisaig where he bought a bottle of lemonade for the drive before continuing his journey. Travelling in the opposite direction the Ford Escort slowly trundled along the A830 along Loch Eil side, Conon's parents were anxious to see their son but they were taking their time enjoying the splendid weather and scenery.

Without knowing it, the fate of the occupants of the two vehicles was sealed and closer and closer they travelled towards each other until at the railway bridge at Beasdale the couple in the Ford Escort slowed down for the bridge and as the sun momentarily blinded him Artur slammed on the brakes at the last second as he saw the giant lorry skid into the bridge out of control, Stan had been distracted for a moment whilst lighting another cigarette and as he glanced up he realised he was too late to brake for the turn and the huge lorry jack knifed as he stood on the brakes, he didn't see the car go under the trailer as the cab of the lorry slammed into the parapet of the bridge. All three were killed instantly.

It was a full fifteen minutes before the next car arrived, they were tourists and very soon the tail backs were hundreds of meters back in both directions. The police, ambulance and fire service had a dreadful job getting through and on their arrival Sergeant Macdonald and PC Davidson had the job of sorting it all out until the traffic unit from Inverness arrived. They found out very quickly though who the three victims were and started preparing themselves for the grim task of telling the next of kin what had happened to their poor loved ones. Before the scene had been examined, cleared and hours later the road reopened, the families of the lorry driver and Sabine who was waiting for her husband and grandson to arrive home and her son and daughter in law to arrive as well had found out when a friend and her husband called in to tell her the terrible news. Sabine fainted and was lifted onto the couch and the doctor was summoned. It would be a terrible day in Morar and Mallaig for many people.

Tomas and Conon fished through the day and caught many trout as they wandered around the loch. About 5 p.m. they decided that as Conon had caught the most and his grandfather had caught the biggest, a nice brown trout just under three pounds in weight, it was time to call the day's events a draw and after breaking their kit down they began the walk home, at least it was almost all downhill. They knew nothing about what was ahead and laughed and joked their way off the hill in the late afternoon sun. As they came through the gate at the back of the croft, Tomas saw all the cars outside the cottage and knew instantly something terrible had happened, Conon saw the angst in his grandfather's face and asked, "What's wrong papa?"

"I don't know Conon but it doesn't look good from here." Their minds raced with possibilities, none of them good, they both knew something terrible had happened and they broke into a jog as they saw Sergeant Macdonald walk from the house and look up the track, obviously looking for them. As they reached the policeman Tomas asked, "Donnie, what is wrong, is Sabine okay?"

The Sergeant glanced at Conon and said, "She's okay Tomas, can we speak privately?"

Conon felt sick, as the two men walked away from the house and he heard his grandfather cry out, "No! Not my boy! My beautiful Lena, this can't be!" as he turned around he saw Conon running towards the house.

"Conon! Conon! Wait I must speak to you! Conon!" Conon never heard his grandfather shout after him and as he ran into the house his Grandmother was sitting at the table crying, her friend Margaret was consoling her and the room was full of people he recognised, some he knew, they all stared at him not knowing he hadn't been told the devastating news. Conon didn't open his mouth but simply scanned the room looking for his mam and dad, he could not see them but he could see the sadness in everybody's eyes. Tomas walked into the room followed by Sergeant Macdonald, Conon turned and looked at his Grandfather, the tears were tumbling down over his cheeks and his shoulders were trembling, "Where are mam and dad Papa?"

"I'm sorry." Was all Tomas managed before he broke down and Conon's world descended into an abyss that just seemed to swallow him up and he just had to escape, he just had to get away from the madness that was happening in his grandparents' house and he ran out of the cottage and passed the dogs who were back in their kennel, he ran until he could run no further, he was so far away from the house he took a few minutes to get his bearings and then he collapsed in a flood of tears. He didn't know his real parents but the mother and father that had brought him up had been taken from him as well and he struggled with the cruel unfairness of what he knew had happened, he knew he had lost his parents, something in his instincts told him so. As he cried he didn't even notice it was getting darker and he drifted off to sleep on the heather bank next to a small stream.

Back at Tomas and Sabine's house the Police did what they had to do and Margaret and others fussed and did anything that they could to help and try and make the time that felt as though it was standing still pass.

"We better go and find Conon, Tomas." Sergeant Macdonald said. Tomas replied,

"Leave him be for now, I know where he'll be, I'll go and get him soon, he'll be okay." The Polish man was well respected and Sergeant Macdonald would do anything for him but he knew the old man had taught young Conon well and that the boy probably was safe but he would prefer to know for certain that he was. Tomas read the Sergeants mind, he kissed his wife gently on the cheek and left the cottage, "I'll be back soon, don't worry." He glanced at Margaret and said, "Look after Sabi until I get back." Margaret just smiled politely and nodded her head.

Tomas took Cruach and Liath from their kennel and began the longest walk of his life and for what seemed like hours he made his way to a spot below Carn a' Ghobhair, there was a Golden Eagles eerie there and he knew it was Conon's favourite place in the whole world and sure enough there he was fast asleep in the heather. Cruach and Liath quietly sniffed around the boy as he woke up, Conon sat up and saw his grandfather standing in front of him. "Come with me Conon it's time to come home, we're all worried about you." Conon stood up and patted the two Labradors and swung his arm around his grandfather's waist as the two of them hugged.

"I'm so sorry Conon, life has been so cruel to us today but we must be strong and you must be even stronger than many your age."

"I know Papa but tell me, are they both gone?"

"Yes, they have both left us."

"Can I stay with you Papa?"

The old man felt his eyes well up again, "Of course you can Conon, forever, of course you can."

Conon and his grandfather began the long walk back to Morar, unusually they didn't speak until they reached the cottage.

"Is Gran okay Papa? I'm scared."

"She is as well as you could think Conon, we are going to be okay and we'll get through this."

Margaret and her husband were still in the house, there was another man there Conon didn't recognise him, he was the undertaker.

Yahweh

Conon hugged his grandmother and again the tears flowed, no one could help themselves, the raw pain of what had happened would take a long time to heal but his grandparents promised him in time things would get better, he hoped so.

The next few days passed in a blur and all of a sudden Conon found himself in the church at Morar surrounded by his grandparents and their very closest friends and before him the two coffins containing his mam and dad. It was a strange feeling to watch them being lowered into the ground later at Morar, in sight of his new home and to think they were gone.

The next few months passed and slowly they laughed again, Conon would check himself, as if it was wrong and as difficult as it was for his grandparents, they gently encouraged him to laugh, it was good to laugh, it didn't mean that he didn't love or didn't miss his mother and father, it just meant he was coping and he would cope, they would all cope, they had to.

A year had almost passed and his parent's old employer, Mr Beattie arrived at the house and Conon found himself strangely happy to see him. He liked Mr Beattie, he was good fun and spoiled Conon, he let him fish and shoot and drive the estate vehicles, and yes it was fair to say he was pleased to see Mr Beattie.

Conon sat at the table with his grandparents and Mr Beattie, they enjoyed a fine lunch and then Conon realised Mr Beattie had come with all of his parent's private belongings. "There are many things there that now belong to you Conon," his grandfather told him, "Your fathers rifles and shotguns, his fishing gear, books, lots of things, we'll sort it out together and Mr Beattie has a favour to ask you."

"Aye Conon, I was wondering, you have some school holidays coming up, how would you like to come up to Wyvis and help me with some Royal Marines that are arriving for some sniper training, I don't know if you'll remember Lieutenant Munro but he remembers you and he's asked specially if you would come and help him, I think he's going to the Commando Training Centre soon and this may be the last time he comes to Wyvis, what do you think?"

Conon looked at his grandparents, they were thrilled to see the excitement in his face and pleased for him, "It would be good for you Conon, get away and have some fun," his grandmother said.

"And of course you'll be paid and Mrs Beattie will look after you when you're staying, if you decide to come?"

"Oh yes, Mr Beattie, I'd love to, when?"

"Your holidays start in two weeks, we'll see you then and get things sorted out for Mr Munro arriving, how's that sound?"

"Fantastic Mr Beattie, thank you."

The young officer, Lieutenant Munro, had asked when he called Mr Beattie if young Conon would be about as he

Yahweh

had made life very difficult for him on his sniper training at Wyvis, the young lad was almost genial in the way he could move about the hill unseen, he was a natural and he wanted to let others see his skills. He was heartfelt sorry when he'd heard of the young boy's sad news and wanted to do anything he could to help.

Two weeks later Conon arrived at Wyvis with his grandparents, they would holiday in the area themselves and stay with Conon at one of the estate cottages until it was time to go home and Cruach and Liath were there too, they would enjoy the break as well.

After week one of the course Conon had sniffed out two Marines who had made the fatal mistake of wearing Avon Skin So Soft, it kept the dreaded midges away but the sweet smell was unmistakeable, they cursed Conon. It was decided that the Marines were going to have a night out in the local town, Alness and as they passed the cottage, two of them grabbed Conon and told him he was being kidnapped. It was all a big laugh until they reached the town and walked into the first bar they saw. The Marines surrounded Conon and propped up one end of the bar, after twenty minutes and several very quick drinks later the inevitable scuffle broke out and the Marines found themselves outside and outnumbered by the angry locals, when the local Police turned up the Sergeant got out and eyed up the Marines, Conon realised it was Sergeant Macdonald, he knew he'd transferred from Mallaig but had no idea where he'd gone.

"Okay lads, it'll be a carry out and back to Wyvis or you're all in the cells for the night, the choice is yours!"

Bellowed the Sergeant. Conon turned thinking about an escape, drawing the Sergeants attention straight towards him, Conon tried to hide his face as the Marine in charge, Shiner Wright, spoke and pulled Conon behind his huge frame. "Yes Sergeant, we have a nominated driver, we'll get a few beers at the off licence and head back to Wyvis."

"Conon? Conon Bridge? Is that you?" The Sergeant asked. Conon looked out from behind Shiner and sporting a bloody nose and a swollen lip he tried to smile and said, "Yes Sergeant Macdonald it's me, I'm sorry."

"Get your arse in that van boy and don't say a word, the rest of you, back to Wyvis now!"

Conon got into the back of the van and hung his head as the Marines wandered off to their minibus overseen by Sergeant Macdonald and Constable Harper, the locals gave them a proper slagging as they left and promises were passed as the young Marines retreated not wishing to be the cause of any further trouble.

The drive back to Wyvis was a very long twenty minutes, all Sergeant Macdonald would say was how disappointed he was. Conon had never been drunk before and was terrified of what his grandparents would say. They arrived at the cottage and were met by Mr Beattie, Lieutenant Munro and Conon's grandparents. Sergeant Macdonald got out of the van and said, "Sabine, Tomas, I have a delivery for you, I'll let you deal with him, fighting and drinking in the town, how old is he?"

Tomas was expressionless, Sabine was horrified, "He's only fifteen!" She said, she was clearly very angry. Conon was more scared of her for the first time ever than his grandfather. "Get inside now you and straight to your bed, after I've checked your face!" "I'm very sorry Sergeant Macdonald."

As Conon trudged into the house Macdonald spoke. "It's okay Sabine, there was no damage, no one hurt other than a few scratches, boys being boys!"

"All the same after all you've done for us and Conon, I'm very ashamed."

"I know how you feel but he's obviously getting on well and he was in good company!" He eyed the Marines however, all stood to attention waiting for the wrath of Munro to descend. "I'll leave these twits to you Mr Munro."

Shiner spoke, "It was nothing to do with the young lad Sir it was us we nabbed him on our way out for a laugh. Don't be hard on him."

Lieutenant Munro ignored Wright and spoke to the Police Sergeant,

"Thank you Sergeant, You lot to your bunks now, 0500 hours start! GO!"

The Marines took their orders from Shiner and doubled off to their accommodation, all of them groaning at the thought of the beasting they would surely get in the morning and the cold swim in the loch to cool down at the end for good measure. Conon listened intently as he sat at the kitchen table.

Tomas and Sabine said goodnight to Sergeant Macdonald who left with Constable Harper, Tomas turned to Lieutenant Munro and smiled and said, "If the boy flies with the crows then he should be shot with the crows." And he winked at the Marine officer who just smiled as the older couple retreated into their cottage. As Tomas shut the door Conon hung his head, he had never let his parents or grandparents down and he had no idea what they would do. His grandmother took out the first aid kit and tended to his cut lip and swollen nose which made Conon wince, "Don't be a baby." She said.

"I hope you remembered everything I taught you Conon?" And he winked at Conon knowing his wife couldn't see his face. Conon smiled.

"Tomas, don't encourage the boy, that's not how we've brought him up!"

"Ach woman, I've a bigger cut in the end of my bird! All young men fight, are you not pleased he is growing up?"

"Achhhh Tomas you know what I mean!" Secretly though, she too was happy that Conon was just a normal boy and his past was not affecting him, "Go to your bed and reflect on what's happened tonight! You've let yourself down and us and Mr Beattie."

Conon glanced at his grandfather who again winked at him as he shuffled off to his bed.

At 0430 hours the bedroom door opened and Conon's grandfather came in, it was daylight. Conon looked up, his eyes full of sleep and he couldn't believe it when his grandfather pulled the duvet back and threw his running shoes a pair of shorts and a tee shirt at him and said very sternly, "Get them on and come with me now!"

Outside Conon saw Mr Beattie in his Land Rover, his grandfather was in the passenger seat, "Get in!"

Conon climbed into the vehicle and they drove the five minute journey up the loch to the Marines accommodation. Outside the Marines were standing to attention in their P.E. gear, waiting for Lieutenant Munro. Conon's grandfather turned around and looked at Conon,

"I think you are made for this kind of life Conon, so let's see? If you think it's fair to let these men be punished because of what happened and you don't see them as friends you can watch and see what happens to men who get caught," before he could finish, Conon opened the door and ran over and stood beside Shiner Wright, his grandfather nodded his head in approval and all Shiner said was, "Good lad."

The beasting was horrendous, none of the Marines gave up though, Shiner was clearly the most powerful and influential of the group a born leader and over the next hour kept everyone going with powerful encouragement, amazingly as Tomas and Mr Beattie watched, Conon actually did himself proud and wasn't last at any of the poundings or exercises that Lieutenant Munro dished out and everyone else noticed too. At the end of the session and after endless corrective advice from Lieutenant Munro they all found themselves in Loch Glass where the near freezing cold water very quickly became a relief and so the joker in Shiner came out and the punishment ended and a free for all ensued with everyone being thrown in and mud being thrown. Even Munro laughed as the group enjoyed the early morning exercise. He walked over to the Land Rover and nodding he said to Tomas, "Do you think he's interested in joining us Tomas?"

"I will do my best to encourage him Mr Munro but I really don't think that will be a struggle."

They all watched as the mayhem continued.

Yahweh

The next few years were good for Conon, he left school with good grades and set off to join the Royal Marines Commandos. He passed with flying colours and won a few trophies on the way, it was Sabine and Tomas's proudest moment watching him pass out of basic training. He was posted to Arbroath where Four Five Commando were based. Every weekend that he could, he went home to Morar.

As the years went by Conon grew in stature amongst his colleagues and he became a well-respected member of his troop in Zulu Company and after only four years he was promoted to Corporal and had completed several courses, parachuting, snipers course, and he was a natural with the communications systems and he'd passed his driving test, then out of the blue one day Conon was called to the Sergeant Majors office, Conon was told his grandfather was out walking on the hill earlier in the day when he simply collapsed. Conon was given compassionate leave and made his way home to Morar to console his grandmother who was heartbroken. "He was old but still very active Conon, he died on the hill where loved to be, poor Cruach and Liath stayed with him until he was found. It's the way he would've wanted to go, not lying, failing in his bed thinking he was being a burden."

Conon listened to his grandmother all night, she told him stories about what they got up to during the war and how much he was admired by everyman that he helped to train, he was a hero in Poland. The funeral arrangements had been made and Conon although sad was proud to have known such a great and humble man. He helped his grandmother to her bed and gave her a kiss on the cheek before saying goodnight. She passed away that night in her sleep and was buried with her beloved Tomas at Morar. Conon was on his own.

They are out there, men and women, some aware, some unaware of what they are ready for, some remember, some have been trained to forget, they are amongst you.

You forget things; don't you?

OPERATION CODENAME "YAHWEH"

During the 1980s it had been realised by several governments throughout the world but more so by the British in collaboration with MI5, MI6 and others that the Peoples Republic of Chinas hunger for natural resources was gathering pace, rapidly; in fact it was unstoppable. The Russians, the Americans and other allied nations were also acutely aware of the need to feed the beast and were moving in on the African continent, forging deals, swapping arms for natural resources and signing lucrative contracts. In the United Kingdom, the government of the day lead by Margaret Thatcher had decided in consultation with the heads of the Armed Forces and Security Services Agencies that the Chinese nation should be closely monitored for any advances in technology or in fact any field where the balance of power or new world order would be tipped in their favour. The Americans continued to keep too much to themselves and although the old alliance appeared outwardly to be as strong as ever, the British top brass and strategic planners were determined neither the Americans or even more worryingly the Chinese would steal a march on them, not this time. Many believed the biggest of threats to the United Kingdom's infrastructure and essentially Christian way of life would come from the Middle East, from Fundamentalists with extreme beliefs, others though were more wary of the rise of the threat from the Far East.

Yahweh was the protector of good against evil and so the operation to oversee the biggest and longest intelligence gathering exercise of all time was born YAHWEH - I am - the protector of all.

Andrew Shepherd

August 11th 2006

The two Royal Marines Commando snipers lay silently in the darkness, their mission was simple, find Bin Laden and the S.A.S. would be tasked to eliminate him. The newly developed suits they were using operationally for the first time were unbelievable, they rendered the wearers next to invisible from above and below, their heat signatures virtually zero, in fact the two men would look like nothing more than a pair of beetles mating on any thermal imaging system. Rumour control had lead the Marines trialling the suits to believe that the British had captured their own alien spacecraft and it was in the process of being reverse engineered at Boscombe Down and the aliens that had been captured had been wearing suits similar to the ones they were now wearing but no one actually, really believed the stories. They had been in position for over a week and they were right on top of the entrance to the cave in the Tora Bora mountains where a band of Taliban guerrillas were in hiding, they believed they had found the bolt hole where Osama Bin Laden was being hidden, they were certain they had at least found where Saif al-Adel, one of Bin Laden's most important operational planners was hiding and they were reporting the movements of the group on an hourly basis by secure means to the drone that was permanently in the air close by, which in turn sent the encrypted messages to a high orbit satellite which in turn beamed the information down to analysts at the Northwood bunker in England where the British Military command analysts reported to the Chiefs of staff of all the British Armed Forces. If the two Royal Marines were captured it would cause a row with the Americans and the Marines would almost certainly be executed by their captors if caught, both men new the consequences should that be the case but both were selected on the basis they had no family and they were two of the best covert operatives the Royal Marines had, both spoke fluent Dari, Russian and a few other useful languages.

In the darkness the two men watched as an eight man team stumbled into the area and headed straight for the entrance to the cave, they were Americans, the sensitive listening equipment they were using picked up the American whispers from almost a hundred meters away. Conon Bridge turned slowly to his colleague and signalled to his colleague that the Americans would face almost certain death if they went much further.

Sergeant Cooper spoke.

"That's not our problem Conon, we can't compromise ourselves here, there's way too much at stake!"

"Are you serious, we can't let them die?"

"We stay put Conon and deal with it!"

Conon was up and gone, Sergeant Cooper cursed under his breath and called in for close air support but the answer came back they were on their own, the R.A.F. had been told to stay well away from the area due to the ongoing operation, the bosses just didn't want Bin Laden spooked if he was there.

Andrew Shepherd

The young look out on a nearby hillside had also spotted the Americans and alerted the rest of his family members, Bin Laden was whisked away deeper into the caves and lead through a catacomb of adjoining chambers and not for the first time spirited away from danger. The fourteen Taliban guerrillas, armed to the teeth made their way to the exit of the main chamber and as soon as the first man stepped out into the inky darkness the explosions and devastating firepower unleashed by Conon took them all by surprise, they fell man on man, the first seven never knew what had happened, they were expecting to get at least fifty meters out of the cave entrance and set a hasty ambush for the Americans, it was a well-rehearsed drill and they could not understand where the ferocity of the attack came from, there were no muzzle flashes giving their attackers positions away. The remainder of the Taliban men left alive shouted at each other that they must protect the Emir at all costs, each man knew they would die protecting him, it was their soul duty in life and so the first man rose to his feet and screamed, "ALLAHU AKBAR!!!" The others followed, all of them screaming out of the cave and firing their AK47's into the darkness at everything but hitting nothing. The rain of death fell upon them and as the last man fell to his knees he saw the shadow of death approach him out of the darkness. The man looked up into the face of the devil before him and in English he said to the dark figure before him, "Meeting death is better than escaping from it." Conon shot the man between the eyes then turned and made his way away from the locus. Sergeant Cooper was furious with Conon, the whole mission had been compromised but as Conon walked past the eight U.S. Marines still taking cover behind the rocks and bushes, the eight men were in awe of the apparition that shimmered in the darkness as he passed them, they had never seen anything quite like it, the soldier, whoever he was had saved their lives but he wasn't one of theirs, his clothing made him seem almost see through, near invisible. Cooper counted fourteen dead and now all he wanted to do was get the out of the place. The U.S. Marines called in for a helicopter extraction lift, they had been well and truly compromised but at least they were still alive, they had no idea that they had narrowly avoided walking into an ambush which had so very nearly been set for them. The team commander asked his ops room if they knew who was operating in the middle of their area, no one knew but the British were the only ones with the capability to get so far behind enemy lines and under cover. The phones were ringing red hot all over the Afghanistan region between the American and British command centres and the messages from the very top were clear, get Bridge out of the region and fast!!

On the hill side watching what had happened the young look out spoke to himself and muttered the word, "Yahweh." The Taliban would very soon have a price on Conon's head, they wanted him dead!

The Americans were furious, yet again Bin Laden had slipped through the noose and this time at the hands of a rogue Royal Marine patrol that had no business being in the area. The Americans wanted answers.

Watching in the wings were a highly covert unit of the British Intelligence Service, S.O.E. Long since believed to be disbanded, they basically worked along the lines of the American Black Ops organisations, money was not traceable, budgets not accountable, almost invisible.

The British had found their man, even if it meant some high level diplomacy to let the Americans think they had won the battle. Conon would be a useful asset for other missions.

Within six hours, Bridge was on a flight heading back to the U.K. They had told him nothing, he didn't ask questions anymore, that was the business he was in, he had no idea what was in store for him over the next few weeks and months.

British Intelligence had for a long time been aware that the Chinese had been working on a new and lethal nerve agent. The Russians and the Americans were both doing their best to capture the information one way or another, the Russians had gone into partnership with the Chinese and using one of their own experimental submarines, they had used a new stealth coating, stumbled upon by the Chinese, to develop one of the most deadly submarines ever to sail the oceans. The Russians who were rumoured to know about the Chinese experiments with nerve agents were not finding it easy though extracting the information from the Chinese who were guarding the exact chemical make-up of the nerve agent and more importantly the antidote very closely. The Americans however appeared to be up to their old tricks, if they couldn't buy it they stole it and so the cogs in the quagmires of espionage turned, slowly. The British did their bit too though, they snooped around in places that didn't really concern them and they watched from afar, this time though they had struck gold, they just needed one man to do the real dirty work for them and now they had their man whether he knew it or not.

Over the next few months Conon lost his drive to fight, to continue. The battles being fought were not for him anymore and anyway he knew he was being made a scapegoat by the very people he had previously fought for. He had always done his best and given his all but when he was offered the option to leave quietly it didn't take long for him to decide what to he wanted to do. He'd had enough of the endless pointless counselling and after a totally unnecessary operation to remove a piece of shrapnel from his left thigh Conon left the Corps and returned to Morar where he had inherited the comfortable family home. He had plenty of savings, he also had the option of work on the estate, an open door, and an opportunity for him to turn civvie and still do something useful with his skills, bizarrely though he joined Strathclyde Police and although his career went well for the first few years, his methods at extracting information from suspects constantly brought him into conflict with his bosses and so after five years on the thin blue line having decided he didn't need the hassle or grief Conon resigned and again returned to Morar and contemplated his future.

Conon arrived on the platform at Morar and looked around, the place was like a breath of fresh air to him. He walked the short distance home and before he'd even made it up the hill his arrival had been noticed.

The work at the estate was a no brainer, it was easy for Conon and he was popular with the guests. He supplemented his income, not that he needed to, by diving with an old Marine he'd met and become friends with. They dived for clams and life was good. He didn't generally go out, if he did it was for a very occasional pint in Fort William but just this once he decided he'd visit the Old Marine bar in Mallaig and see how much it had changed.

For the first time in nearly ten years Conon walked into the aptly named Marine Bar, the lighting was dingy and the air was filled with the smell of beer and whisky and just a hint of hash, oddly too, even though nowadays it was illegal, cigarette smoke hung the atmosphere. Every head in the bar turned around and looked at Conon as he walked through the door, there was probably about thirty or so mixed groups of men and women, they all turned and cast a glance at the stranger. After a quick look around and seeing only a few faces he recognised Conon stepped up to the bar and asked for a bottle of Miller lager and a glass of Black Bottle whisky. The jukebox was playing Queens Crazy Little Thing Called Love. No one lingered on the stranger at the bar, most of them were fishermen in their twenties and there were a few younger girls. The guys over to his right continued their game of pool and then there was the noise of a chair getting pushed back over the wooden floor from the end of the bar to his left, the first move. He expected to see someone he used to know, a reaction. The large shadowy figure loomed up on his left as Conon sipped on his whisky.

"Well, well, well, so you think you can just walk in here and buy yourself a drink you cheeky bastard!"

The voice was unmistakeably that of Donald Stone, a hard man twenty years ago, now a drunk who lived on memories, who scared wee boys with his tales and his party trick, biting the sides out of pint glasses. His surname wasn't Stone of course, he was simply called Stone on account of the rumour that whilst he was at school he was supposedly "rock hard". Stone continued as Conon chose to ignore him.

"I used to respect you! Now you're nothing but a fucking pig! And coming in here, you cheeky fucking bastard!"

Conon knew Stone was playing to the now silent crowd who probably had no idea who he was, slowly he turned around to his old smoking and drinking buddy and finished his dram. Stone was wearing an old donkey jacket, jeans that were stained, probably with his own piss, old scuffed black leather boots and an old torn tee shirt, his hair was greasy and his teeth were long past rotten. Stone grinned menacingly at Conon then he punched Conon square on the side of his jaw, Conon rocked, he put a finger inside his mouth and pulled out the dislodged filled tooth, he handed it to Stone who looked down at the tooth in the palm of his hand, Stone grinned as Conon spoke,

"I hear you're getting found lying in puddles of your own piss and shit Donald so why the fuck should I care what a turd like you thinks of me?" Stone was still staring at the tooth as Conon head butted him right on the bridge of his nose bursting it. Stone collapsed onto the floor unconscious, blood oozing from his yet again broken nose. Everyone in the bar sat or stood where they were not knowing what to do, one girl knelt down and tended to Stone. Conon picked up his bottle of Miller lager and took a sip. A few heads quickly got together pondering some form of revenge for Stone, but who was this stranger? Conon looked at the junkies and drunks who were in the bar,

"If any of you think you're big enough, I suggest you have another few drinks, you've already taken too long to get your fat arses out of your seats!"

No one moved, Conon left.

Unknown to Conon, Stone would keep the tooth for reasons known only to him, probably as trophy of sorts, but unwittingly he had done Conon a huge favour and would do for years to come.

Yahweh

Five Years Later

The Antaeus (half giant son of the God Poseidon) was the latest state of the art submarine, the pride of the Russian fleet, slipped past the point of Ardnamurchan and into the NATO exercise area, the Antaeus was a miniature Kursk, built with new stealth technology, the naval hierarchy had decreed after the disaster in 2000 that never again would they build such vessels and the emerging world powers, India and China were prepared to pay handsomely for such technology. She was only forty meters long but nuclear powered and bristling with the latest weapons, communication systems and a new top secret silent hydro propulsion system, the Antaeus and her crew of twenty men could simply not be heard or seen thanks to her top secret hull coating and propulsion system. It was 0030 hours, Captain Zaitsev, a direct descendant of the Great Russian sniper Vasily Zaitsev gave the command to shut off all propulsion and ordered silence among the crew, the sonar operator informed him, "Captain we appear to be over a cable of some kind, it's directly beneath us there's no power of any kind going through it."

The clam boat had slipped quietly out of the harbour at 2355 hours, no one knew where they were going but everyone in Mallaig knew that the motor vessel Worthy, one side painted red the other side painted blue was heading out to fish for razor clams in the sound. Dougal and Shory were pushing their luck again, twice that year already the fishery officers had confiscated all their gear believing they were electrocuting the clams but as no one ever knew where they were in the dead of night with their lights off of course no one could prove it and they always saw the danger coming. Onwards into the darkness the Worthy slipped, the men heading for a mark they knew well, where in no more than thirty meters of water the near kilometre of copper cable lay on the bottom. They found the mark easily with the GPS on board and threw the grappling hook out and connected with the buoy and line first time, two minutes later the copper cable was aboard and connected to the generator, a quick blast of two hundred and forty volts later the power was shut off the cable remained connected as Dougal rigged up for the first dive and entered the water, he attached himself to the Worthy with a rope that was so strong, he could pull the boat down with it before it would snap, then he slipped quietly into the water. The darkness had always bothered him but in a few moments he'd picked up the faint glow of the green light remotely operated by Shory on the marker buoy ten meters under the surface. Downwards he swam until he hit the bottom, still attached to the Worthy. He clipped onto the copper cable so as not to lose it if his torch failed. There was a rope bound to the cable and at one hundred meter intervals they had caribinas spliced into the rope, they unclipped the marker buoy and slid it along the rope until they reached the next one and that was the start of the next dive. When they reached the end of the rope they towed the copper cable to the next spot, always in twenty or thirty meters of water, always next to a big feature to avoid their gear getting hauled up buy the local clam dredgers. At twenty three meters, he had about thirty minutes bottom time, already in the light of his head torch he could see the clams strewn all over the seabed either side of the copper cable, he smiled & started gathering clams thinking only of the money. After twenty five minutes Dougal surfaced and handed the line to Shory, who was drunk again. Dougal drank a warm mug of tea, it felt good after being in the water but an hour and a half later it was time to dive again and he watched as Shory struggled drunkenly in the darkness to fire up the generator again, another blast of two hundred and forty volts and Dougal got back into the water and headed for the bottom again.

On board the Antaeus the sonar operator spoke to Zaitsev, "Captain, the small vessel we've been monitoring, it's above us now, and she's stationary in the water." Captain Zaitzev looked at his executive officer & announced.

"Probably some hydro cable being laid and as yet uncharted, stupid Brits." Both men laughed as Zaitzev ordered everyone to return to their duties quietly, the ship rested on the sandy bottom and the crew fell silent and waited to carry out their spying mission deep inside British territorial waters, then every alarm on the ship went off, Zaitzev asked calmly for a status report, the sonar operator announced calmly.

"Sir the cable it's just gone live!" Zaitzev looked at the propulsions systems Officer and told him.

"Get us off the bottom and out of here" the sonar operator shouted out.

"We've fowled the cable sir it's been sucked into the port side jet!" Zaitzev ordered, "Shut it down now!"

It was too late! They tried the starboard engine but the static in the cable practically drew it into the propulsion

Andrew Shepherd

system by itself, they were without knowing it moments away from being securely attached to the Worthy and they were in very shallow water. Almost every circuit on board had been fried by the sudden pulse of raw electricity & both engines had shut themselves down. The Antaeus's achilles heel had been exposed, the handpicked crew were aware of it but never thought that they would be exposed to such electric power in such a manner. They were virtually powerless, the only option was to switch to the auxiliary system would mean they could easily be detected.

After five minutes or so Dougal thought he heard something, no one else would be out at this time, he must've imagined it and carried on, then again a very faint buzz somewhere about him but where? He checked his air and his time, both good, and then again another buzzing sound definitely, he carried on another few meters another, just in the light of his torch in the dark inky night water he could see what he thought was a whale resting on the bottom, he knew it couldn't be but curiosity drew him forwards, so onwards Dougal swam. His eyes could barely take in what he was seeing but the copper cable under him was lifting off the seabed as he again heard the buzzing noise, it was coming from the object ahead of him which appeared to have been fouled by the cable, he couldn't make it out properly but getting closer he shone his torch along the length of the object until he came to the middle of the object and realised he was looking at a submarine; one with a red star on the low conning tower he could now make out and one which he realised was somehow sucking their cable into its propulsion system. He turned and started for the surface, he was panicking trying to make sense of it all and in the blackness he forgot to unclip himself.

Zaitzev gave the order to switch to battery power & auxiliary propulsion and head for deeper water, "Sir!!" the executive shouted out looking at his charts, "There's a sunken U-boat about 500 meters away we should lie alongside it for now, it's charted and may throw the Royal Navy off our scent for a while it'll give us thinking time?" Zaitzev looked at his executive nodded and gave the order to execute the command to the sonar and propulsion systems officers. As the Antaeus lifted off the bottom of Sound of Sleat, Dougal clambered aboard the Worthy as Shory fastened the lines to the cable around the stern cleats, they were now secured to the Antaeus, both men watched in horror as the line tightened and the stern of the Worthy lurched round throwing both of them across the deck, Shory shouted at Dougal.

"What the fucks going on?" Dougal screamed back as the stern of the Worthy started to disappear under the water.

"Cut the fucking line!" But it was too late as the stern of the Worthy was now five feet under the water, the boat started moaning and creaking in the dark as the two men scrambled backwards on their backsides towards the wheel house, Dougal fumbled in the dark and found a life jacket and ordered Shory to get it on, he was in a dry suit so would be safe with the air now trapped in it. The two men found a length of rope and lashed themselves together as the Worthy slipped beneath the waves. The two men clung to each other,

"Ok so now do you want to tell me what the fuck that was all about?" asked Shory, sobering up very quickly.

As the two men began the swim towards Traigh beach, Dougal did his best to tell Shory about the encounter.

"Listen bud the boats not insured, no fucker will believe us so let's just shut the fuck up about the whole thing, we'll end up being spirited away to some fucking unknown prison hell hole for looney bins knowing our luck anyway, Dougal agreed with his friend.

Two hours later Dougal and Shory stumbled ashore and started off across the moor towards Mallaig.

"Captain screamed the sonar operator the ship above us, we're pulling her down!"

Zaitzev asked for comms to report any mayday calls but there was nothing, after what seemed an eternity both vessels lay on the bottom. Zaitzev ordered the boomer buoy to be floated this would let them listen into all the local VHF radio transmissions. He gave the order to deploy the dive team and clear the cable fouling their propulsion system, the divers made ready and within fifteen minutes the two men were exiting the hull of the Antaeus via the forward dive chamber. Zaitsev asked for the comms team to send a flash message to the Northern Fleet Headquarters at Severomorsk, Murmansk and to simply let them know they had encountered a problem and were moving out of the NATO exercise area and heading for international waters. The emergency communications float was launched and within seconds the Russian

Yahweh

satellite had received the scrambled message, relayed it to NFHQ, the heat was about to turn up and not just aboard the Antaeus, the situation was about to become far more complicated and dangerous for everyone.

As soon as the divers reached the cable they could see it had gouged into the thick rubber based coating on the upper side of the port induction vent, both men struggled to replace the section of rubber but eventually with a massive amount of brute force the section returned to the formed shape of the hull, they checked that the cable attached to the fishing boat was freed and not still connected to the Antaeus, they wouldn't cut the cable unless they had to, that would mean if the boat was ever found someone would see the cut and Royal Naval Intelligence would know someone had been there that shouldn't have been. Almost twenty minutes later they made their way back to the dive hatch and as the number two diver was about to enter the Antaeus neither he nor his diving partner could believe it as his pressure gauge erupted and both of them became blinded by the air escaping from the airline, his air was venting straight out of his bottle. The two divers shared air for the few minutes it took for the dive chamber to empty but the horror was evident as they looked at the gear and saw that the gauge had disappeared, they were safe though and were back on board, soon they were giving Captain Zaitsev a full report, "Well we'll have to take a chance that the gauge will not be found any time soon gentlemen we simply cannot hang about to see if it'll turn up."

After thirty minutes there were no maydays, no life boat launch, no problem with the Royal Navy sniffing around for now. Zaitsev hoped the integrity of the hull was sound but he couldn't afford to hang around, not now. The electronics crew were frantically working at over-riding the circuitry in an attempt to restore power to the hydro propulsion system, finally the green lights were glowing across the main switch systems nearly one hour after the near catastrophe had occurred, the propulsions officer reported to Captain Zaitsev the systems appeared to show all was well however he wouldn't be able to tell if that was the case until they were underway. Zaitsev spoke to the whole crew.

"Comrades we have had a very lucky escape tonight and it is my intention to head for the Atlantic and back to Murmansk and allow our experts to examine the ship, I have orders and a duty to ensure the safety of the crew and ship at all times, we will be home in six days as long as we do not encounter or discover any problems on the way, carry on with your duties." "A wise decision Captain, obviously our report will show that we had no idea that the surface ship was using some kind of electrical system that disabled our ship?"

"Obviously." replied Zaitsev but his mind was already contemplating how some innocuous vessel barely registering on his ships systems could nearly destroy them.

The Antaeus lifted off the sea bed, this time there were no problems and the order was given to steer a course south of the Isle of Eigg and make for the open ocean, the Antaeus slowly, silently and stealthily made her way out of the Sound of Sleat, ten knots was what Zaitsev asked for.

Yahweh

"For now let's just take things nice and easy and make sure we have no problems."

Shory and Dougal arrived at Dougals flat after a long cold and wet hour trudging across the moor. They got out of their wet gear and showered, as soon as Dougal was out of the shower Shory washed himself warm and when he reached the living room with a warm set of dry clothes on Dougal had poured him a large dram, "We don't let on to anyone about tonight," said Shory. The two friends agreed that they would say they ended up taking on water, tried to sort out the problem and ended up being sunk before they had a chance to even get off a mayday call, it wasn't a completely implausible scenario after all. They drank some more and finished the bottle before falling asleep on the sofa and chair in the sparsely furnished flat. Below them the flat tenant Eric Ubych had heard the two men come in later than normal but fell back to sleep after checking his watch and seeing 03.15 a.m. He had another couple of hours to go before he had to get up himself and get to his own boat for a day's fishing. Outside no one stirred in the small west coast fishing village, in another hour or so some of the local crews would arrive at the boats in the harbour and get set for the days fishing, some would be out for a few days but most knew that the radar systems and radio equipment would be interfered with thanks to the ongoing NATO exercise, it caused the same problems every year but the fishermen still had to get out and make a living regardless of the problems the Royal Navy caused, they never gave any concessions, never, it angered most of the men who never seemed to get anywhere with the Admiralty, they just bullied their way about the Isle of Skye and the North west of Scotland every year.

At an altitude of nearly thirty six thousand kilometres the high orbit satellite, Highball had been monitoring the Joint Warrior NATO exercise area within the Sound of Sleat, nothing was seen or heard at sea level but the Royal Air Force data intelligence officer had seen some kind of anomaly on his screen, it was similar to the kind of signature given off by the power systems running between some of the North Sea oil installations, he just wasn't sure about it though, it lasted for no more than a minute then disappeared then a strange pulsing was heard on the sonic detection system, sonar buoys preplaced in the exercise area by the Royal Navy were sending data to Highball continuously; the satellite had been launched by the British a year earlier on the same rocket as a communications satellite, quietly and without any pomp or ceremony. Unnoticed Pilot Officer Sid Walsh printed off his findings and went to his Flight Officer, the two men mused over the signals sent to the listening station, a bunker deep underground at the now supposedly defunct RAF Kinloss, "It's probably nothing Sid, having said that though neither sounds are anything like I've ever heard before, subsea for sure, I'll run it by the old man, it may be that one of the P3 Orion's heading over from the States, for the exercise can have a sniff around and see if they can come up with anything, one's due to be in the area in about two hours. Good work, well done."

Flight Lieutenant Griffin knocked on the OC's door, "Come in," came the reply, Griffin entered and waved the papers in front of Squadron Leader McDonnell and informed him there was something unexplainable in the signals being sent back from Highball, McDonnell knew Highball was currently being used to monitor the NATO exercise about to start off the west coast of Scotland in two days' time, he glanced up at Griffin and asked him to explain. "Well Sir it looks like some kind of electrical anomaly but it only lasted a minute then Sid noticed something else, on their own probably not much but so close together, well it's probably a coincidence but we thought you should know about it?"

"Sid?" Enquired the Squadron Leader sitting behind the desk, "Yes sir, Sid Walsh he's just joined us, has a degree in astrophysics a bit of a whizz kid, nice, not geeky just head down type."

"Ah yes I know the lad, what do you think?"

"Well we've got one P3 about two hours west of Barra heading our way for the exercise, they should have enough fuel for a loiter of say an hour or so, the crew will be pissed off but if there's anything there we should know about they should find it? Then we have another two P3s, one Norwegian one Danish currently at Lossiemouth just in case there's anything to follow up?"

"Ok I'll see if we can get in touch with the U.S. naval command at Jacksonville and ask if they'll retask before their guys land, you can get in touch with Lossiemouth and ask them to give the Dutch & Danish crew bosses the heads up, the Navy are sending up a couple of Merlins tomorrow but they won't be at Gannet until 1200 hours and the Navy won't tell us if they have any black assets in the area but if they do and they get a whiff of something abnormal out there I'm sure they'll let their boys know."

"Yes Sir, I'll get onto it straight away." Griffin turned and left the office. McDonnell lifted his secure phone and dialled one of his colleagues, Gordon Young, at Northwood. He'd left there two years ago to come back to the Kinloss area where he intended retiring soon, quietly. "Hello its Kevin here, McDonnell, Kevin McDonnell."

"Kevin how the hell are you?" The men who had joined the Royal Air Force together remained friends despite the difference in their ranks, they exchanged pleasantries for a short time then Gordon asked if there was anything Kevin wanted he sensed a tinge of urgency in the other man's voice.

"Gordon it's probably bugger all but one of our analysts has picked up on a couple of spurious signals being sent back to Highball from the Joint Warrior NATO exercise area in the Sound of Sleat, it's monitoring. He's a bit of a whizz kid by all accounts and I was wondering if you can talk to US Naval Command and ask if one of their P3s that should be west of Barra just now to drop some sonar buoys in and check it out just in case anyone is sniffing about?"

"Consider it done Kevin, by the way do you remember about two years ago just before you retired?" The two men laughed, "There was a newspaper article in one of the Scottish Sunday tabloids about Russian subs spying in our waters just off the Moray coast?"

"Yes of course I remember it but no one ever really bottomed the source for that story out, didn't we think it was just some hack generating a story, news was a bit lean at the time?"

"Yes that's right," replied Young, "but an RAF crew flying one of the new MR4 Nimrods at the time, that allegedly never flew only one did but in the dark, reckon there was something similar to a giant squid in the area off Lossiemouth, it was all they could come up with at the time to get the press of their backs. It was reported, filed and forgotten about, apparently the new systems on board were "too sensitive" then it transpires that some guy placed in Murmansk two years earlier by the Chinese to spy on the Russians was captured by the Ruskies. There were rumours circulating soon afterwards that they, the Russians were building some kind of mini super sub with a hydro propulsion system, we know very little else about it, so who knows old boy?"

"Ok Gordon speak to the yanks we'll listen out for them up here anyway,"

"Will do, cheers for now." The telephone call ended but the start of a long night had just begun for Group Captain Young.

On-board the US navy P3, call-sign Casper 1 the radio operator took the scrambled message, "Proceed to British OS map 3-9 area and commence search for any subsea activity heading for open water, more details to follow." The lieutenant handed the message to a captain who spoke directly to the pilot, orders were orders they'd been flying for seven hours but could still stay out another three and it sounded like the Brits were twitching about something or the exercise was going live forty eight hours early. Life on board the P3, Casper 1, the cartoon ghost character was painted on the tail of the aircraft, was comfortable, toilet, food and rest area if needed were all there so another hour wouldn't kill them. The pilot adjusted his course and waited further instruction from his crew chief. Further back in the command area, the brains of the aircraft, the crew joked as they swung into action and sorted out the co-ordinates for the search pattern.

On-board the Antaeus the sonar operator called out to the Captain, "Sir we have a P3 about ten miles out and it just adjusted course and now appears to be following a search pattern, they're currently on a heading of 1.5.0. Degrees and will cross the north end of the Island of Coll in exactly..................

12 minutes." Commander Zaitsev thanked the sonar operator and told him to let him know immediately the American aircraft changed his course again. Zaitsev knew the NATO exercise wasn't due to start for about another forty six hours but he was suspicious of the naval submarine hunters behaviour, as he instinctively should be, it was highly unlikely the Royal Navy had a hunter killer in the area but not impossible so had the accident with the small vessel earlier raised alarms? Had the crew survived and made it ashore and alerted the authorities? No, not possible, the local Mallaig lifeboat would've been launched, the coastguard helicopter or a Sea King from Gannet would be sniffing around, not to mention several ships from the NATO flotilla now arriving around the Isle of Rum north of them, there was nothing apart from one P3 Orion which appeared to have diverted off its

course for Lossiemouth. It was enough to give Zaitsev cause for concern, he ordered all crew to be vigilant. The Antaeus continued on her course of 2-4-0 degrees towards the open ocean but she and her crew were still a long way from international waters, Zaitsev gave the order to maintain a steady fifteen knots. Unknown to the crew the rubber coating damaged by the encounter with the cable lifted six inches and was gently oscillating as the jet of salt water was pushed through the chamber changing the dynamics of the ship on any sonar from a knitting needle to a comparably sized corkscrew.

"Sir the P3, it's just dropped a sonar buoy, it's currently active and about three kilometres away from us on our port side." The whole crew fell silent as Zaitsev looked around and knew instinctively these men did not need to be told to be quiet at this time, "Continue on our course maintain fifteen knots, steady as she goes," he whispered into his microphone, the propulsions officer standing behind the crewman handling the boat merely squeezed the junior officers shoulder, both crew men knew exactly what they were doing and the ship was itself so smart that the on-board counter measures had already detected the sonar device and began masking any trace of the Antaeus. Above the waves the P3 was beginning a wide lazy ninety degree turn and starting to change course for near Sanna Point, on the Ardnamurchan Peninsula it would take less than five minutes to get to the next turn and start leg three of the search, the sensor operators on board monitored the screens but nothing out of the ordinary was jumping out at them. The most experienced systems operator on-board, Captain Eadie McLean had over twenty years on-board P3s she was nearing the end of her service and was on the so called jolly so at the end of the exercise she could go and visit her ancestral home, Swordlands on the shores of Loch Morar, it had taken years of research but it had been worth it and here she was searching the waters a stone's throw away from the place. The P3 passed Sanna Point and began a turn to port, McLean spoke to the pilot directly and asked him to turn through 125' and onto a heading of 3-0-0 degrees, this would cut diagonally across the initial box pattern and if anything was out there, watching or listening out for Casper then stepping out of the box a little may just be enough of a surprise to catch them out. None of the crew said anything they just sat monitoring the screens, no one questioned McLean, it was a no brainer she knew what she was doing, and she was probably one of the best acoustic systems operators in the Navy. Casper flew on now heading directly for Barra.

On board the Antaeus the sonar operator called out to commander Zaitsev, "Sir, the P3 he's gone out of the normal search pattern, he's cutting the box at 45 degrees and now heading 3-0-0 degrees the sonar buoy hasn't picked us up but the MAD boom has been deployed. Zaitsev knew the Magnetic Anomaly Detection boom, the large probe at the rear of the P3 was highly sensitive but the new stealth systems on board his ship had managed to help them evade two Tu.95 Bears on their initial sea trials, the Bear crews actually said at a debrief they could see nothing, not even a ripple in the water when the Antaeus slipped along at fifteen knots, fifteen meters beneath the surface, the sonar operator advised of a wreck very close to them, the fishing vessel Republic, she was last recorded at 83 meters, they would hide alongside the vessel, they were not only silent they were invisible at the best of times, they were however not yet aquatinted with Chief Eadie McLean. As Casper crossed the midway point of the third leg McLean asked for the SDO to jettison a Prowler pod. Prowler was a new stealth subsea search system, smart and instantly capable of making its own, almost completely autonomous decisions when seeking or searching for anything out of the ordinary in the murky waters and what they really liked about Prowler was the fact that once dropped there were numerous options to retrieve it, helicopters, ships or even submarines could handle the system easily. McLean spotted the flicker on her screen, it was there for no more than a second but long enough for Mclean to mark the spot, she punched a few buttons and in another few moments she was talking to the pilot giving him a new course to fly. The P3 slowly moved into position, the aircrafts movements were being watched by the analysts on-board the Antaeus who were keeping their Captain informed, the P3 was less than five minutes from flying rite down their throats and they were still at least three hours from safety. Zaitsev gave the order from the executive officer to drop the Antaeus quietly onto the sandy bottom and keep all noise to a complete minimum, the orders were followed to the letter and the submarine slowly glided to a halt and drifted very slowly downwards towards the bottom eighty odd meters below. The Captain gave the order to brace for the bottom and hoped that no one would hear the Antaeus settle on the sand.

Above them Mclean watched the systems in front of her and saw that the Prowler sonar system had heard the crump as the vessel settled, the Prowler stopped almost dead in the water listening to its prey about one hundred and fifty meters away in the murky water, "Got you, you son of a bitch!" she exclaimed out loud. "Okay guys, we've got some one hiding down there we need to know for sure that the Royal Navy aren't trying to pull a fast one here."

"I'm on it Eadie." The signals operator flicked some switches on his terminal that effectively scrambled everything that was being said and he contacted his command centre at The Naval Air Station Patuxent River, U.S.A. he then asked the simple question, "Are the Royal Navy testing our systems? We have something showing up here but we need to confirm that this is a NO DUFF exercise." The message came back almost instantly, "Whatever is down there it doesn't belong to us or the Brits so just keep an eye on it, don't let it out of your sight whatever it is!"

The signaler passed the message back to Mclean who in turn spoke to the pilot who was ultimately in charge of the aircraft and then to the senior officer on board, Captain Pimmy Roberts, Roberts was the chief navigator on board and had dealt with numerous cat mouse games with the Russians…….. French, Chinese, Germans and at times worryingly even the Royal Navy sitting off the eastern seaboard listening in to everything and anything. None of these previous cat and mouse games had ever been publicised, it wasn't good for international relations and in any case it kept everyone on their toes. This time though it really did seem as though someone was technologically, as difficult as it was to believe, one impossible step ahead of them. They really had to find out more about who or what was down there.

Mclean sent the signal to the Prowler system to move in closer in an ever decreasing circle and instantly it locked onto the hull of the Antaeus and was sending information back to the systems operators on the Orion, "Eadie, it looks like we've got two objects on the bottom about one hundred and fifty meters away from Prowler."

"The charts show a wreck, a fishing boat sunk in 1985 but there's no way there's two wrecks, ones our little friend and he's a sneaky fucker, trying to hide on me are you? Who are you?" Mclean asked.

The Prowler slowly moved in whilst all the time the sonar operator onboard Antaeus watched the spy come closer and closer. Slowly the Prowler approached and at one hundred meters from Antaeus Mclean gave the order for the probe to hold station, they needed more info from the Royal Navy and from their own command, it was obvious that they were now dealing with a live situation and something was out there not wanting to be found. Mclean marked her target and armed two torpedo's, she conversed with Captain Roberts and the Pilot, all three agreed that they should at least be prepared for the unthinkable. Below them the sonar operator onboard Antaeus pointed to his screen with Zaitzev looking over his shoulder reading the information which told him the American aircraft had just armed two torpedo's, he had to hold his nerve, the crew would spot any weakness and panic was the last thing he wanted although he knew panic from one of the most experienced Russian Navy Submarine crews was highly unlikely, Zaitzev leaned forward and nodded to the sonar operator that he had fully understood the message. For now they sat tight and played the waiting game. Now was when Zaitzev found out who had nerve and courage.

The crew of the Antaeus all manned their stations, Zaitsev had ordered complete silence whilst the sub lay on the bottom, eighty five meters below the surface, they all knew that the hull of the ship was damaged and that they were not now invisible, clearly the Orion was hunting them and only luck would now see them reach the safety of international waters. Zaitsev knew the sensor put into the water by the Americans was searching for them and that it must have detected them but he had to hold out and use every trick in the book to evade capture. The sonar operator watched as the Prowler approached downwards in an ever decreasing circle, Zaitsev stood behind him watching the sensor on the screen getting closer and closer. Both men stared at the screen as the American probe appeared to stop and hold station about one hundred meters off the port side of the submarine and hover about twenty meters from the seabed. The Prowler had found them and would stick to them like a limpet.

Yahweh

Aboard the Antaeus, Zaitzev and the crew knew only too well that the American search probe, which also had the ability to blow them to kingdom come, was sending vital information about them back to the analysts above them flying the P3 Orion, they had to think fast in order to even attempt an escape, if escape from the situation they were now in was even possible. Zaitzev though, was already planning his next almost unbelievable move, his crew would not like what he was going to do next, they weren't going to like it one little bit but he had been prepared for just such an eventuality and asked for a coded message to be sent to Russian Naval Command at Severomorsk. It was a straightforward signal which to the crew gave nothing away but when decoded back at Severomorsk the hierarchy would be incandescent with rage at what had occurred. Zaitzev knew his career was effectively over but at least he could save the crew and the ship, and with any luck himself as well. The signal was sent.

Above the waves and flying at two hundred knots the Orion crew were currently dealing with the flurry of information being sent back to their terminals from the Prowler, Mclean and the rest of the crew knew there was something lying on the bottom trying to appear silent and invisible, there was also a wreck near the anomaly showing up on the bottom. Mclean asked the man next to her what was down there.

"Looks like multiple heartbeats Ma'am, looks like it's a sub."

"Well they definitely aren't ghosts, that's for sure."

Mclean spoke to the man in charge who was now leaning over her shoulder, Captain Ryan.

"We need to speak to the Royal Navy pronto boss, it's not ours and if it's not one of theirs then we've got something down there that shouldn't be there at all!"

Captain Ryan was on it and speaking to his bosses back at their home base in the States, the alarm bells were ringing all the way back to Northwood, England, within ten minutes. The British had a major problem on their doorstep.

The Lieutenant Commander hurriedly made his way along the corridor and knocked on the Admirals door and walked straight in without waiting for an invite, Admiral Currie was on the phone, the Lieutenant Commander stood with the sheet of paper in his hand, Currie looked up and excused himself from his call and placed the receiver back on the phone. "What is it Irvine?" The Intelligence Officer leaned forward and placed the sheet on the Admirals desk. "Sir, Group Captain Young has asked that you be informed of this immediately, he's waiting for further instruction."

Currie looked at the report, it was from The United States Naval Command at Norfolk, Virginia Naval Air Wing.

After looking at Irvine, Currie read the signal and mulled over its content, it would require a rapid meeting of several heads of the Defence departments. "Okay Irvine get everyone together ASAP and find out what assets we have locally and discretely of course give them the heads up."

Yahweh

"Yes Sir, I'll get on it right away, I'll leave the signal with you."

Currie quickly read the signal again.

It was worrying reading to say the least.

Andrew Shepherd

TOP SECRET

Copy - Royal Navy Operations Head Quarters, Northwood, England.

From - Admiral Fitsimmons Head of North Atlantic Fleet Operations, U.S. Navy.

Be advised that at 0145 hours GMT a US Naval P3 Orion, call sign "Casper 1" on exercises in The Sound of Sleat, south of the Isle of Skye, appears to have detected an unidentified submerged object and we recommend that you take all necessary steps to identify this vessel which is unknown to our data and appears to be a submarine of unknown origins. Our assets are briefed to stand by and assist with all measures at their disposal and should you require any further assistance we have been authorised from the highest levels to offer any equipment at our disposal to expedite your orders.

Message ends.

"How long ago did this kick off Irvine?"

"It appears that its ongoing Sir and it looks like it kicked off about two hours ago."

Currie picked up his phone and asked his secretary to arrange for all heads of departments to meet with him in the briefing room in five minutes and he asked her to get the Secretary of State for Defence on the phone immediately. "Follow me Irvine, it looks like the proverbial is about to hit the fan!"

In the briefing room Admiral Currie sat waiting, it wasn't long before General Matheson arrived closely followed by Group Captain Young, each with their small entourage of staff officers. "Ok gentlemen here's what we have so far." Currie gave his brief address to the watching and listening heads of staff and asked if anyone could put any meat on the bones of what he had just given them. Group Captain Young coughed, cleared his throat and spoke, "Gentlemen, about two and a half hours ago an analyst spotted something unusual in the Sound of Sleat off the Isle of Skye, we contacted the U.S Navy and asked for a P3 on transit from Patuxent River USA to have a snoop around just to cover our arses, however it looks like the aircraft has picked up something that we're not altogether sure about, that is to say it's not ours it's not American and we don't know who it is down there."

Admiral Currie looked around the table and could see that no one appeared to have a clue about what was going on, "Ok gents, let's just firm up on one or two facts here, am I correct in assuming that it's not one of our subs or some wild card entry thrown in by the French or the Canadians?" The faces stared back blankly at him, clearly no one knew what was in the water off the Isle of Skye. The phone rang, the Secretary for Defence was on the line and after a quick appraisal was up to speed on what was going on. Group Captain Young advised that although there was an American aircraft in the area and it was monitoring the situation, perhaps a suitably equipped Tornado from R.A.F. Lossiemouth should be scrambled, at least then if there was any "dirty" work to be done then if anything was to be blown out of the water the Americans wouldn't get any fingers pointed at them and whatever it was, it was well inside British territorial waters. The Secretary for Defence agreed and left to inform the relevant government personnel, Young left the table to send the message to Lossiemouth, and he imagined that the famous 617 Dam Busters Squadron would be called upon to carry out the mission, an obvious choice given their locality and experience.

At a hurriedly arranged meeting with the Prime Minister, the Secretary of State for Defence advised the Prime Minister of what was ongoing off the Isle of Skye and after a very brief discussion all parties present agreed that they should send the Tornados from Lossiemouth armed with the necessary persuasion. If the Russians or anyone else uninvited was snooping around inside British Territorial waters, the Royal Air Force backed up by the Royal Navy would let them know they weren't welcome.

The signal was sent and Young went to his office to call the Commanding officer at Lossiemouth, the two men were old friends although they flew different types of aircraft,

Young had essentially flown in helicopters, where Gale had been a fast jet pilot. Group Captain Gale, Windy to his staff, was waiting for the call, "Hello Group Captain Young, Gale here, I've received the signal and we have two Tornado crews getting kitted up, two aircraft are being armed, I just wondered if there was any more info, I'm heading to the ops room to brief them personally and head the flight?"

Young spoke and informed Gale that they really had no idea who was out there and that the Orion P3 was on station but was going to need to land very soon as they had no airborne refuelling assets close enough so one of the other crews would need to head out to provide the necessary cover for them.

On board the Orion the crew circled above the Sound of Sleat, the Prowler probe held station in the water sending info back to the crew above. Mclean and the rest of the crew were intrigued, who or what was down there, the R.A.F. would arrive on scene within thirty minutes and then they suspected the sparks would fly, the Royal Navy had also been alerted and amongst several surface ships heading for the Sound of Sleat at full steam they also had H.M.S. Ambush an Astute class attack submarine heading in their direction, ironically she was watching a Russian Klondyker that was hanging around outside British waters like a bad smell, every ship in the area was on alert and heading with purpose for the sea off the Isle of Skye, it was about to become a very busy place.

In the briefing room, which was adjacent to the ops room at R.A.F. Lossiemouth, Windy Gale walked in accompanied by the intelligence officer and the Wing Commander of 617 squadron, waiting in the briefing room were three other aircrew, one pilot and two navigators who also handled the weapons systems. The air crew sat and listened as the Station Commander gave his brief, flying with him was the best navigator in the squadron, Squadron Leader Brearly, nicknamed Amos after the Emmerdale farm character. The other two crew were Ug Urquhart and Joe Slater, they were the last crew to fly a Buccaneer into Lossiemouth when the aircraft retired from service.

"You will head for the Sound of Sleat and liaise with the Orion on station, the Norwegian crew were scrambled some time ago and are almost at the scene and they will take over from the U.S.Navy Orion but for now it looks like someone is snooping about in the waters off the Sound of Sleat and they shouldn't be there." Flying Officer Urquhart, Ug to his friends was flying on the Station Commanders wing and it sounded like it was going to be an interesting morning. Fifteen minutes later the two Tornados sat at the end of the runway, Urquhart and Gale hit full throttle and the afterburners kicked in, it was still dark as the twin blue jet blasts lit up the darkness at the end of the runway as the Two Tornados thundered down the strip and were air born heading for Inverness to the west then a dash through Glen Affric, then it was straight over the hills at Arnisdale and a drop down to sea level and they were in the Sound of Sleat. Both aircraft were armed with Stingray homing torpedoes once programmed capable of following the terrain on the seabed and searching out their targets. The aircraft flew on through the morning darkness, hugging the terrain at two hundred and fifty feet, Urquhart following Gale about three hundred meters behind the lead aircraft, Urquhart spoke to his navigator who was punching in the information into the first of their two Stingray torpedoes. "How's it going back there?" Joe Slater spoke back, her voice was firm and confident, "We're ready to launch as soon as Casper gives us their co-ordinates and that'll be any minute,"

"Good we're just about five minutes out now so get ready for some fun!" The two Tornados pulled hard upwards and crested the top of Ben Sgritheall, clearing it by only fifty feet it was only 0300 hours and the world was still asleep, visibility was good and as the two aircraft dropped down to sea level they passed the two Royal Navy minesweepers the Hurworth and Quorn, steaming at full speed through Kyle Rhea, the headsets crackled and the American accent came through on the frequency, "Tall Boy and Grand Slam this is Casper do you read me over?" Gale, call sign Grand Slam called back, "Casper this is Grand Slam, have you got figures for us?"

"Grand Slam your target is on the sea bed at 52.467'N 6'262W." Gale's navigator returned the call, "Casper this is Grand Slam we have 52.467'N 6'262W,"

Slater called in, "confirming 52.467'N 6'262W from Tall Boy!"

"This is Casper that's confirmed, the target is all yours."

As the two Tornados circled at one hundred feet above the sea the crew of the Antaeus new their time was up, they had sat silent for over an hour hoping that the Americans would give up, maybe think that their Prowler had gone faulty and that they just wouldn't believe there could be a submarine from the Russian Navy so far inside their territorial waters but they were if nothing else, professional and Chief Eadie Mclean was not one for being fooled, Zaitsev looked at his Executive officer who whispered, "If they launch a Stingray torpedo we're finished, they have two minesweepers thirty minutes away which will throw depth charges at us and there is another P3 on route from Lossiemouth now, Norwegian, it's almost here, our friends will not let us go easily my friend." The crew watched on as the sonar confirmed the Tornado aircraft were climbing and levelling off at five hundred feet, Zaitsev looked around his crew, "We can live to fight another day men or, die now and never be heard of again." One junior member of the crew looked at Zaitsev and spoke. "Captain, we are done for anyway we should fight our way out!"

Gale gave the order for Urquhart and Slater call sign Tall Boy to launch the first Stingray torpedo.

Aboard the Orion, a translator signalman gave Mclean a running commentary of what the Russian crew were saying and at that time in one instant, the mood aboard the American aircraft was almost euphoric, in the midst of what was well after the end of the "Cold War" they had flushed out a Russian submarine, spying in British waters.

Yahweh

Zaitsev smiled at the crewman as the sonar operator spoke out, "Captain, we have one Stingray in the water, its propulsion system is initiating!" The Stingray jettisoned its parachute and the prop began turning, the gyroscopic navigation systems began searching as it sped towards its target, five hundred meters away, it was armed and seeking out the Antaeus. Zaitsev could not be responsible for the deaths of thirty men he grabbed the microphone from the radio operator and spoke clearly in excellent English, the crew watched in stunned silence, "Casper 1, this is Antaeus, I present you with the submarine Antaeus and ask you now to detonate your torpedo." Mclean gave out the order clearly and calmly as everyone listened in, "Grand Slam, detonate your torpedo." In the back seat of the Tornado call sign Tall Boy with her finger already on the button Slater pressed down on the switch twice and the Stingray torpedo shut down all systems and simply sank to the bottom, one hundred meters away from the Antaeus, such an expensive piece of hardware would be retrieved later, not destroyed.

Zaitzev stood looking around at his crew who all stared back at him aghast at what had just happened, here they all were aboard the most advanced submarine in the world and about to become prisoners to the British, it was impossible that the most experienced submarine Commander in the Russian Navy could have allowed this to happen but in reality their fate had been sealed by two drunken Mallaig fishermen poaching for razor clams. Zaitzev summoned the executive officer and ordered him to follow him along with the Political officer to his quarters. Once there Zaitzev told the two men of his intention to give the Royal Navy the appearance that the

Andrew Shepherd

Antaeus had been scuttled with him on board and also appearing to have fired its one experimental missile off so as not to fall into enemy hands, they on the other hand would know the truth, that Zaitzev had concealed himself within an escape compartment on top of the missile and he would be picked up at sea by the Russian Navy away from prying eyes and that hopefully the Antaeus would return to its home port virtually by herself, only Zaitzev and the Executive Officer would know exactly what would happen, the crew would be completely unaware of the submarines true fate.

Yahweh

The Tornados soared to five thousand feet and circled above the clouds waiting for further instructions whilst HMS Hurworth and HMS Quorn steamed down the Sound of Sleat, the signals were flying back and forth as the Norwegian P3 Orion, call sign Troll man, flew at ten thousand feet towards what was now the hottest airspace in the world. The Prime minister and all other Cabinet members at the Cobra committee meeting sat at the cabinet table waiting for feedback from the Highlands, the briefing from Group Captain Young had been succinct and to the point, the R.A.F. had discovered something anomalous, the U.S. Navy, in the form of an Orion P3 ASW aircraft had pinpointed it and the R.A.F had been briefed essentially to blow it out of the water using two Tornados from the Dam Busters Squadron, and when the Stingray torpedo went active the Captain of the Russian Submarine had thrown his hands up instantly and now a diplomatic nightmare was about to unfold, none of them was prepared for what they were about to hear from the Secretary of State for Defence.................

"Ladies, gentlemen, we have just heard that a Russian submarine has after encountering some difficulties surrendered to us in the Inner Hebrides waters halfway between the Islands of Coll and Muck we have two minesweepers steaming towards the submarine which is still underwater, but the minesweepers are still in The Sound of Sleat and barely capable of dealing with the situation, our next nearest assets are hours away!"

Stunned silence pervaded throughout the room but only for a few seconds, the Prime Minister spoke, "Ok who the hell is it, I mean are we sure it's the Russians, what is it doing in our waters and what the hell do we do next?" The Foreign Minister spoke, "We know very little at this stage there have been no communications between the Russians and ourselves, the Chinese appear to be asleep or being conspicuously dormant and as for who, what and as for what we do next, we don't know, we don't know and we throw everything we've got in there and surround the bugger and pin him down until we have some more answers!" The Secretary for Defence was next, "We have a submarine, Russian that much we think we know and several aircraft in the area which have essentially flushed it out, the Captain has surrendered, we know not why, we don't know if there are any nuclear issues, reactors missiles or whatever else on-board and we have no idea how on earth this has all happened!"

"Are we certain this thing is Russian?" asked the Prime Minister again.

"Yes Sir," replied the Defence Secretary, the Prime Minister blasted back, "Then waken up our Russian Embassy friends and get Illiev over here now!!"

The Foreign secretary left the Cobra meeting room and as he arrived at his office the staff who were on duty at that time were clearly busy dealing with the influx of telephone calls from the Russian Embassy, the Foreign secretary asked his staff man to call Petre Illiev immediately and invite him over for a face to face talk. When Illievs mobile phone was dialled he answered almost immediately, "Miles, I am on my way I'll be about ten minutes and tell your boss we want a complete press black out, no paparazzi outside when I arrive and please also tell him we have a Klondyker heading from the mid-Atlantic to try and mop this unforeseen, Illiev coughed, problem up." Illiev hung up and gritted his teeth, the bosses in Moscow were incandescent with rage and heading for orbit, how could Zaitsev have been so stupid? They were all asking the same question, what was he playing at?

On board the Antaeus the crew all stood or sat at their stations, they could not believe what their Captain was saying, he was surrendering the vessel, their vessel, to the Royal Navy, he couldn't, even under the circumstances such treachery just wasn't an option and they all, to a man thought exactly the same. Zaitsev spoke quietly to all of the crew, "Gentlemen, I am going to surface and order you all to abandon ship, when everyone has left the ship I will remain on board and scuttle her and by the time she is resting on the bottom there will be absolutely nothing useful for the British or the Americans to salvage." The executive officer spoke, "Sir, you will receive the order of Lenin for this, I will see to it." Zaitsev smiled, he had no intention of getting himself killed or suffering the humiliation of being seen on international television. He gave the order to surface.

The Norwegian Air Force Orion arrived on scene as Casper's crew bugged out heading straight for RAF Lossiemouth to refuel and rest the crew, they were all rather disappointed though, the situation was just getting interesting but the Norwegians would have to stand watch over the unfolding drama now or they were going to fall out of the sky, simple, no fuel, no power they fell out of the sky. All of the data was electronically transferred from Casper to the Norwegian P3 and with a message of good luck, the United States Navy P3 Casper 1 left the area. The crew of Troll man called the RAF Tornados, "Grand Slam and Tall Boy from Troll man, how much loiter time do you have left?" The call came back from Grand Slam, "We have at least another thirty minutes of loiter time but there's a VC10 heading our way to refuel us, they should be on station in about fifteen minutes, we'll be cutting it fine but unfortunately our options are limited.

It was still just dark and as the Antaeus surfaced, the Norwegian P3 swooped low across the water at just one hundred feet, the radio operator on board advised the two RAF crews and Gale gave the order for Tall Boy to remain at five thousand feet and wait for the tanker whilst they would get down to sea level and show face over the Russian submarine. The Norwegians screamed over the Antaeus as the crew launched the life rafts, every camera on board the Norwegian P3 clicked furiously snapping thousands of images of the submarine as she held station in the water and just as the Norwegian anti-submarine aircraft cleared the Antaeus it seemed to the Russian sailors on the topside of their ship that thunder was approaching rapidly, Grand Slam was heading for them at five hundred knots at just fifty feet above the waves, Gale wanted to show the Russian crew the RAF were here in force and meant business, the eighteen sailors all threw themselves on the deck as the Tornado screamed over the top of them pulling up a maelstrom of seawater in its wake as Gale pulled the aircraft into a vertical climb and hit the afterburners directly over the Russian submarine to punch his message home good and proper, above the VC10 was arriving and Tall Boy was beginning his refuelling run, in under a minute Urquhart

Yahweh

and Slater were joined by Gale and Amos. Urquhart asked the Station Commander how his fly by went. "These old tubs are still capable of packing a punch young man and scaring the shit out of the odd Rusky or two yet." The air crackled with laughter. Fifteen minutes later the VC10 had departed and Gale called the Norwegian P3 crew, "Troll man from Grand Slam that's us refuelled and we can hang around for another few hours."

"Roger Grand Slam."

So far any watching eyes would have seen nothing unusual, it was after all one of the busiest air exercise areas in the United Kingdom and it wasn't the first time in recent years that a submarine had surfaced unexpectedly in or around the waters off the Isle of Skye.

Zaitsev stood in the conning tower, just ten feet above the deck and watched his men scrambling for their life rafts, the Russian Navy were sending a spy ship disguised as a Klondyker fishing vessel to rescue the men, they would be afloat in the water north of the Isle of Coll for at least eight hours, they just had to hope that the local ferry ship from Oban wouldn't spot them and alert the Coast Guard, if they did the British had the situation all under control though and the Coast Guard station at Stornoway would be briefed that the RAF were exercising in the area and would transfer the crew from the life rafts to the ocean going fishing vessel. On board the ship the Russian sailors would be tended to by the Doctors on board and thus their escape would be less of an embarrassment to the Russian authorities. Zaitsev saluted to the men in the two life rafts and descended into the Antaeus closing the watertight hatch after him. Once inside the vessel he checked all of the monitors which showed all systems were functioning and then he readied himself for an escape the like of which had never been seen before anywhere in the world. Zaitsev had been made aware when training, before actually taking command of the Antaeus that one of the four mini ballistic "Hammer" missiles on board was actually an escape rocket, the pod on top was just big enough to allow one crew member, him, to essentially scuttle the ship if danger was imminent, if as they were in this case, spying in another countries waters. Zaitzev could launch the escape missile and destroy the ship remotely. He had hoped he'd never have to use the system but this was the moment for sure, he carried on dressing himself in a life support suit, essentially a space suit and with the turn of a key in the control panel and a code punched into the launch control system, he initiated the countdown system that would lead to the destruction of the ships propulsion and control systems, or so he thought and he then made his way forward to the number two tube and entered the escape capsule. After securing the hatch he punched in the code needed to ignite the whole process, he tightened the straps on the seat and prayed he would survive but he knew if he didn't he had destroyed the Antaeus and gone down with his ship, an honourable end to a glorious career.

Above the waves as the Antaeus began to submerge the crew watched on in stunned silence as they floated away from the whirlpools of water left by the submarine as Captain Zaitsev took her down, the Norwegian P3 called out over the radio for the Antaeus to resurface but although Zaitsev could hear the commands he had no intention of doing as he was told, the Norwegian frantically called for guidance from the Royal Air Force command centre, RAF Kinloss were listening in and as Squadron Leader McDonnell and Flight Lieutenants Griffin and Ryan were watching the picture unfold, the Prime Ministers voice boomed over the secure TV link to the command centre, "Expedite."

The message was passed to the Norwegian and to Grand Slam and Tall Boy, the two Tornados began their descent from five thousand feet as Troll man turned around and headed back towards the now submerged Antaeus, they would get the first crack at the submarine. As the rocket motors ignited beneath Zaitsev every system on board the Antaeus clicked the wheels had begun turning and the computer navigation systems began plotting the ships route out, even Zaitsev was not aware of what was going on underneath him. He felt a jolt and suddenly he was being pushed backwards into the seat with great force as the rocket motors propelled him in his escape pod out of the submarines number two tube. The crew looked on as the water erupted about two hundred meters away from them and the Hammer missile cleared the water and shot skywards into the semi darkness, "The Captain has fired a missile at the British!! God save his soul," screamed the executive officer. As the Tornados swooped down the crews watched in horror as they saw what was obviously a missile launch from the submerged submarine, "Holy Fuck!" was all Ug said as Slater armed their only other Stingray torpedo, she also worked furiously at reprogramming the Stingray sitting on the bottom. The Norwegians dropped a storm of depth charges over the last known spot of the Antaeus but her automated navigation systems had taken over and although the crew and Zaitsev believed the ship had self-destructed the Antaeus was heading away from the scene at a depth of forty meters and a speed of fifty knots, her counter measures worked at confusing the Stingray which had woken up again and was searching for the Antaeus, but as she passed through twenty nine knots the force of the water streaming over her hull forced the rubber coating back into place and she became invisible again, she would make her own way home to Severomorsk. The Stingray swam in circles unable to lock onto the escaping submarine.

Zaitsev rode the missile and soared into the stratosphere before the capsule separated from the main body of the missile, now he had to hope that the GPS system would work and the Russian Navy would find him when he landed in the North Atlantic and before he perished. Unfortunately Zaitsev was about to become the first victim of the whole affair and six minutes after leaving the Antaeus he felt the parachute deploy and only hoped he was over international waters. After touching down in the capsule Zaitsev could feel the water beginning to lap up around him and rather than wait to drown he fumbled his way out of the capsule and inflated the life raft and waited to be picked up by the Klondyker which he knew was heading to rescue his crew. Aboard the M.V. Oleg Yeltsin the crew monitored Zaitsevs life support systems and noted his position, he would be picked up within the hour and as long as his suit stayed intact all he would have to worry about would life in the gulags of Siberia from now on.

Yahweh

The Royal Navy minesweepers were ordered to make good speed to the area where the survivors of the Antaeus were and to then head for a meet in the Atlantic Ocean with the Russian Klondyker, way beyond the Outer Hebrides and away from prying eyes, where the crew would be handed over and all on board would be briefed and ordered to never speak about the events of the last few hours.

It never happened.

Petre Iliev was ushered into the Prime Minister's office, the Secretary for Defence was also present, "What the hell is going on Iliev?" asked the Prime Minister, today he was in no mood for ceremony.

"Mr Cameron, firstly on behalf of my Government may I offer our sincerest apologies for this wholly unexpected situation, we had no idea that the crew of the vessel Antaeus had gone rogue and due to the, ehhh, capabilities of the vessel we could not actually locate her for some considerable time." The truth was something Iliev himself didn't quite actually understand, he had not been briefed on the mission the submarine was actually on and he didn't have any real working knowledge of the Russian Navy, powers and pay scales way above his head were at work and he had been briefed to simply apologise and assure the British government that the crew of the rogue submarine were mutineers and that the Russian Navy and Government had no idea of what was going on such was the stealth capabilities of the vessel. He asked the Prime Minister for informal permission for several Russian vessels to enter British waters to retrieve the missile that had been launched as it was simply an escape capsule that may possibly have one man on board, the permission was granted for one week. "Now get out of my office Iliev and go tell your all powerful, over inflated pay scaled Kremlin goofs that Red October is a bloody fantasy and we will find your submarine and if we find your man in his can before you we'll be finding out a lot more!" As soon as Illiev was back in his car he used his secure phone to inform his bosses at home that the U.K. government were allowing the search and recovery of the capsule but the British would obviously be looking for it themselves in the meantime.

The two Tornados loitered for another hour, they still had two Stingray missiles but the on board systems failed to show any targets at all and the torpedoes were shut down. The Norwegian P3 searched for the Antaeus for two more hours but found nothing, the Tornados from Lossiemouth had returned to base and as the sun began to rise the crew of the Antaeus were taken aboard HMS Quorn, the ship then headed for the open ocean to deliver her cargo to the Russians. Everyone aboard the Royal Navy ships were also briefed and ordered never to speak of the events again.

Five miles south west of Berneray the Antaeus began her dive into the abyss still running at fifty knots she was just too fast for anything to capture any sign of her, once she had reached a depth of five hundred meters her speed would be increased to seventy knots at which time she would follow the mid-Atlantic ridge all the way North, if anything out there was capable of picking her up hopefully the information would be dismissed as some kind of seismic activity from the subsea volcanic ridge that was constantly rumbling away beneath the waves.

Yahweh

Within days she would be back in her home port, and berthed within a completely covered and secure dry dock alongside two other vessels of her type under development, ready for her systems to be interrogated and her hull to be inspected by the engineers.

About seventy miles west of the Isle of Barra, Zaitsev was being thrown around rather more than he would have liked but he was still alive, he just had to sit and wait and hopefully he would be picked up by the Russian spy ship soon, then he was aware of lights on the horizon, he watched the lights, clearly a ship and heading for him. An hour later Zaitsev was aboard the Oleg Yeltsin, he was taken to the Captain's cabin. Zaitsev was given a large glass of brandy and a meal, he was then told that his crew were to be picked up shortly, they would be surprised no doubt to discover that their Captain had survived the encounter, none of them were or ever would be aware that the Antaeus was still in one piece, their days as secret submariners was over. Zaitsev was taken to his cabin and told to wait there until the recovery of the crew was complete. Zaitsev knew he would never command a submarine again but at least he was safe and more importantly so were his crew.

Andrew Shepherd

Two months later

Conon was no more than ten minutes into his dive when he saw an unusual shape ahead of him, he wasn't one hundred percent sure but it looked like a boat. He was over unfamiliar ground but he knew of no wrecks in the area, none of the charts showed a wreck of any kind out here, the closer he swam in the light and clear water on the bottom he could see the Worthy beginning to become clearer in his view, quickly he circled the boat and surprisingly, apart from the fact the Worthy was here, there was no gaping hole in her side as had been claimed by Shory and Dougal, Conon tied his bag onto the deck of the boat and started his ascent, Jack and Rex weren't going to believe him, slowly he ascended up the line until he reached the surface, he hoped that the others on the boat would be watching out for him, the biggest problem he had right now was that he was early getting to the surface and if they were keeping an eye out for him they would probably think that he a problem, he didn't. Jack Campbell was hard at work on the old compressor filling bottles for the days diving when old Rex Newlands came out of the wheel house and shouted "I think we've got a problem!" Jack pulled off his ear muffs to hear the old man better & saw him point at the buoy where Conon had surfaced, he was early, way to early he should've been down for at least another twenty minutes. Jack helped Conon on-board which he didn't normally do and he asked the younger man what was wrong, Conon looked at him as he clambered over the side of the dive boat and said, "Get your gear ready you're never going to believe this, I've just found the Worthy!" Old Rex rolled his eyes and said to Jack as he helped Conon over the side of the boat, "He's been smoking that whacky backy again, the Worthy went down miles away from here!"

"I know what you're thinking Rex but I'm telling you I know what I saw down there and you just wait and see! Jack will back me up, now where's my cup of tea you grumpy old fart?"

After a mug of warm tea and a rest and an account of what he had found on the bottom Conon was ready for the water again. It was a bright, late spring day and the water was dormant and calm, almost flat calm. They didn't normally venture this far out of Mallaig but the local hotels were screaming for fresh hand dived clams and the boys aboard The M.V. Poacher were it, they were the only team of divers who would still sell their catch at the back door it was all illegal of course and the fact that Conon was an ex copper made it all the funnier for everyone involved, he'd joined up hastily, lasted two years in the world of policing, it wasn't for him. They dived out of sight of as many prying eyes as possible, then they sold the scallops and with any luck they made a little money, the fact that Conon and Jack were both ex Royal Marines also played a little part in the local fisheries officers being less inclined to bother them. Conon and Jack often did some poaching for salmon as well and it amused them immensely when they read the menus all the local restaurants posted outside their eateries, they would read, "Fresh Poached Salmon" on the dish of the day specials. Conon sat drinking his tea as Jack and Rex listened to his story, they believed him sure enough but they just couldn't put it all together, understand why the wreck Conon appeared to be describing was where he said it was, it should be miles away from the spot they were over. No one had found it yet, not that anyone was really making a concerted effort to find it but then the prawn boats didn't really go near to where Dougal and Shory said the boat went down and for some reason no one ever went near where they were diving today. Dougal and Shorys boat went down about ten miles away or so they said at the time. "I'm telling you both its the Worthy, I've never been surer in my life, ok it's covered in shit and growth but we all know what the boat looked like and there's no gaping hole in the bow like they said there was, it's undamaged, if I didn't know better I'd say it looks like it was pulled down there! You know as well as I do Jack, you've seen enough wrecks in your time and so have you Rex to know when a boats been pulled down or scuttled."

"Well Conon we'll have a better idea of what's happened in a wee while but let's just make sure there's no gaping hole, it'll mean getting inside her and we can check if she's been scuttled as well then and if she has, not another word, we don't even mention it to Shory or Dougal, some other bastard can have that onerous job if they ever find it but we'll stay out of it. It's making me wonder though, if there is no hole and it is the Worthy, why would Dougal and Shory make up such a fantastic story?"

Conon stood nodding his head in complete agreement with the older man.

"Coz no bugger would believe them if it was pulled down there," said Rex, "we all know there's subs down there all the time and it would be easier to believe that they hit a rock somewhere and scrambled ashore and anyways if it was a Royal Navy sub they'd just deny it wouldn't they, so of course shutting their mouths would be less hassle for the two of them. That pair of dopey bastards would just talk themselves into trouble as well no doubt." Conon and Jack laughed at the old man's cynicism, there was as he said submarines exercising in the area regularly but they skilfully avoided the local fishing boats, especially after the sinking of the Antares back in 1990. The likelihood of a Royal Navy submarine being responsible was extremely low.

"Ok Conon I'm ready let's get down for butchers at her." The two men donned their gear, checked each other and in minutes they were clambering over the side of the boat as Rex watched, "Careful down there boys you never know what's going on and if Conon's right that boat shouldn't be there!" The two divers nodded at Rex. The old man watched as the two divers disappeared into the spewm of compressed air bubbles and water, Rex was ex Royal Navy, a diver on a bomb disposal team nearly thirty years ago but he was always suspicious, he'd seen enough in his time to know that darker forces were at work around the inner isles, submarines used the area to train in, even now and every now and then some very out of place vessels turned up to "fish" in the Sound of Sleat.

The two divers descended into the green murky water, the rays of sunshine reflecting off the plankton lead the way downwards, Jack was about two meters under Conon, he turned and looked back as the younger man gave the hand signal for all was ok, Jack returned the signal and both men continued their descent. Slowly they fell towards the sea bed, after a few moments features began to appear on the bottom on which they could focus, their spacial awareness kicked in and both men became completely aware of their surroundings. Conon glanced at his gauges and watch, twenty two meters, he glanced to his left and saw Jack move slowly towards him as he scrunched his shoulders up and showed his open palms to Conon, as if to say, ok where now, Conon pointed over to his right where a rise on the sea floor sat like a huge camel's back and he moved off towards it as Jack followed. As the two men crested over the rise on the sea floor, there in front of them they could be clearly see the lines leading off in the slack water towards the murky shape a further ten meters or so below them of what was unmistakably a small fishing vessel. As the two divers made their way along the ropes which were lying slack in the water and just resting on the bottom, Jack pulled lightly on one of them, the rope rose slightly under tension and Jack started to pull his way along the rope towards the sunken vessel, then he became aware of a sticky feeling on his gloves, he could feel resistance as his gloved hands stopped gliding easily along the rope and as he looked down he could see a black residue on the line but didn't give it another thought. As they went through thirty meters the water darkened visibly but the sunlight was still brilliant enough at that depth for the two men to see clearly all around themselves for about twenty meters. Jack and Conon made their way towards the sunken boat and Jack turned and gave Conon a huge thumbs up as he saw for the first time the name, "Worthy" painted on the back of the sunken wreck, he pointed at the name plate and glanced at Jack, who he could tell was smiling under his mask and mouth piece.

Yahweh

The two men floated and bobbed around the boat for over twenty minutes, there was as Conon had said earlier, absolutely no sign of any holes in the hull of the boat as Dougal and Shory had claimed there was, after they had hit rocks at the north end of the Isle of Eigg after trying to get home drunk. The boat was, apart from the sea weed and rubbish caught in her rigging in near perfect condition but they were about ten miles away from where the boys claimed they had sunk the boat, someone was lying!! Shory and Dougal were drunks yes, but there was no way they would ever have got themselves so badly out of place and why did they say the boat had been holed when it was so obviously sound? It was a mystery but nothing about the boat gave either Jack or Conon any clues. The two divers made their way onto the deck of the boat taking out their knives as they entered into the rigging that was still hanging from the mast, they moved very carefully towards the doorway leading into the wheel house constantly checking each other to ensure neither of them became entangled. Once safely inside the wheel house, Conon stopped at the doorway leading down into the galley and crew bunks area, he shone his torch and looked back at Jack who gave him the thumbs up to let him know it was safe to go further into the bowels of the boat. Conon finned slowly through the enclosed space trying not to stir up any silt that had found its way into the galley, he slowly opened all of the cupboard doors that he could locate and apart from a few fish and crabs there was nothing, absolutely nothing to give them any clues as to why the Worthy lay on the bottom of the ocean floor, there was certainly no signs of any holes in the hull as far as either of the men could tell and both were very experienced divers. Jack signalled to Conon to surface,

Conon acknowledged and both men left the wheel house and once clear of the rigging they checked their gauges before starting the ascent. Then just as Conon turned for a last look at the Worthy, he caught a glint out of the corner of his eye about ten meters off the stern of the boat, he swam quickly towards Jack and caught one of his fins as the other diver started his ascent, Jack turned and Conon pointed at the sea floor, he showed Jack two fingers, Jack understood that Conon had spotted something and he watched as Conon descended back towards the sea floor. Conon could see the object just protruding from the sandy bottom, it was out of place and as he swept his hand over it he saw the chrome outer frame of something circular glint in the faint beam of sunlight, then he could make out the white round face of some kind of disc. Jack watched and then saw Conon pluck something out of the sand and turn towards him and raise his find upwards towards him, showing him, then Conon began to ascend again, whatever it was Conon was clearly excited by his find. Jack waited and as Conon approached him he stretched out his hand and the younger man passed the object to him which fitted into the palm of his gloved hand. Jack opened his hand and examined the object, it was obviously a pressure gauge that had ruptured off the airline it had previously been attached to but more importantly the writing on it was celeric, Russian, both men looked at each other in the water and they both gave each other huge thumbs up signals and they kicked for the surface.

About a hundred and fifty miles away on a remote beach not far from the Butt of Ness on the Isle of Lewis a lone man walked his dog in the early morning sun, in the distance on the shore line he could see some sort of barrel shaped object as he approached it the old man saw there was a panel just big enough for someone to get in and out of, it was definitely a hatch, he'd been in the Royal Navy during the war and it was definitely a hatch but it looked on closer inspection like one of the American space capsules from the Apollo missions only smaller, then as he checked the far side of the strange object he saw strange writing on a small red triangle, he thought it was maybe Russian but he wasn't sure. The tide was going out so it was going nowhere, the old man turned and picked his pace up, the collie dog ran after the ball his master threw. As soon as old Donnie Macleod arrived at the single man Police station at Ness he found Constable McKean in his garden, he explained what he'd found and McKean simply told him to go home and keep it to himself for now but even as the words came out of his mouth McKean knew old Donnie would never shut up after the first dram had gone over his lips. He left his lawnmower where it was and went for the keys of the Land Rover and made his way out to Eoropie Dunes, the "Top Secret" papers mistakenly sent to him weeks ago about Russian ships being in British Territorial waters was beginning to make sense to him now but he'd been told by the Chief Inspector at Stornoway to say nothing and bring the papers to his office where the Chief Inspector would get to the bottom of the strange mail package. McKean realised, this was probably what the Russians were looking for all the time, rather than checking the salinity levels of the sea water and warning about strange coloured lights at strange times of the day and night, he wondered at the time why on earth the British would let the Russians that close to the U.K. coast when they could easily do the research for themselves, oh well hopefully it would be a straight forward found property exercise he laughed to himself, he really wanted nothing to do with anything so apparently cloak and dagger like. As soon as McKean arrived at the beach he quickly inspected the capsule and called Stornoway Police station on his radio, he asked for the Chief Inspector to be patched through to him on point to point so no one else could hear the conversation. The Chief Inspector ordered him to cordon off the beach and not let anyone within two miles of the place, he'd send assistance from Stornoway and he was told that under no circumstances were any photos to be taken of the object.

Two hours later a Chinook helicopter was on its way to Eoropie Dunes with a full complement of SBS swimmer canoeists on board. The men were the most trusted of all British Special forces, they would all do their jobs and say nothing. Four hours after old Donnie had told McKean about the find the Chinook touched down and the team of men immediately began the task of recovering the capsule, it would be taken to Boscombe Down for inspection by the Royal Air Force boffins. The police were told it was an old mine that had probably been lost overboard from a Russian Naval ship. The capsule was quickly and out of the sight of Constable McKean and the other police officers present, loaded into the back of the Chinook helicopter, the beach around the area where the capsule had lain was primed with enough explosives to start a small war and the man in charge fired the switch. Three miles away the windows rattled in old Donnie's house, he thought nothing of it and carried on with his cup of tea, which was fortified with a large tot of rum.

Yahweh

The man in charge looked at McKean, "New chap on the explosives, didn't quite get the required amount right Constable." McKean smiled. The demolition team gathered their equipment up and as the Officer in charge said his farewells to the local Police officers and thanked them for their help McKean watched from a distance as he saw four men run up the ramp of the Chinook helicopter, he couldn't make it out clearly but it certainly looked like the capsule inside the helicopter, it was though none of his business now, as long as it was off his beach and away from prying eyes he didn't care two hoots where they took it or what they did with it, McKean just wanted a quiet life. The Special Boat Squadron officer in charge just said, "Some sneaky beaky equipment old boy, hush hush stuff best not discuss it with anyone." The man who appeared to be in charge shook McKean's hand and wished him good luck then ran towards the Chinook that was winding up its huge rotor blades and within two minutes they had gone, the stiff breeze drowning out the sound of the blades thudding through the air. McKean walked towards the beach and shouted at his colleagues to wait until he checked all was well, he mused to himself that the guy who appeared to be in charge from the EOD team hadn't even said it was safe to remove the cordon or anything for that matter about local safety. McKean cleared the top of the dunes and looked down at the sand where the capsule had washed up, there wasn't a damn thing left but a hole in the sand that the tide was already beginning to wash over, six hours from now no one would ever know what had happened there and already the Chinook was out of sight and not a sound could be heard above the breeze.

Aboard the Chinook the team went about covering up and securing the capsule to the pallet they had strapped it to, Cooper the man in charge as well as the others on the team knew they had found the missing Russian capsule and now all they had to do was get it to Boscombe Down where it would be handed over to the R.A.F. boffins for a much more detailed inspection.

Rex watched as the two men surfaced, he wasn't happy, he didn't like what Conon had told them earlier and yes he liked his rum and he ranted on about strange goings on out in the Sound but no one ever listened to him so he said nothing. The two men, ex Royal Marines descended down into the murky, dark water but even Rex knew Royal Marines weren't bullet proof, for the next half hour he sat and kept an eye on the buoy and sipped on his hip flask of rum and as the time was about up for Conon and Jack's dive he put the kettle on. Five minutes after the kettle had boiled Jack and Conon clambered aboard the Poacher and took their gear off and sat down as Rex handed each of them a mug of hot tea, the two men were staring at the object in Conon's hand, "What's that you got there Conon?" asked Rex. Jack looked up at Rex and said, "Time for us to fuck off out of here Rex and for me to make a couple of phone calls when we get back, it's a pressure gauge off a dive set but it's Russian! Special Forces!" The old man heard what Jack said but didn't want to believe his ears, he turned back into the wheel house and fired the old boat up, muttering to himself about, no good coming of all this nonsense, Conon on the other hand heard exactly what Jack had said and wondered what he meant by "phone calls" he suspected Jack was a bit more than just a booty in the Corps but he never asked and Jack never gave any more away, Conon never told the truth about his own past in the Marines, no one needed to know and the chances of anyone from the past catching up with him were at best slight, or at least that was the case until about an hour ago and Conon knew depending on who Jack was calling his hiding place was about to be uncovered, the truth though was, they knew where he was all along and they were watching him, closer than he realised. Rex fired the engine up and they turned and set sail for Mallaig, an hour away. As they steamed back to Mallaig they watched as they saw several local fishing boats working away plying their trade, some trawling for scallops, some trawling for prawns, the best of West Coast of Scotland langoustine. Rex kept an eye on what was about him he didn't want to get in anyone's way, the boys on the trawlers put up with them and left the really shallow clams to him and his divers, everybody had to make a living after all and it was no use falling out with anybody over a few bags of clams.

About a mile away the fishing boat Plentiful was finished for the day and crew had stowed all the gear and were starting the process of tailing some of the prawns on the way back to the harbour, one of the crew was down below making a cup of coffee for the rest of his crew mates. Aeric Ubych was a crewman aboard the Plentiful, he'd arrived in Mallaig about a month ago, spoke good English and worked hard, he always went for a few beers in the Marine Bar when the boat tied up and said nothing to any one unless he was spoken to and it was fair to say he was liked. Aeric had found a cheap flat to rent in East Bay at Mallaig, it overlooked the harbour and he didn't draw attention to himself, it was just as is handler had briefed him and it was just as they liked it. About two months ago something had happened in the Sound of Sleat, he didn't know what and he didn't ask, it wasn't in his brief, he was, for the time being just a low level listener, he wasn't the sort of spy you read about in James Bond novels, he was put to Mallaig to listen, that was al, he was told if anything of interest came out of the woodwork, the village was so small he would hear about it very quickly. Kyle McGavin was the

Yahweh

skipper of the Plentiful he could see the Poacher cruising slowly back towards Mallaig about a mile off his starboard side then the radio crackled into life, "Aye McGavin you listening boy?" Kyle spoke back to old Rex on the radio, "Hey dad, how's business today? Kyle for some reason always called old Rex Dad, it caused much hilarity over the years, "You guys are heading in early is everything ok?" Aeric appeared at Kyle's side and tapped his shoulder with a mug of tea. "No nothing wrong, Conon found something interesting today so we're just heading in early to check it out, Jack wants to make a couple of calls, we'll see you ashore."

"Aye cheers dad, see you in the Marine in an hour."

Aeric had overheard that the two divers on Rex's boat, who he knew dived for scallops and were both ex Royal Marines Commandos had found something interesting, he wondered what it could be and Jack, the older of the two men wanted to make some calls, who to? It sounded just like the kind of information his handlers were looking for from him. Aeric made a mental note of where old Rex's boat was, she was close to the "Twin Peaks" feature, that was the direction she was travelling from and he went back to the deck to carry on stowing the gear for arrival at Mallaig and to make a further note of landmarks, he wanted to be sure the information he gave his handler was good quality. Aeric didn't mind working in Scotland, the people were nice, friendly and very hospitable but there were other more desirable places he could be posted to, this might be his ticket to one of those places he thought.

Jack sat looking at the depth gauge in his hand and wished they hadn't found it, he had been asked quietly to keep an eye on Conon days after he arrived in Mallaig and he knew now through no fault of his own, very soon life would get very awkward for him and Rex and probably more so for Conon. Jack and Conon sat and watched a Royal Air Force Chinook fly overhead going south, the Royal Air Force trained in the Highlands all the time with the giant helicopters, it was impressive but not an unusual sight. Once ashore Rex went straight to the Marine Bar with some scallops for the owner and the first of many dark rums was put on the bar for him, it was mid-day on Friday afternoon and Rex was the only customer in. Jack and Conon were still on board and were talking about the find. Jack wanted to speak to a few old contacts about the find but he knew Conon was suspicious and wanted to say nothing about it to anyone,

"Jack it's Russian and that boat was pulled down, you know it was, I know it was, there's no way that gauge just coincidentally landed there. You must know there's something dodgy going on and I'd rather not have anything to do with the calls to the Royal Marines, it's not smart to go poking our noses in!"

"I know Conon but at least let me make a couple of calls and we need to decide if we tell the fisheries guys about the wreck or shut up and we really need to speak to Dougal and Shory as well, if they have got any crack about it that they haven't been telling anyone then they fucking sure as hell will now! Yes, you know as well as I do there's always dodgy shit going on about here, the Royal Navy have subs in and out of here all the time and they say fuck all, you can hear them when you're down there if they pass close enough, chances are it was one of ours that pulled the Worthy to the bottom and that pair of idiots were probably so pissed they wouldn't have known what was going on." Conon agreed to say nothing to the fisheries guys or to Dougal and Shory for now and the two men left the boat, Jack told Conon he was off to phone one of his old mates at Royal Marines Poole, Conon didn't ask any more questions, he knew how they operated and suspected lots of awkward questions in the days ahead if the Marines showed any interest in what Jack had to say. He just wanted to avoid all contact with them at all costs, they after all had discarded him and he was in no rush to help them out on some wild goose chase.

Jack arrived home and checked around the house first before making his phone call, he wanted to be sure no one else was at home, he made the call and he talked with his friend, he explained all about the boat going down and how it was supposedly ten miles away from its last known position and how they'd stumbled upon it and how they'd found a Russian divers Invicta depth gauge, Jack was simply asked to keep everything very quiet for now and to make sure that no harm came to Conon, watch his back so to speak. The man at Poole spoke quietly, the line was secure, he asked Jack how long he'd been inactive although he already knew the answer, Jack replied, "About seven years," the man on the other end of the phone simply said, "You do know about Yahweh and how you were put where you are to keep your ears to the ground for anything that could be of use Jack." Jack knew exactly what it meant and repeated the word down the telephone line, "Yahweh, yes I understand completely." The Major on the other end of the phone explained to Jack that his remit, which up until now was to keep an eye out for Conon Bridge and any unusual boats snooping around the Isle of Skye where the Special Boat Squadron trialled a lot of new equipment and where they did a lot of training, had just got much more complicated. The Major further explained he knew who Jack dived with and Conon may have believed he was off the reservation but the bottom line was a man with his skills and language expertise was just too valuable to be allowed to disappear, the Ministry of Defence had invested hugely in him so that if the time ever came, they knew they had just who they'd need for the specific job that Conon and a few others were capable of taking on, the implant inserted in a filling in one of his molars had given his position away on an almost daily basis, or so they thought. Both men ended the telephone call but Jack knew the watch over Conon was nearly at an end and Conon was about to be reactivated, whether he liked it or not. The man at Poole left his office.

Jack sat down at his living room window which overlooked the sound of Sleat, ironically there was a Chinook helicopter hovering out around the mid channel and he watched through a set of high magnification Zeiss binoculars as a dive team dropped from the massive helicopter and after it had flown off the modern rigid raiders appeared, powered by jet engines, the Corps were so much more high tech nowadays it was scary. Jack watched as the team were scooped up and sat aboard the craft, it was a very slick operation, in daylight at least, he imagined for the guys in the team that had little or no experience a night time lift would be a totally different exercise. He wondered what the outcome of his call to Munro at Poole would bring, he knew that "YAHWEH" had something to do with the Chinese and that there were actually several different interpretations for the actual word, the main one being, "Devine Warrior" but he knew the British Government were spying on the Chinese who were rapidly catching up in the arms technology race and in lots of cases they had overtaken the Americans, which didn't best please the allies. It wasn't broadcast openly but it was a well-known fact in military circles that the British were also spying on the Americans as well as the Chinese and the Russians amongst others but then, so were the French, the Germans and the joke was that Royal Navy submarines spent more time off the Eastern seaboard of the United States than they did it the Barents or North Atlantic Oceans. They were all trying to get one up or over on each other and from time to time American, Los Angeles class submarines would have mid water collisions with Russian, British and Chinese submarines, the press was when required, drip fed on stories of, "Navigation training exercises gone wrong, or had run into difficulties," people in the know knew fine that H.M.S. Astute had been trying to avoid hitting an unidentified submarine in the Inner Sound off Kyleakin in 2010 but what the Royal Navy weren't telling anyone was they suspected it was a Russian Navy submarine and not a United States Navy submarine as some suspected. And so the games of cat and mouse under the oceans of the world continued. The country who could develop a super stealth submarine would have a huge advantage.

Major Ben Munro R.M. made his way to the ops and Intel room, several signallers and three of his team were sitting in the intelligence cell watching Sky News, CNN,

Al Jazeera, anything that would give them a heads up something was kicking off somewhere, they had men and women on the ground all over the world but the press still got there first sometimes so it paid to watch the news. In a world scrutinised and relayed by the media in real time, nothing was sacred to the press, they were like fleas on a dog, unavoidable, you couldn't see them all the time but they were there and once one appeared unless you dealt with it robustly and got rid of it they spread. The three man team were simply sitting and waiting, none of the men within room stood up but politely acknowledged Munro, they were all equals and only when there was a need to was rank given the outward show of respect it deserved, Munro made his way into his office and closed the door.

The three man team all looked at each other nothing was being highlighted or came to anyone's attention on any of the major news channels that warranted any excitement for them but Munro turning up and shutting his office door; that was not normal at all. The three men knew something was on and the adrenalin began to course through all of them, they were all Special Boat Squadron men, hardened swimmer canoeists, all were veterans of several tours in Afghanistan and anywhere else in the world where there were troubles, British or not, the UK government sent them anywhere to gain experience and train hard, very hard. Donnie was the first to speak,

"Tenner says we're off somewhere fucking cold!" The man next to him Scouse Mcleas laughed back at him,

"Nah we're heading for Afreeeka maaan dem boys in Somalia are fuckin about too much they needs them ass's kicken maaan!" The scoucers attempts at a Jamaican accent were woeful. The third man Mack, lifted his head and added his tupensworth, "I reckon we're heading for closer to home girls, much closer to home." Donnie was the sniper, Scouse was the communications expert, Mack was the explosives and paramedic man, Munro the boss, as he was called, did all the rest.

"Why the fuck do you reckon we're heading for close to home Mack?" asked Donnie,

"Well there's fuck all going on anywhere else and no one is sticking their head above the parapets anywhere so it smacks of being so quiet that the old man is on the blower to Northwood right now speaking to the knobs underground about something very, very hush hush." The other two men looked at each other and wiggled their fingers under their chins and squealed, "OOOOOO very, very hush hush," the room filled with laughter.

Munro could hear the laughter from the team room and tried to ignore it as he was transferred to the Head of Operations office at Northwood and knew the boys were second guessing what was going on, he waited to be connected to Air vice Marshall Young's phone. The voice came through, loud and clear, "Good evening Major Munro, I gather you have something urgent for me?"

"Yes sir an old colleague who is aware of the code word YAHWEH has contacted me." There was a pregnant pause as Young tried to take in the seriousness of the seemingly innocuous comment that had just been made and he asked Major Munro one question, "Where is your man?"

"Mallaig Sir, North west Scotland." Young knew where Mallaig was and simply told Munro to get the ball rolling at his end and wait for further instructions.

Conon pulled the laces tight in his trainers and put the key under the door mat as usual then he picked it up again and looked about, there was no one about but he didn't have a good feeling about what was going on and as he stuck the key in his jacket pocket he pondered whether or not leaving the area might be a good idea, he'd get work and he'd get by but he liked it here, he closed the door and began his long run out onto the moor and to the foot path, which although boggy took you all the way out to Loch Morar where he played and learned his skills as a young boy taught by his grandfather, it took a good hour and it always cleared his head, this time his mind raced about what was going on, would he be further embroiled in some stupid plot over which he would have little or no control over or would he never hear another word about it all, god, who knew. He switched on his iPod and started his run, uphill and out of the village away from everyone, prying eyes and gossips, he kept himself very much to himself.

Yahweh

Munro, made two further phone calls, one to the Head of Special Forces Operations at Whitehall, he spoke directly to General Angus who was going to brief the Ministry of Defence members who needed to be briefed, he was told two men, both ex Royal Marines had whilst diving in the Sound of Sleat off the Isle of Skye, found a Russian Special Forces diving gauge, it was what they had been looking for, a clue as to the where about of the Antaeus, it had been on the agenda for some time but despite their best and most discrete efforts there was no trace, no trace of the submarine at all. The only clue they had was some kind of missile launch at the time of the apparent ships scuttling, the missile had landed in the North Atlantic after separating from the forward section or had it fragmented? The debris had landed in one of the deepest parts of the ocean and so unless luck gave them any clues the remains of the missile would lay where they had fallen for ever. They were almost caught out some years ago when testing one of their escape systems in the area close to Ullapool, several people, gamekeepers, coast guard crew on one of their cutters and a local crofter had all reported a strange light in the sky over Loch Broom. The Ministry of Defence had been contacted but conveniently brushed the incident under the carpet to spare their blushes, luckily the Police officer who took the calls chose not to make any enquiries that would cause embarrassment, he had simply let the incident be buried.

And the two men, it appeared from early indications that one of them was a sleeper or at least in hiding, the other was a watcher, no particular brief, just a safe pair of hands with open eyes and listening ears, watching for anything out of the ordinary and listening for the same.

The second call was to Porton Down, to the head of a small team of men, led by Professor Smith, Head of Research at Porton Down, he had for several years been monitoring a small team of men, ex armed forces, all of whom had been singled out as assets with specific qualities that if required could one day be put to use as covert operatives for the most dangerous and extreme of specialist operations. They were individuals who had no families, they were the fittest of the British Forces and all were expendable, operatives who not so long ago had each and every one of them disgraced themselves in some way and after being quietly discharged from the services of their country, were asked to volunteer for a second chance to redeem themselves, it may take a long time for their country to call on them again and for some the call may never come but if they were needed they each understood after undergoing certain tests at Porton Down, the results of which they would not be completely aware of, they would be called upon, unfortunately part of the procedures meant none of the subjects used for the experiment would know that almost complete memory loss was a distinct and highly likely possibility.

As Munro made his second phone call which was directly sanctioned by Major General Kyle, he had no idea who he was speaking to or what the person on the other end of the phone did but he simply said the word, "Yahweh" to the male voice who answered the phone and hung up. Even Munro had never been involved in anything quite so apparently farfetched and that was saying something. The man who he had been speaking to was the Head of Research at Porton Down Chemical and Medical Research Branch, only officially the department didn't exist. For the last ten years or so everything had gone very quietly, very smoothly, the team just monitored the seven subjects they had experimented with, some years previously and waited for the moment when they would be called upon to take this particular technology to the next level, only then would they know if the microchips, implanted into the adrenal glands of the seven volunteers would work. And so Professor Smith excused himself from dinner and told his wife he would be late as something had come up at work, she didn't ask any questions as this sort of thing happened from time to time and she simply saw her husband out of the house and returned to the dinner table. Professor Smith drove to the office he had worked in for the last twenty years and as soon as he logged onto his computer he was able to tell in an instant that the operative who had been out of active service for just over five years was Conon Bridge, the Professor smiled to himself, he wondered how co-operative, Bridge would be when the team eventually met up with him again, it had been a long time. He remembered Bridge was one of the more thoughtful of the subjects he'd been fortunate to work with and he was in a lot of ways grateful that it was Conon Bridge who would be the first to have the opportunity to see if the experiment had been a success. Professor Smith called his assistant Doctor Pedro Silva, after a very quick call Silva was on his way and by the time he reached the office Smith had taken a further two calls and found out that their transport, a helicopter from Royal Marines Poole was already on route.

At Poole Munro had briefed his men in the ops room and was able to tell them that they were going to carry out some dives on a sunken boat that had disappeared some months ago off the west coast of Scotland, near the Isle of Skye and that one of the divers who had located the wreck was one of their own, Conon Bridge. Munro also told his team they would be calling in at Porton Down on the way North to uplift a couple of very important persons. The guys had all heard of Bridge before, he was the guy who had gone AWOL from a hide in the foothills of the Tora Bora region of Eastern Afghanistan about ten years ago, he had apparently suffered a complete breakdown and went on a single handed rampage killing fourteen Al-Qaeda operatives as they emerged from one of the cave complexes armed to the teeth, ready to ambush an American Marine foot patrol searching the area for Osama Bin Laden. Unfortunately at the time the Americans were totally unaware the British were operating in the area and it caused a real problem with the American Military hierarchy, they were desperate for Bin Laden's head after all. Bridge had been hurriedly flown out of Afghanistan and was taken to a hospital for the mentally ill, where he was held for a few more years, at the behest of the Americans to appease them and then he just seemed to disappear according to records. Munro, Donnie, Scouse and Mack all sat in the helicopter and began checking the gear as it flew northwards heading first of all for Porton Down.

The helicopter arrived at Porton Down and Munro marshalled the waiting men, Smith and Silva towards the open door, inside the helicopter the rest of the team having finished checking their gear tried to get some shut eye, Munro had told them what was going to happen, they would fly north and refuel at the Royal Naval station at Prestwick, HMS Gannet, from there after Munro had spoken to the man keeping an eye on things in Mallaig, they would fly out to Ardentigh, the owner was friendly and they would be well away from prying eyes.

The phone rang in Jack's house, he answered it and Munro spoke, "Hello Jack its Munro here, are you well?

"Hello, yes all's well, are you on your way?"

"Yes we're well on our way now but we need to chat, we were thinking about meeting up for a meal tomorrow." Jack acknowledged the invitation and asked the Royal Marines officer what time he should arrange the meal for, "About 1900 hours should do it, and make sure Conon is with you, I'll have some friends I'd like to introduce him to."

"We'll meet you off the pontoon, we'll see you then." Both men hung up, Jack sat and stared at his phone, he knew something was way wrong with what was going on and obviously he liked Conon but feared the meeting may not go well. He knew he had to be there but he'd far rather he didn't have to be.

The Sikorsky S92 helicopter flew on through the night, it was the same aircraft operated by the Coast guard but the one they all flew in was inconspicuously painted and looked like it was just some other civvie chopper, although this one was extensively modified to run nearly silently by comparison. The crew had set their course to arrive at Mallaig about 0200 hours and from there it was a quick five minute detour up Loch Nevis to the outdoor centre at Ardintigh, the facilities were basic but all of the team had visited the place at least twice before for basic selection courses and escape and evasion exercises, the owner was ex SAS, one quick call to him and no one would bother them for a few days at least, maybe the odd hill walker or shepherd out searching for sheep, they popped in for a brew now and again but generally as it was so remote no one really visited the place. Ardentigh was not officially the reserve of the British armed forces but it was the next best thing. At 0210 hours the helicopter touched down and the team decamped and quickly cleared the downwash from the S92, they huddled over their kit as the chopper took off again and disappeared into the darkness and breeze which woke everyone up. The men gathered their kit and headed for the main galley where the kettle was turned on and they sat and listened to Professor Smith as he lead them through the plan after a potted history about the work he and his team had developed and how the man they were all going to meet tomorrow was probably the most promising of the guinea pigs but potentially the hardest to re-harness so to speak. The four Special Boat Squadron men sat and listened, they all knew that Conon Bridge had gone off the rails during operations in the Tora Bora mountains over ten years ago, or at least that was the official line on the story; and his prowess within the elite SBS was something of legend, each of the team all entertained the idea of slaughtering several Talibanis in an ambush but to walk out of an observation post in the middle of the night and take on fourteen armed to the teeth Talibanis himself was an awesome feat, so much so the rumour was that the Taliban had put a price of $1.000.000.00 on his head, they didn't know it at the time but it had really pissed Bridge off that the price on him wasn't in pounds sterling. Smith continued and told the team how there was a special interest in Bridge because he had managed even after a relatively short time away from Porton Down to periodically vanish although he shouldn't have been able to and he was clearly resourceful enough to never have used identifiable bank accounts or anything obvious that would give his identity away, he simply drifted away from what he knew and started a new life, it would appear in Mallaig in the north west Highlands of Scotland. Strangely though, just now and again Conon would slip the net and appear in places when the team watching him just didn't expect it.

Smith was careful to tell the Marines that he only wished to do some catch up work with Bridge but the four men were not stupid, they knew there had to be a hidden agenda but they all knew that it was none of their business and it wasn't in their remit to ask any questions about what happened to the guy next, once they had snatched him and taken him back to Ardentigh for the good doctors to do their magic, their job was done. The truth was actually well outside Professor Smith and Doctor Silvas remit also but that wasn't their concern, they were briefed to deal with Bridge, now that they knew where he was and get him to volunteer to come back into the fold, they were paid for by the British governments black ops budget which officially didn't exist, they never asked questions, it just wasn't their concern. They would all head to Mallaig tomorrow evening, Tuesday, it would be quiet, they would meet with Bridge and Campbell, also an ex-Marine and Smith, Silva and Munro would have a meal with the two men, drug Bridge and the other three would be tasked with getting him out of the bar, onto the rib boat and back to Ardentigh. The Professor commented, "Nothing could be simpler gentlemen." Smith and Silva bid the Marines goodnight and left the galley hut and went to their beds in a bothy hut nearby.

"I fucking hate it when some shiny arse says shit like, "nothing could be simpler!" Sure as shit stinks something will go fucking wrong, it all sounds way too straight forward." Donnie wasn't happy but the others looked at Munro who just said, "We're all tired guys, let's get some kip and see what the morning brings, it does sound as if our role here is pretty straight forward." The four Marines got up and went to their beds, they all slept well.

The following morning Jack phoned Conon, "Hi Con, some guys who are friends of ours have come up for a few days on the strength of that phone call I made, they want to meet us in the Marine Bar about 1900 for a meal and a chat, they're paying, what do you say?"

"Not a fucking chance Jack, men from the dark side appearing from where, wanting to have meal and a chat, you're on your own bud, count me out." Jack wasn't happy anyway, he'd smelled a rat when he spoke to Munro the day before but he knew there was something far more important than just a meal and a chat involved and he knew that if he ever heard certain words in certain contexts then personal friendships were put to one side, it was the life he chose, no matter how much he liked Conon he had to get him to that meeting. "Con, listen mate, I know you don't want to have anything to do with these guys, I know they fucked you over and binned you but they're talking big bucks to show them the wreck site, to get their hands on the pressure gauge, even if you don't need the money, come on, what have you got to lose?" Conon listened, the silence was deafening, "They want to shut us the fuck up Jack because you know as well as I do that gauge is Russian Special Forces issue and what the fuck was it doing on the sea bed off Eigg? I was happy to say fuck all any way, you made the phone call, you enjoy the dinner, you can have the bounty and just tell them I signed the Official Secrets Act the day I joined the Corps. I'm not interested and that's my final offer." Conon laughed as he listened to Jack, "Con, please, I wouldn't ask you like this but we're a team mate and I'd prefer you there to keep an eye on my back, come on man just sit and eat and say fuck all if you want but do it for me and whether you go or not half the dosh is yours." Conon hated refusing Jack, "Ok, but the split second I smell a rat, I'll be getting out of the place, by whatever means I have to use!"

"Good man, I'll pick you up about 1830 shipmate." The two men hung up, Scouse, pulled his head phones off and from the side of the galley hut told Munro and the others the meet for tonight was on.

Jack and Conon walked into the Marine bar and were greeted by the grand total of three revellers, Shory and Dougal, the two guys who owned the boat they'd found and who didn't know it had been found yet and Aeric Lenz, a Polish guy who turned up a couple of months ago and worked on young Rexs boat. Jesus, Conon thought to himself, if it wasn't dodgy enough meeting spooks from the dark side, Shory and Dougal were here too, "Easy Conon, they know fuck all about this." Jack sensed Conon's unease, he bought a coke for himself and a fresh orange and lemonade for Conon and they sat down near the door. Conon sat so he could see who was coming and going. About ten minutes later Conon saw the six men arrive outside the bar they were all fit, three younger guys in their twenties and without a shadow of a doubt, squaddies, there were three older men with them, Conon went to get out of his seat, Jack put his hand on the younger man's forearm, "Easy tiger, let's just wait and see what the story is and then if you still feel the same I'll back you all the way." Outside Smith and Silva nodded towards the four Marines and walked passed them and into the bar, Conon was mildly surprised but still nervous, the first guy that walked into the bar was vaguely familiar but he couldn't think why, he was probably some birdwatcher that had been in the village sometime before and Conon knew he had a fantastic memory for faces in particular but he wasn't sure about this man and in that instant his defences kicked in again, he didn't know the man, neither of the men and he had to remember why he was here with Jack. Munro, Scouse, Donnie and Mack all walked in and sat down at the bar, Conon got it, they were the muscle and the other two were the brains, he recognised Munro instantly. Munro bought a round and walked over to the table where Jack and Conon sat, he stuck his hand out, "Jack, long time how are you?" Jack half stood up, shook Munro's hand and replied, "I'm well, and life's good, can't complain Munro. So let me introduce Conon Bridge." Conon didn't get up, he shook Munro's hand, "We've known each other a very long time Conon, I'm honoured, you're a legend in the Corps now, you look like you've kept yourself in good shape."

"Thanks, it pays to stay sharp sometimes, you're not looking so shabby yourself." Conon glanced at the three men over Munros shoulder and looked at Munro straight in the eye. "Muck me about and I'll demolish the lot of you." Munro cleared his throat and told Conon they were here to dive on the wreck, check out the dive gauge, there was no hidden agenda, nothing else to it. Conon didn't like it or believe it but he settled into his seat as Munro beckoned Smith and Silva over, the five men sat down together. Munro introduced Smith and Silva, they looked at the menus, all but Conon, he wasn't eating. "So Conon have you lived here long?" asked Smith. Conon heard the words but they weren't computing and just then he saw Munro move his hand and then he knew that he was about to be done over, it was a strangely amateurish attempt, he saw the tablet in Munros fingers and before Munro had even realised and thought to look up he was being propelled backwards with a force unleashed by Conon's hands and feet that he had never felt before, the other three men leapt from their bar stools but their attempts to overpower Conon were pointless within fifteen seconds the four Marines were crushed, Jack grabbed the two scientists and dragged them outside, "I suggest we get the fuck out of here quickly gents," the three men staggered passed the melee and watched in horror as Conon Bridge literally walked through the Marines and left them and the bar in a mess, he singlehandedly wrecked the bar, Munro lay on the floor flat on his back, Scouse and Donnie were either side of a pool table and Mack was somewhere behind the bar, all four were unconscious. As Conon left he threw a wad of twenty pound notes on the bar and shouted at the barman he'd pay for any damage as he walked quickly through the door and out onto the street. As Conon walked along the pavement away from the bar, he felt the sharp searing pain in the back of his neck, he saw the ground rush up at him and his head was beginning to spin, he was losing control, his balance had gone, he tried to make sense of it and stabilise, but none of the goons in the bar got a slap at him so why had the ground rushed up at him so quickly, he tried to roll over and push himself up but as he looked up he saw Jack!! Jack was standing over him, he saw Jack's hands reach out to grab him and thought he was going to help him up and then his world turned completely upsides down as he heard Jack say sorry, "Sorry Conon," and he watched in disbelief as the older ex-Marine punched him square on the jaw and knocked him out cold.

Yahweh

Mack came round first and after quickly assessing the scene in the bar, he realised he'd only been out cold for about a minute, the two drunks in the corner were scratching their heads like a scene from a Laurel and Hardy movie, the others were all beginning to move and the groaning was getting louder, Mack realised there was a third guy in the bar moments ago but he had gone, he'd probably shit himself and legged it. Munro pushed himself to his feet as Smith crashed through the door, "You guys better get outside quick." As Munro pushed out through the door he saw Jack standing over the limp frame of Conon Bridge who was apparently unconscious, Munro was joined by the others who quickly scooped Conon up, they used tie wraps to secure his hands and feet and started along the roadway towards the pontoons where their rib was berthed, the unconscious man was heavy but between them they managed the couple of hundred meters in quick time, Smith and Silva actually struggled to keep up, Jack jogged along at the rear keeping an eye out for any nosey bastards. At the boat Silva gave Conon a quick check over, he was still breathing and had a good pulse, Smith readied the injection which would put Conon to sleep for a few more hours and then gave Silva the nod as the Marines made sure Conon was secure. Silva wafted the smelling salts under the unconscious man's nose and within a second Conon was kicking and lashing out with all he had but he quickly realised it was pointless, Smith loomed over him, "Try not to struggle Conon it'll be much easier for everybody if you try to relax." Smith scratched Conon's arm with the needle, Conon growled as he felt the needle being pushed into his arm. All he heard was Smith saying, "You're going to help us Conon that's all, just help us." As he drifted off all Conon could muster was a very slurred, "Fuck youuuuu."

The four Marines man handled Conon onto the rib and tied him securely to one of the seats and strapped themselves in, Smith and Silva were already in place ready to leave Mallaig as quickly as possible, Munro beckoned to Jack to speak to him over the gurgling of the two huge outboard engines, "Keep an eye out for anything out of the ordinary Jack, you know what I mean, I don't need to teach to how to suck eggs!" "No problem, when he comes round tell him I'm sorry, I doubt I'll be seeing him myself for a while?"

"If all goes to plan, probably not Jack but he'll need somewhere to come back to." Jack threw the lines onto the rib and cast them off, he watched as Donnie throttled the rib to a quick idle, the boat cleared the end of the pontoon in about five seconds and as soon as the boat was clear Donnie looked over his shoulder and rammed the throttle fully forwards and the rib seemed to almost launch itself out of the water as both 200 hp outboards propelled the boat onto her plain and before they were passing the end of the inner harbour they were doing over fifty five knots and skimming along on the near flat calm waters, they disappeared into the darkness, Jack shivered and turned to walk home, he wasn't happy at all.

A short distance away unnoticed in the shadows of the old fish market Aeric Ubych had watched the whole series of events unfold and he knew it was what he had been waiting for, he waited until he was sure Jack had driven away in his car and he quietly walked out of the shadows and home to his flat. Once inside he lifted a small corner of carpet and removed a floor board and reached into the void for his satellite phone, it was secure and had only one function. He dialled the memorised number and a woman spoke, "Yes what is it?" Aeric explained exactly what had happened. The two local divers, both ex Royal Marines Commandos had met with two men who were backed up by another four who were obviously special forces and after a very short discussion one of the ex-Marines had beaten up the four special ops guys with ease before leaving, Aeric then left the bar unnoticed. Outside the older ex-Marine floored the younger man and then knocked him out before helping to tie him up and then he was taken away on a fast rib to god knows where? "Good work Aeric, don't ask any probing questions just wait and see if anything else comes out of the wood work and report back to me as soon as you see or hear anything." The line went dead, Aeric concealed his satellite phone again and rolled a joint which he enjoyed with a mug of strong coffee and some Abernethy biscuits, he liked them.

Two thousand miles away at the Russian Naval base at Severomorsk, Sonny Yvonyv, Commander and personal assistant to Admiral Tonesky knocked on her superiors door, she walked straight in, the Admiral lifted his head, "What is it Commander?"

"Admiral, it looks like some ex Royal Marines Commandos diving in the Sound of Sleat off the Isle of Skye in Scotland may have found one of our divers depth gauges, one was lost when the Antaeus was snagged on the fishing boat it pulled under just over two months ago during the NATO exercise there."

"Do we have anything else Commander?"

"Yes Sir, it appears a small team of operatives, possibly from the British Special Forces arrived in Mallaig shortly after the two ex-Royal Marines found the gauge and forcibly took the younger of the two away, they kidnapped him and from what our watcher has told me the older man was in league with the team doing the kidnapping. I've instructed our man to continue to keep a watching brief and not ask any questions, the locals will talk, they always do."

"Yes, but are the two ex-Royal Marines locals? We need to know, if they're not they'll say nothing and we'll be none the wiser, one of them at least appears to be a very special man, or at least be of a special interest to our friends."

"We could have someone else put in place, someone with more appropriate skills?"

"Hmmmm, Commander, where would these other men, probably SBS take this so called ex Royal Marine?"

"Leave it with me, I'll have a look at google earth and see if there is anywhere that would be obviously quiet that would fit the bill. The Royal Navy are still at Kyle of Lochalsh but they wouldn't want to draw any attention to their operations there, to what they may be doing by taking him there, I suspect there may be somewhere nearer that will be quiet and out of the way."

"Good Sonny, keep me informed." As Commander Yvonyv was about to leave the Admirals office he called out

Yahweh

to her at the door, "Commander you mentioned sending in someone with more surveillance experience, or should I say, more appropriate skills," the Admiral scratched his chin and laughed to himself as he asked, "Have you any one in mind?" Yvonyv turned and smiled, she was a stunning blonde and an expert in explosives, diving, reconnaissance, escape and evasion and communications, she'd been injured about a year ago escaping American forces in the Iraqi desert and was now almost fully fit, she was here to train for her next promotion and Tonesky knew who she had in mind for her mission. Yvonyv turned and looked at her boss, "Sir, me of course." As Yvonyv left the room Tonesky grinned, God help any man who crossed her.

An hour later Yvonyv was back in the Admirals office, she placed the paperwork on Tonesky's desk, "There Sir, Ardentigh, it's a sort of outward bounds centre that it would appear is regularly used by the British armed forces, mainly Special Forces and the owner is ex SAS. That's where our guys are I'll bet a fortune on it." Admiral Tonesky spoke, "Get me the head of redeployment on the phone Yvonyv and tell him we need to re-direct a satellite for twenty four hours and we need it quickly, the last thing we need now is the British piecing things together and discovering the Antaeus is back in Murmansk and the coating is being manufactured by our Chinese friends as part of a deal to share our technologies, if they find even a small piece of the coating from the hull of the Antaeus on the wreck of that fucking sunken boat their boffins will know very quickly one of the elements is one which can only be mined in China, and get yourself booked onto the first flight into Heathrow, you know what to do from there." Within five minutes Tonesky was talking to the head of the FSS, the Federal Security Service and within two minutes the head of the FSS Mr Bortnikov had waved his hand and handed a piece of paper to his secretary instructing him to see to the re-deployment of the next satellite available. "Tonesky, you do realise that if, and it's a huge if, that if the British decide to go searching China for the source of this wonder materiel they won't get anywhere near Luxi Dao, God help all mankind if they do, not only is that where the stealth coating for our submarines is being manufactured, it's also where something far more sinister is kept." Tonesky had heard rumours of an underground laboratory somewhere in China where they, the yellow people had developed a nerve agent of the most lethally known proportions, VX1, it was, ridiculously one step on from VX and the only known antidote, was a closely guarded secret by the Chinese, it was believed that thousands of Chinese soldiers, Mongolian conscripts, had died testing the agent until their scientists had found the answer to the problem and they weren't sharing it with anyone, certainly not the west and not yet with the Russians.

Conon woke up and immediately realised he wasn't tied up but lying on a camp bed, it was getting bright outside, about 0600 hours he reckoned, he rubbed the sleep from his face and sat up on the bed and swung his feet around and onto the floor, he was still fully clothed and had his boots on, he stood up and walked towards the door, he knew he was at Ardentigh he recognised the scenery through the window of the bothy hut he was in, as he stepped through the door he saw Mack and Scouse sitting on chairs at either side of the porch, both men were battle

Yahweh

scarred with each sporting black eyes and Scouse had a large plaster over his left cheek bone. "Good morning gents," said Conon, Mack replied,

"Good morning Conon, how's about a cup of tea?"

"Yeah, sounds very civilised." Conon knew both of the guys would be armed under their warm down jackets and he also knew that they wouldn't be as easy as they were the night before, or was it the night before? He followed Mack down to the main mess hut as Scouse walked along beside him, as he climbed the broad steps of the main building on the site, he caught a glimpse of the rest of the men inside the hut and he could smell the fresh coffee and bacon. He stepped into the room and studied the rest of the team, the others had got off lighter than the other two, Munro's face was covered in scratches and Donnie hadn't a mark on him, nor did the two older men. Conon was again sure he recognised the older man but he couldn't remember where from, it was Munro who spoke first was. "Hello Conon," Conon knew Munro from old but they had never worked together, "Hello again Munro and so, to what do I owe this pleasure?"

The older man introduced himself "Professor Smith, I'm so sorry we didn't get the chance to chat properly last night," Conon looked at the man standing with his hand outstretched and shook it as the other man who was with him in the Marine Bar last night appeared from the galley area with a tray full of bacon rolls. Conon shook Smith's hand and looked around, everyone seemed very chilled out and relaxed but there was obviously a very good reason for the team assembled to have dealt with him the way they did last night and why? Silva sat down at one of the main tables and Donnie appeared with another tray full of mugs and makings for tea and coffee. Smith beckoned for Conon to sit down, he was well and truly cornered so he sat. Donnie asked if Conon took tea, coffee, milk and sugar. "Tea, just milk." Donnie handed him a mug and told him to help himself to a roll. Conon noticed the pot of boiling tea was kept just out of his arms reach. Professor Smith spoke again, "Conon do you remember me at all?"

"Yes," replied Conon, "but I just can't place where from?" Conon looked around the room again and picked up a bacon roll, all eyes were on him, "Well Conon you're, you were and you still are very much a very special person, that's what I'm here to explain and to do that these guys have been sent here to assist me, help me, help you to help us."

"Sounds like a stitch up but I'll hear you out before I leave." Conon looked around the room again and knew he would probably have to go through a window to escape but what was the point, he'd only be running for how long? God only knew, before they caught up with him again, at least if he sat and listened he might find out why they were so interested in him. He knew he was an ex Royal Marines Commando and he knew he'd been used as a scapegoat in Afghanistan but if he hadn't ambushed those Taliban operatives they would have slaughtered the whole American Marine patrol, eight men and how the hell was he supposed to know they were just about to step on top of Bin Laden's hidey hole, the Yanks had said nothing to the Brits about it, he was very soon to find out that that wasn't the only thing the Americans had been keeping from the British. Again Smith spoke, "I'm going to ask these other men to leave us alone, naturally they'll be just outside but essentially none of them are cleared to hear what I have to say to you, there is however one other person on his way with the highest clearance who will explain things to you exactly." "Who?" asked Conon.

"The Prime Minister!" Smith looked towards Scouse who was listening to a VHF radio.

"They're Five minutes out Sir," Munro ordered the rest of the team outside and left Smith, Silva and Conon in the mess hut.

The noise of the helicopter grew louder, it wasn't at all unusual in that part of the world though, some very rich people lived in some of the remotest estates dotted up and down Loch Nevis and on the other side of the Loch on the Knoydart peninsula, so another helicopter flying up the Loch was hardly going to attract anyone's attention. The helicopter touched down, David Cameron stepped out and was ushered towards the mess hut by two close protection officers, one other man followed them. The door opened and the Prime Minister walked in with the other man, Conon did not recognise the other man. David Cameron spoke, "Hello, Professor Smith." the two men shook hands and turned towards Conon.

"Mr Cameron, this is Conon, Conon Bridge." Conon stood up and shook the PMs hand, he was the Prime Minister after all.

"Mr Bridge, nice to meet you, I gather you've been a bit difficult to pin down, have you had any kind of explanation as to what's going on, why we are so especially interested in you?"

"No Sir, I have no idea at all." Mr Cameron beckoned for the three men to sit down, he looked at the other man he'd arrived with and invited him to sit in the soft chair beside him.

"Well I suppose that's a good start. This Mr Bridge; May I call you Conon?"

"Yes that's fine by me Sir,"

"Conon, this is uhhhh, Mr Black, he doesn't exist, essentially he is one of the top men within an organisation that works pretty much along the lines of the United States black ops kind of business but the Americans as far as we know still don't know about our set up, there are some things we still do better than the Americans. So Conon I'll let Professor Smith speak and then we'll tell you exactly what it is we need help with, how does that sound?"

"I suppose the fact that you've come all the way up here to speak to me with a man who doesn't exist and sending a team of Special Forces here to corner me kind of gets my attention!" The PM smiled.

"Good Conon, now let's all sit back and try and absorb as much of the next hour or so as possible." Smith began to tell Conon about how he'd been delivered to a hospital for soldiers with Post Traumatic Stress after he'd been quickly extracted from operations in Afghanistan and how he'd volunteered for an experiment which meant he would be retrained and have selected parts of his memory concealed to him, he'd be brainwashed essentially and that after some very specialised training and with the use of newly developed drugs essentially based on a synthetic adrenalin and an implant, which was currently in place but inactive, he would with some very minor procedures, be able to endure unimaginable pain and would have physical endurance beyond what was thought humanly possible, the drugs were self-administered. Conon laughed at him, he looked at the Prime Minister and at Mr Black and then Silva, none of them were laughing, at least some of the gaps were beginning to be filled in. David Cameron spoke. "Conon you may find it all very hard to believe but it's all true, it will all be explained to you in great detail by Professor Smith and Doctor Silva over the next few days, if you agree to assist us with a huge problem we have........"

"I'm listening!" Conon interrupted. The PM looked at Mr Black and invited the so far silent man to give his input. "Conon, about ten years ago we started hearing stories coming out of China about huge numbers of soldiers being killed during experiments being carried out at a very remote island base, Luxi Dao, there's a very small air force base there, a standard sized runway disguised as a road but our satellite surveillance tends to suggest that there is a huge subterranean network on the island and it's continually supplied by ships. The aircraft activity is insignificant so we're beginning to think everything's going in and out by boat. You're probably wondering how do we know any of this, the answer's simple, a Chinese Air Force Pilot defected about the time the rumours started to appear and it's claimed he had been involved in flying one of their new stealth bombers. He told his American handlers they were testing a weapon that was being developed on the Island, all the info was being stored on the mainframe of a computer within the Luxi Dao Research Centre. The Chinese have it dressed up as a fishery research establishment but that's a load of baloney. The Chinese pilot was then handed over to the British government, he asked to be given asylum in the U.K. for some reason and naturally our guys had a pop at him first. He also told us they are developing a new nerve agent that only the Chinese had the antidote for despite the Russians best efforts to get involved. It would be used to wipe out the rest of mankind if the need arose. The only problem was that about seven thousand soldiers had been killed whilst the experiments were being carried out, almost all of them Mongolian conscripts. The information mostly dried up then, we're not sure why. The Americans of course know all this. Then around a month ago one of our Astute class submarines picked up a communication being sent into the C.I.A. headquarters at Langley which our boffins at GCHQ were able to decipher. The message basically read that one of their operatives, it was claimed an American spy, in case you're not following the plot, had been captured on Luxi Dao trying to steal the antidote to the nerve agent and that he was days away from being executed. The only thing saving him at the moment is that the Americans have threatened to go public about the nerve agent and the most God awful row has broken out between the Chinese and the Americans. So far they have no idea we've been spying on them, the Americans and the Chinese satellite technology really is incredibly easy to piggy back, we've been listening in on them for bloody years using one of our own AWACS aircraft, specially modified of course, but flying over NATO airspace and there's nothing they can do about it." Conon sat in disbelief, he was fit, he was trained to do the kind of mission that would be needed to carry out a reconnaissance of the island but to single handily infiltrate a base that was probably tighter than a ducks arse in the middle of the Pacific Ocean, it was as close to suicide as he could imagine. The Prime Minister spoke, "So Conon that's what we need you for, I've been briefed on your capabilities, I've been told you speak several languages and I have no doubt what we're asking you to do is extremely dangerous but if you agree, you'll be looked after for the rest of your life, right now Conon as cheesy as it sounds, your country really does need you!" The words were resonating in his head and he was trying to take it all in when Scouse knocked on the door and came in, he addressed the Prime Minister "Sir, we can't let you move from this building for at least thirty minutes, there's a Russian satellite just about to pop over the horizon, we know it's a Naval intelligence spy satellite but it's well off its recent search parameters." "Excellent, Scouse." The Prime minister said. "Yes Conon the Russians are definitely trying to shoehorn their way into this somehow but we're just not too sure how heavily involved they are yet." The Prime Minister spoke to Scouse, "Send in Captain Munro would you." Munro walked in, the rest of his team had concealed themselves for the next half hour whilst the satellite passed overhead, he was invited to sit down by the PM. "Well Munro,

Conon has listened with great patience to what we had to say....."

"I'll do it." interrupted Conon, he liked the thought of the challenge. The PM smiled, "I love it when something goes well, Munro, you'll be spending a lot of time with Conon over the next few weeks as will you Professor Smith, Mr Black will also re-introduce himself, Conon you are now officially reinstated into the Royal Marines. Munro, the satellite, is it possible that someone may have been telling our Russian friends that you are here and something is going down?" Munro replied, "It certainly sounds like it Mr Cameron." "Then as Conon is no longer a concern of yours may I suggest that you take your team and eliminate whoever is watching what we're up to here?"

"It will be a pleasure Sir, the boys will be glad to do some arm twisting I'm sure." Munro and the rest of the men sat around the fire that had been lit and finished the tea, coffee and bacon rolls.

An hour later and after the sky was clear the PM left with his team aboard his helicopter, he shook Conon's hand as he left and wished him well on his mission. As the PM strapped himself into his seat on-board the helicopter he was thoughtful about how amazing Conon's life was going to become over the next few weeks and he looked forward to his mission being a success.

At 1725 hours the flight from Moscow had touched down at London Heathrow Airport and Commander Yvonyv was met at the arrivals lounge by a junior Ambassador named Brigsonov and driven straight to the Russian

Embassy at Kensington Palace Gardens, of course they were being watched. From there she wasted no time in gathering the minimal equipment she needed and after a shower and a meal they left via a rear door, she was driven to Gatwick Airport for the connecting flight to Inverness, she boarded the flight under a Polish identification, it was easy. Yvonyv arrived at Dalcross airport on the outskirts of Inverness and picked up the keys for her hire car, a basic silver Vauxhall Astra, she left the terminal and saw the Police dog handler walking away from the terminal, the German Shepherd he walked with was unusually dark and big she thought as she loaded her case into the boot of the car, from there it was a few hours' drive to Fort William employing counter surveillance methods all the way and then onto Mallaig where she would meet with Ubych, hopefully in the early hours of the morning, if anyone saw her arrive they would think she was Eric's girlfriend on a visit from Poland, she shuddered at the thought. Yvonyv had only one purpose for being anywhere near someone like Eric, she needed to find out who was in Mallaig and what exactly they were looking for, she had no idea Eric had been compromised.

Mack, Donnie and Scouse had their orders, they had one last task before leaving, they knew someone was watching in Mallaig but they weren't sure who, so one last visit was needed.

The three men arrived in Mallaig on the rib, it was just gone seven pm, they tied the boat up and they made their way straight to the Marine bar. Mack ordered a round of drinks and they all sat down to enjoy their pint, choosing a seat near the door. Eric Ubych sat at the end of the bar and noticed the guys who'd just walked in were the same three guys from the night before. He tried not to make it obvious that he was watching them and also listening to every word they said. Donnie sat with a full view of the bar before him, he leaned forward and quietly told Scouse and Mack the guy at the end of the bar was the same dude that had been in the previous evening he'd been sitting next to Laurel and Hardy when the scrapping started and he was keeping an eye on them now, he was their man. The three Royal Marines sat quietly and exchanged banter with each other until Eric made his first and last mistake, he stood up from his bar stool and walked to the toilet, eager to make his presence appear normal but he fooled no one, as soon as he'd gone through the door Scouse rose from his chair and announced it was his round. He went to the bar and asked the barmaid for three large Glenmorangies, then as soon as she'd turned away he squirted a syringe of highly potent and tasteless sedative into Eric's half empty glass of lager. The barmaid had just finished pouring the whisky when Eric reappeared, Scouse said hello to him as he paid for the drinks then gathered them up and sat back down at the table, no one had seen a thing apart from "Cheers" as the three Royal Marines downed their drams. Eric supped from his glass and within two minutes he could sense something wasn't right, he felt slightly nauseous and he got up to leave, sensing he was in trouble, his legs wobbled slightly beneath him and as he tried to focus on the tree men sitting near the door, now he knew he really was in trouble. As he walked towards the door the barmaid shouted after him, "Eric, are you okay, do you need a taxi?"

Yahweh

"No I'm fine I'm just going to walk home round the bay, I'm going to get some fresh air," he replied trying to feign a laugh as he slipped out of the bar and into the cool night air; one minute later Eric was followed by the three Royal Marines who had left virtually unnoticed by the dozen or so people in the bar, it was Mallaig and strangers were an ever present in the village, all year round.

Eric staggered along the road, as he did so he had it in his head all he wanted to do, all he needed to do was get home, he knew he had been drugged and the three guys in the bar were probably responsible, yes, the guy who was buying the whisky's it must have been him when he'd gone to the toilet, stupid, stupid, stupid fool for making such a basic error. Eric staggered on and stopped for a few seconds and leaned against the wall at the old R.N.L.I. parking sign to try and clear his head, he breathed deeply and then looked around and saw no one about, so far so good, he was sure he would make it to the flat and safety. The three Royal Marines skulked in the shadows seen by no one, they watched as their target made his way towards the area about the pontoons where their boat lay. Eric pushed himself off the wall and attempted to put his left foot out to take another step towards his flat but his head filled up with a horrible, out of control feeling, his head spun and as his eyes closed and before he had even hit the ground he was scooped up by Mack and Scouse, Donnie had side stepped the whole capture and sprinted to the rib and was firing the engines up, the lines had been cast off and as he watched the limp figure being carried down the ramp he scanned the area, no one was about and no one had seen them. Eric was unceremoniously dropped in the bottom of the boat with Mack and Scouse watching over him and as soon as they cleared the pontoon Donnie hit full throttle and the rib shot onto her plain and the cleared the green outer harbour buoy at nearly fifty knots. Ten minutes later the rib and its cargo were arriving at Ardentigh.

Eric was tied up and placed in a chair with a bag over his head, standard practice and a little bit of added fear factor for when he regained consciousness once Munro had injected him with the antidote to the sedative, it was only a matter of time before he would talk, assuming he had something to say. Conon walked into the room, he saw the man with his hands and feet tied up, the bag over his head, he remembered the scenario well from his own training, "A new recruit?" he asked Munro, who laughed.

"No, Conon, this is the guy we think may have been responsible for re-routing the Russian satellite, watch and learn, you may find some of this useful." Munro removed the bag from Eric's head which was slumped to the right, he was still out cold. Conon spoke, "Its Eric Ubych!"

"You know this man?" asked Munro.

"Yes he works on one of the fishing boats here, he appeared about a month or so ago, he's Polish I think, lives in a flat on East Bay, he keeps himself to himself and works hard, he doesn't bother anyone."

"I'll bet he doesn't, he's a low grade listener, a spy Conon, you see we know the Russians have been snooping around here for years, the Navy have been testing torpedoes and sonar equipment since the end of the second world war and as you know, other equipment in the Sound of Sleat and we suspect one of their experimental subs sank in or around the Minches about two months ago, that would've coincided with the sinking of a small fishing vessel, the one you've found and the pressure gauge you picked up. For some reason the Russians don't want us finding that boat, probably because whilst their submarine was operating in our waters we had absolutely no idea it was out there. We're guessing but it's beginning to look like the Chinese and the Russians are working on something top secret, we think it's a stealth submarine but we can't figure out why the Russians would want to lie in bed with the Chinese and share their technology with them but then we got a whisper that maybe the Chinese have some kind of new super nerve agent, we think they maybe together on it or the Russians want in on the deal and the Chinese aren't keen but the Island where we think it's all happening is beginning to look conspicuously quiet, answers on a postage stamp please." Conon laughed as he watched Munro push the injection into Eric's arm.

Within seconds Eric was coming round, he slowly lifted his head and scanned the room, he saw Munro sitting on a chair in front of him, he saw another man sitting at the far side of the table in the middle of the room, he was using what looked like a lap top computer, he tried to look over his shoulder but a sharp slap across his face concentrated his attention. "Never mind who's behind you Eric, try and concentrate on me, my name is Munro." Eric wiggled his jaw and felt his skin sting after being slapped by Donnie, Conon sat well back, watching and saying nothing. "Ok Eric, let's start shall we? Who do you work for?" Eric laughed and told Munro the truth.

"Rex, Rex Newlands, I work as a deck hand on his boat, what the fuck is all this about, why am I tied up, who are you people?"

"Now, now Eric, we all know that's a lie so let's not waste any more time. We know who you are we just need to know who you're really working for? Now be a sensible lad and just tell us, we'll find out anyway."

"Then find out if you're so smart!" Munro nodded towards Donnie, Mack was also there and the two men took a firm hold of Eric's right arm, Eric tried to struggle for a second but he quickly realised it was pointless, he would however not tell the strangers anything they wanted to know voluntarily, they would have to extract any information from him the old fashioned way. Munro found the vein in Eric's arm easily and injected the sodium pentothal into his system, he would be singing like a bird inside a few minutes. Eric had the bag replaced over his head and was left for a while for the drug to take effect, none of the Marines spoke during the next ten minutes. Munro signalled to Donnie and Mack to remove the bag from Eric's head and sure enough after only a few brief moments Munro was amazed that the Russian had gone into melt down as easily as he did. Eric told Munro how he had been sent to Mallaig about two months ago to listen out for any information about anything that had happened out in the Sound of Sleat around that time, they didn't tell him what, that meant he could listen with open ears, to anything important, he told them he was a low grade operative and that he was expecting someone to make contact with him soon to take over from him. He'd realised the men around him were British Special forces and that they must've discovered something, that's what all the activity was about. So Munro and his team knew the Russians were snooping around looking for the same clues as them, all they needed to do now was get rid of Eric, do a reconnaissance dive on the Worthy and then get Conon out of the area and start preparing him for his mission.

Eric was sedated again and taken back to Mallaig, he had served his purpose, by his own admission he was going to be replaced so there was no need to dispose of him permanently and by the time his handlers realised he'd talked, everyone would have moved on. The rib arrived in Mallaig under the cover of darkness again and this time the Marines simply carried Eric up a few steps at the end of the old pier, they left him on the steps, still unconscious, they were careful not to clear the pier itself as there were cameras on the harbour.

Yvonyv had a clear view from Eric's window and watched the two men carry the limp figure up the steps, the third man stayed on board the rib, she couldn't see if it was Eric they left on the steps but she suspected it was and she also knew if it was he'd probably been drugged and would have given the British all the information they wanted. She watched the rib leave slowly and quietly before leaving the flat and made her way round to the pier end, the walk took only ten minutes. As Yvonyv approached the steps she looked around and made sure no one else was about, she'd seen the camera on the end of the Harbour office building but her face was concealed, she would look like just another tourist walking on the pier and anyway by the time Eric's body was discovered she'd be long gone.

She climbed down the steps and found Eric unconscious, sitting on the steps near the bottom, the tide was almost at his feet, she checked his pulse and after making sure he was still alive she pulled his head back and injected him under his tongue with a undetectable drug which would paralyse him, then she pushed him over the end of the steps, it would look like he'd drowned and that would be enough to throw the local Police off the scent for a good while, they'd probably never find out the truth about how Eric had really died.

Yvonyv made her way back to the flat and cleared it of everything that could give the Police any clues about who Eric really was then she sat and watched as the early morning fishermen started to appear on the harbour and cast off the boats for the early morning trip to sea. It was little over an hour since she had disposed of Eric. The Silver Dawn was first out and almost as soon as the fishing boat cleared the end of the inner harbour Yvonyv watched the crewman at the stern of the boat throw his cigarette butt into the water and start shouting at the skipper, he pointed furiously at the water and the Silver Dawn's engines were thrown into reverse, Gus the skipper hung out of the wheel house and shouted at the crewman to grab the boat hook then Yvonyv watched as Eric's limp body was dragged over the side of the trawler and the harbour became alive with men running to see what had happened. Within minutes an ambulance arrived as the Silver Dawn tied up against the end of the pier, as the man who everyone now knew was Eric was being checked for signs of life by the paramedics in the back of the ambulance.

Yvonyv then watched as the Police car turned up, the two officers went into the ambulance and Yvonyv left the flat and got into the hire car, a non-descript Vauxhall Astra, no one would notice her driving around the bay amidst all the excitement and confusion. Yvonyv slipped quietly out of Mallaig unnoticed and headed back towards Glasgow, she would return to the embassy from there.

Three hours later Yvonyv sat in the departure lounge at Glasgow airport and watched the regional news broadcast at 0755 hours, the news reader spoke about how a Polish fisherman had been pulled out of the harbour at Mallaig, he was thought to have drowned after a night of drinking at a local bar, local sources were believed to have reported that the fisherman was probably trying to find his way back to his boat and probably slipped on the harbour and drowned. Local police were still investigating the death but believed it was a tragic accident and they didn't think there were any suspicious circumstances surrounding the man's death, his name was not being released until next of kin had been informed. Yvonyv smiled to herself and sipped on her coffee. At Ardentigh Munro and his team also watched the bulletin, Professor Smith looked at Munro and asked if his team were responsible, not that he really cared. Munro was emphatic that his men had left Eric in a safe place, somewhere where he would come round and get home from and probably be returned to Russia where he'd probably end up working at a prison camp in Siberia for the rest of his days, no chance of promotion, no prospects and as much a prisoner as the men he'd probably end up guarding.

"Well," said Smith, "Someone got to him!" Munro looked around the table, "Gentlemen, I think it's time we finished up our work here and quietly leave the area so we can get on with our other business elsewhere."

The Marines and Conon loaded the dive gear into the rib and left for the spot where the Worthy lay on the ocean floor. It was a twenty minute ride on the fast boat and by mid-day Conon, Mack, Donnie and Scouse were in the water, Munro was staying on the boat, the gear they used for their reconnaissance was standard civilian dive kit, the Marines didn't want anyone seeing anything unusual or knowing they were any more than just a bunch of guys on a recreational dive.

There was very little time and within the hour the four men sat on the rib ready to dive, Munro was at the helm minding all of the other business on board the craft, and at 1200 hours, the four divers descended into the green water, it took them about five minutes to free fall onto the sea bed, at ten meters from the bottom the features started to appear and after swimming a short distance the Worthy appeared out of the murkiness. She was untouched and still looked like she could fire up her engine and just move off, Mack, who was teamed up with Conon began to swim down the port side of the craft whilst Scouse and Donnie swam down her starboard side, the Marines took hundreds of photos and inspected everything that was easily accessible, then all four men arrived at the stern of the craft and the thick net hauling rope was lying on the bottom, seaweed and growth just starting to take a hold, it was quite amazing actually and it occurred to all four divers just how little growth there was on the boat.

Yahweh

Conon swam out past the stern of the boat towards where he'd found the dial and looked backwards to see the three Royal Marines all following him, he pointed at the sand and Mack lifted the rope from the sea bed and shook the sand and debris off it, he looked at the others and pointed into the murky water, towards where the end would be, Donnie and Scouse went back towards the stern of the boat and cut it at the hauler and tied it to a rope that lead up to the rib. As Mack swam out with Conon he ran the rope through his gloved hand and about forty meters away from the Worthy the rope changed colour, it was so obvious but it wasn't normal and on closer inspection about four meters of the rope appeared to be covered in a black residue, they'd found another clue. As they surfaced Conon glanced down on the Worthy and he knew she would probably lie where she was for ever more, she would become a home for fish and crabs and other like creatures.

Twenty minutes later the men were back on board and heading back to Ardentigh, the rope concealed in a compartment in the hull, it would be kept wet until it could be examined by the boffins at Porton Down.

Conon sat down by the shore line on a flat rock looking out across the Loch with a mug of hot tea, he didn't really care that Eric Ubych had died, it wasn't his problem but it did focus him, just a bit more, he was thinking about the probable difficulties that lay ahead and although he was no stranger to death, killing or the depths some would go to to survive, he wondered just what did lie ahead, the Prime Minister himself had basically arrived to ask him for help, it was a bit much to take in, even for him, Professor Smith came and sat beside him.

"What a stunning view, eh Conon?"

The water across Loch Nevis was almost flat calm as they watched the boat arrive at the fish farm a short distance down the loch from them, the crew on board took no heed of what was going on at Ardentigh, helicopters and soldiers were a common sight up there.

"Yes Sir, I was just contemplating when or even if, I'll ever get to enjoy it again."

"Not anytime soon Conon and that's being completely honest with you, it'll be a while before you're ready for your mission, then once your mission is over, assuming you're successful there will have to be debriefs and probably an enforced period of rest somewhere very out of the way."

"That part sounds fine as long as it's warm and not the South Pole." Both men laughed but Conon knew the hard work was just about to start, the Chinook was due to arrive in about an hour, he was told he wouldn't get to go back to his home to collect any of his belongings,

Yahweh

everything he needed would be provided and it would be the best of kit, he was however allowed to make one phone call and he knew who he wanted to speak to. As soon as Conon reached the training camp at Royal Marines Poole he would be allowed to make his call, obviously it would be monitored and recorded but at least he was being allowed one call, the secrecy of the mission was paramount. The Chinook could be heard approaching from some distance away, the Marines had their kit ready, Professor Smith and Doctor Silva were also packed ready to go, Conon stood in the clothes he had arrived in and watched the lumbering twin rotored helicopter, its blades thudding through the morning air, it cleared the headland a short distance away, it threw up huge clouds of spray as the pilot began his approach to land on the fore shore. Five minutes later they were on board and heading back down Loch Nevis towards Mallaig, as the chopper turned to fly round the outer harbour, Conon sat and looked out of his window and saw Rex's boat heading out, Rex and Jack were as usual heading out for the first dive of the day, he hoped he would be back on the boat with them one day. On board the boat Jack looked up and watched the big RAF helicopter swoop past the outer harbour and he wondered if Conon was on board, he'd been there and done most of it but he knew that Conon was on his way to carry out a mission that only a very select few men or women were ever chosen for, he had no idea what it was Conon would actually be doing over the next few months but he knew it would scare the shit out of just about everyone else on the planet, he waved up at the Chinook and carried on with getting his gear ready for the days diving as the helicopter disappeared out of view.

Just after 0800 hours the Chinook touched down at HMS Gannet at Prestwick and the Marines and the Doctors all left the aircraft, within another ten minutes they were on board an HS125 aircraft and heading for Bournemouth Airport, it was far more comfortable and the Marines and the rest of the team actually managed to get some sleep, not much though, it wasn't long before the pilot let them know they were beginning their descent and they were all required to fasten their seat belts. Three unmarked Range Rovers were waiting for the team, nobody gave them a second glance and in no time they were heading for Poole.

By midday they were driving through the main gate at Royal Marines Poole, Hamworthy, Conon couldn't believe the changes to the place, new buildings, it barely resembled the base he'd last seen about ten years ago, as they pulled up outside an office block Munro turned and spoke to Conon, "Just follow me for now Conon, we'll get you sorted out with clothes, kit and a room if there's anything else just ask,"

"My one phone call and some money, I assume I'll be allowed to buy myself some things in the NAAFI?"

"Yes of course, it's in the same place and anything else you need we'll have one of the lads go into town with you and uhhhh just make sure that you're ok."

"You mean keep an eye on me?"

"Well not quite like that but there's a lot resting on your shoulders and we don't want to mess anything up now, do we?"

"Don't worry about me Munro, some toilet gear a towel, clean socks, tee shirt, boxers and that'll just about do me for now, point me in the direction of my bed and if it's ok I'll just get some sleep."

"No problem, probably best that you sleep as much as possible for now." Conon followed Munro into the office block as the rest of the guys unloaded their gear and took care of the weapons and stores they had with them.

Munro ushered Conon into his office and sat him at the opposite side of his desk. "Time for your call Conon, just mind your P's and Q's and I won't state the obvious," he then stood up and handed Conon the phone, "dial nine for an outside line, then just dial your number."

As soon as Munro had left the room and closed the door Conon stared at the phone for a few seconds before lifting the receiver, he dialled Jacks mobile number, it rang for a few moments then the voice he knew well spoke from the other end.

"Hello."

"Hello Jack, how are you?"

"Conon, how are you? I'm fine, listen I'm......" Conon cut him off,

"I know Jack, it's okay, you had to do it you had no choice."

"Well, something like that, seriously are you okay though?"

"Yes, honestly mate I'm fine life's about to get very interesting but if it all works out then that boat and compressor I fancied are definitely on the cards."

"That's good news Conon, listen I know they'll be listening to this and I'm not going to ask anything and you'll not be able to say anything, I'm happy you're okay and I know that if you didn't want to be there you wouldn't be there but don't worry about a thing, I know where the key is for your place, me and the missus will look after the house for you and take care of everything here until you get back."

"Thanks Jack, I couldn't ask for more, just open any mail and take care of any bills, electric, any crap like that, you know where to find all my financial stuff and where I have my money stashed."

"Consider it done mate, now you get off and don't do anything I wouldn't do!"

Conon laughed, "Yeah, we never really told each other the truth about what we've both done in the past, maybe we will when I get home eh? Anyway, take care Jack, I'll see you soon and tell that old bastard Rex I was saying hello."

"I will, Conon and yes we'll have a good talk when you get back and I'll keep an eye out for a good boat for you."

The two men hung up and Conon replaced the receiver, he was happy that Jack knew he was ok, his business at home was being looked after and more importantly that he and Jack were good. He could concentrate on what was ahead of him now and not be concerned in any way

Yahweh

about what was behind him. Munro walked back into the room, "You knew we'd be listening Conon so no point in pretending." He sat down again.

"You knew I'd phone him as well didn't you?"

"Yes, but to be totally honest, we knew he'd say nothing and we knew you'd say even less, we've just got to be careful that's all. Anyway now we need to sort out money and a bed for you and some rest. Just don't get too cosy and remember from here on in, always expect the unexpected." Conon thought the last comment sounded like it was straight out of the training manual, he winced inwardly.

Munro lead Conon out of the office and took him to the accommodation block where he would be staying, on the same floor Scouse, Donnie and Mack all had rooms next to Conon, he was simply told they'll look after you and they will be training with you, they are a cracking bunch of lads, Conon had no doubt about that. As he looked around his room he could see across the sports ground and across to where the quarry pit was, where many men had been broken and lost their nerve in the muddy lake, not him though, he'd survived as had the others he was about to get to know much better as well.

Conon lay back on his bed and his thoughts drifted back to Jack, they'd befriended each other not long after he'd arrived back in Mallaig, Conon needed to settle and Jack had spoken to him on the pier one morning as he wandered about looking at the fishing boats contemplating which one he may think about asking to work on, if the estate work dried up when Jack in his usual smiling way said good morning and they just started talking. Conon was no stranger to the Mallaig area, he had grown up there.

Jack and his wife Denise were very close to being surrogate parents, Conon confided in Jack, he was the older man, the steadying influence in his life at a time when he could easily have ended up drinking his life away, he reminded him of a character in a book called, "Archies Way" written by a man called Richard E. Probert, Jack said he'd met him once in Mallaig and spoke to him at the harbour, Mr Probert had told him he was sailing around Scotland and he was an Orchestral Conductor, a Professor of music no less and that he had written a book. Jack had found the book, read it and gave it to Conon whom he'd told to read it as he found it inspiring, it was a great read. As he drifted off into a deep sleep Conon thought of Loch Glass and of Morar and Mallaig, he'd surely find his way back to those places one day.

Conon awoke from his sleep and after checking his watch realised it was seven in the morning, it was the noise of someone in the next room that woke him. There was a knock at the door, he got up and opened it, Scouse stood outside with a big grin on his face, "Morning, just thought you might fancy some breakfast?"

"Yes that'd be great give me a minute to wash my face and I'll be right with you." Conon turned and left the door open, Scouse stepped in and as Conon washed he saw Scouse in the mirror standing at the window looking out across the sports field, he looked to be a million miles away. Conon stepped out of the shower room. "A penny for them?" He asked Scouse, who turned around to speak.

"Ah nothing really, just you know we've all heard of you and what you did was awesome back in Afghanistan, we were talking last night, as you do and we were just wondering what the hell was going on? None of us has a bloody clue and we didn't even know it was you we were collecting until you walked into the Marine bar."

"Well Scouse, maybe today we'll all find out just a bit more but walls have ears and all that crap so we'd better not say anything about any of it just now."

Scouse smiled, "Yeah, definitely best to keep ones mouth shut, anyway come on the galleys still in the same place and the scran is still the best you'll get, unless you're visiting an R.A.F. base of course!" The Liverpudlian joked.

"Aye some things never change, eh?" said Conon as the two men headed for the galley.

Once they'd arrived at the galley the head chef, a Colour Sergeant was standing behind the counter encouraging the Marines to eat as much as they could, it was still as Conon remembered it, anywhere else the head chef was counting how many sausages or rashers of bacon you had on your plate, not here, it was a different world. Conon and Scouse found Donnie and Mack and went and sat with them. Donnie spoke, "Well old man looks like you've caused a stir, some of the Wrens have been chatting about the legend that is Conon Bridge arriving here sometime soon." Conon smiled and as discreetly as he could he checked out if anyone was actually taking any notice of him, no one that he could obviously see. Here he was no one special, at least in his own mind and everyone in the place was sensible enough to know that you didn't stare and you didn't ask questions about anything if it didn't concern you. What Conon didn't realise was that everyone in the room, bar none, around seventy to eighty Marines and Wrens knew who he was, no one apart from him though knew why he was there.

The four men sat enjoying their breakfast, Donnie didn't shut his mouth the whole time, Conon wondered how he managed to keep his food in his mouth he talked so much but he was funny, a natural comic, he left the table briefly to get the wets in, Conon laughed at the use of naval phraseology, wets he reminded himself was the term used for tea or coffee, he'd moved away from speaking in Pussers lingo but he'd get into the swing of it again quickly enough, then a Wren came into the galley, she looked about and made a beeline for the four men. "Good morning lads, Major Munro wonders if you'd point Conon in the direction of his office for 0830 hours, he has to collect some cash I believe." Scouse acknowledged her politely, and as the Wren turned away Donnie was standing in her path. He was smitten by Petty Officer Donna Slace, it was pronounced Slachee, it was a Slavic name, and she knew the effect she had on him but she would never entertain him or any other squaddie for that matter. Donnie smiled at her, like a school boy he stood blushing trying his best to be polite, Scouse alerted everyone else at the table of the young man's plight. Slace stood looking at the Marine standing in her way, she was completely in control, "Good morning Donna." He said.

Slace looked at him up and down, she leaned into his ear and said, "Donnie, your flies undone." As the young Marine quickly looked down the Wren gently stroked him under the chin and teasing him she whispered in his ear, "You wish," as she drifted around him brushing against him with her breasts, the tray of wets toppled sending the four mugs of tea and coffee all over the floor. The galley erupted in laughter as Slace made her way out and down the stairs, Donnie stood like a scarlet rose but he was smitten and didn't care as the head chef handed him a mop and bucket, he might be in the Special Boat Squadron but Colours wasn't going to have one of his team cleaning up after Donnie.

Conon was delivered safely to the Majors office where after a few moments he followed Munro along the corridor, into the admin office, there they went straight into the small imprest office and Munro spoke to the Wren behind the desk, it was the Petty Officer from the galley earlier at breakfast time. Munro asked her for the agreed advance to be given to Mr Bridge, as he referred to him, which both Conon and Petty officer Slace thought was strange, she went through a file on her computer and opened a locked drawer and counted out a thousand pounds. The money was signed over to Conon and Munro just said, "Buy what you need for yourself but don't buy any kit, we'll be supplying everything you need." Conon then headed for his accommodation block via the NAFFI where he had a look around and bought a good pair of trainers and a pair of shorts, some toiletries. Conon had been given a single room, clean bedding and some towels, that would do him for now, he made his way back to his room and put on the pair of trainers and shorts and a tee shirt he had be given by one of the lads and he took himself out for a run around the perimeter of the base, that part hadn't changed much and after a couple of laps exploring the place, stopping a couple of times to take it all in, he decided that as he wasn't pencilled in for anything when he got back to his room he'd have himself a nice warm shower and a good scrub, then it was into a nice fresh clean bed for a couple of hours shut eye. His eyes closed and about ten seconds later or so it seemed at the time, although three hours had passed, he woke up with a start to find a tall man looming over his bed and in a slow American drawl the tall man just said, "Get your running gear on son and lets have you outside in three minutes." Conon looked at his watch it was only one p.m. but he was shattered

Yahweh

and struggled to wake up, sleep deprivation was one of the things he hated most when training for anything. Outside he was surprised to see Munro, Scouse, Mack and Donnie all in the front support press up position, the tall American man shouted at him, "Move you're fucking ass Mr Bridge, these men are waiting on you!!" the other four men, like Conon had seen all this before but Gunny Herman, a US navy seal on secondment to the SBS took his part in the training set up very seriously, the guys nicknamed him Clunt on account of him looking uncannily like Clint Eastwood and because he could be a real hard task master. The beasting lasted only five minutes, it didn't matter that Conon arrived ten seconds early Clunts job was to switch him on and over the next four weeks he would achieve his part of the objective. The rain began to fall as the six men ran through the main gate and headed for the pond, it was a place where many men were broken but these five men knew how to survive, the others were there to give Conon some support initially but it soon became apparent to them and Clunt he had lost none of his fitness and that was before the doctors got to work in him Munro thought. After over two hours of aquatic beasting Clunt ordered the men out of the water, the run back to the base was short and sweet, they were dismissed and as the guys headed for a shower and a hot meal, Clunt made for the training wing where he and Munro spoke about the last few hours and the next few weeks. Over the next week it was obvious that Conon's basic fitness, weapons handling, navigation and communication skills were sound, they only really needed to firm up on up to date computer training, hacking, escape techniques and Scouse would train with Conon on the new and latest signals equipment, training was going well, everything was on schedule. Scouse and Conon worked endlessly through weeks two and three, a lot had changed in nearly ten years but Conon's basic knowledge of most communication's systems was way above average. Munro, Mack and Donnie only had to bring Conon up to speed on the technical issues that might get in his way whilst trying to get into Luxi Dao. The kit Conon may have used for similar types of incursions in the past had been improved considerably, the directional explosive devices were smaller, meaning they could carry more and they packed a far greater punch and the one thing which Conon was delighted to find out was that the camouflage suits that he had worn all those years ago rendering the wearer almost invisible had also been improved.

And then at the end of week three one of the funniest men Conon had ever met was brought to the base escorted by two burly prison guards all the way from Wormwood Scrubs. Rumour had it Ewan Kerr could pick any lock, open handcuffs and just about anything that could be locked, he was a modern day Harry Houdini, so how had he ended up in prison the guys wanted to know? Easy, he could beat any alarm and even if he couldn't he could tell you to the second how long he had before the police would know he was in a building but, how was he supposed to know the last gaff he'd blagged was guarded internally by a pet tiger, Kerr was hilarious and the two days he spent with Conon and his training team were a welcome distraction. By the time Kerr was leaving he'd made four new friends and joked with them as he left. "If you ever need me lads just call me, my secretary will deal with any requests!" And he was gone. Conon was called to Munro's office, he was enjoying the training but week four was rapidly approaching and it was time for testing.

Professor Smith arrived on Thursday morning along with another medical officer and gave Conon a full and rigorous medical, he was actually exhausted by the end of it and was delighted when he was told that he was in exceptionally good shape, exceptionally good. It was during the examination the medical team discovered the M2 molar with the locator transmitter fitted in a routine dental appointment for a filling had been knocked out, Conon remembered the short scrap with Stone and Professor Smith chuckled and told Conon that Stone would probably be getting some emergency dental treatment very soon. The professor was delighted and asked to be left alone with Conon, the next hour or two would determine whether or not he was mentally ready for the highly dangerous and sensitive mission ahead. "So Conon, you have an idea of what we need you for, what we need help with but are you ready for it? Have you thought about what could happen if you're captured?"

"I assume death will feature Prof? Let's just hope that if it does come my way it'll be quick. We've all suffered the degradation of the crap they put us through on the selection courses for us and the S.A.S."

"That's just it Conon, if you're captured it will probably be the longest most drawn out night mare imaginable. To that end you have to be ready to pay the ultimate sacrifice, whether any of us likes it or not and we need to get this thing going quickly, so I'm sorry to come across so bluntly. Anyway there's no way the British Government can have you being captured and tortured, they will deny all connections with you and......."

"Yeah, yeah, yeah, Prof, I know just a tool in the grand big scheme of things, but hey look on the bright side, if I do make it and I intend to, then the government get what they want so badly and I'm rich beyond my wildest dreams eh? And I'll be relocated in a nice warm part of the world with a new identity and I'll never be bothered again, right?" The Professor held a small ceramic vile in his hand about the size of a grain of corn, "Well Conon, this goes under the skin and if the going gets too tough you know what you have to do with it." Only when he actually commenced the mission or just before the start point, the vile would be inserted under his skin probably under an armpit where even if he fell or was struck by a weapon or something similar the vile would remain fairly well protected, only if it was removed, using a knife or blade and crushed between two teeth would the ceramic outer shell burst and instant death would follow. Conon understood, but he didn't intend failing.

Professor Smith then spoke about how an implant, inserted into his femur several years ago needed to be kick started basically, if it still worked then the effects of fatigue and build-up of lactic acid causing muscle failure would be virtually non-existent, he didn't go into the science, he just gave it to Conon in layman's terms. There was a tiny optic fibre connecting the implant to the vagus nerve running almost the length of his body, which when activated would turn on his pain resistance by telling his body he wasn't feeling any pain, he might need to self-administer some drugs to help things along but who knows maybe he wouldn't even need to do that depending on how well the chip worked.

The Professor called Doctor Silva, who had been preparing the surgical equipment at the medical centre, everything was ready and the two men left the exam room they were in and arrived at the medical centre minutes later. Conon was asked to lie back and relax, easier said than done, not knowing what was really going on but he managed. The two scientists busied about the room and all Conon was aware of was Professor Smith holding a box about the size of a pint of milk that sounded like a Geiger counter next to his left thigh, he felt nothing and ten minutes after entering the room Conon was told to sit up. There was a knock at the door and Munro walked in. "How'd it go then?"

"It's all going extremely well." replied the Professor.

"Conon, we need to run a basic fitness test," said Munro. "You, over a measured distance carrying some basic kit, essentially an endurance run."

"Yeah, no worries Munro, I get it."

"We'll run you with Scouse, Donnie and Mack, they will beat you, they're three of the fittest guys out there but tomorrows another day." Munro smirked and Conon thought, so did Professor Smith, they knew what was happening after all so they knew what to expect.

Two hours later the four men stood at the start line, Donnie was the joker and was goading the others about how he was going to whoop their asses and at roughly ten years his junior, so he should at least beat him Conon thought to himself. The course was easy to follow, two miles of running with about forty pounds of kit on, then two miles of various tunnels, obstacles high and low and water lots of water, then a straight two mile run back to the base, easy...... Donnie stretched away from everyone right from the start but Conon stayed with the other two and even helped them through the tunnels, there were several PTi's posted along the course for safety reasons but they weren't needed, the only time they stepped in was to aide Donnie at one of the water tunnels. On the run for home Conon felt great, he was thoroughly enjoying the little jaunt and so he decided it was time to wind the little shit in, he tucked his head down and thought about anything but his aching chest, arms, legs and shoulders. With just under half a mile to go, just as he came onto a straight stretch of track about two hundred meters long Conon saw Donnie who was charging on oblivious to anyone behind him, the adrenalin started to kick in again and Conon felt his body ease up a gear and he began to reel the younger man in. Three hundred meters from home and Donnie glanced over his shoulder to see Conon fifty meters behind him, the young man nearly fell over when he saw the old guy, as he called him, so close to him. The rouse was up though and Donnie made his last blast for home, even when Clunt appeared out of the bushes at the side of the road and tried to shoulder charge him he still managed to stay on his feet, "ALWAYS EXPECT THE UNEXPECTED YOU FUCKING TURD!!" The US Navy Seals calls rang out for all to hear and Conon dug in even harder but now only a hundred meters from the finish line he wasn't going to catch the young gun.

Yahweh

As Conon ran over the line he patted Donnie on the back, Donnie was doubled over wretching and belching like he'd just been chased for his life, the old man had surprised him and nearly caught him, he'd be ready for Conon the next time.

Scouse and Mack came home just over two minutes later and together, forty three minutes and twenty seconds, an awesome time, the two men knew Donnie would beat them, he always did the little shit but they were in awe of Conon, almost ten years older than them but still able to run at an incredible pace, it was an awesome display. They all shook hands and guzzled on the bottles of water provided by the support team of Major Munro and several PTI's. The four men were congratulated on their efforts and given the rest of the day to themselves, Scouse suggested they give Conon a tour of the Op's room after they'd freshened up as they all walked back to the accommodation block. After showering and a huge meal the four men all went to the main ops room, Conon had been cleared to get access and the team showed him around, explained how they gathered all the Intelligence they could from ongoing events, nationally and worldwide and how the TV channels were superb at breaking high profile news long before they really should, journalists as Mack explained were gob shites that just couldn't hold their water, they would do just about anything to get the story out first and only very rarely would the top brass step in and request that they hold off for a certain period of time before running with a story. That usually only happened when it was obvious that lives could be lost or undercover operatives could be compromised if anything was leaked or published too soon. What Conon did find surprising though was that when certain weather forecasters were presenting they had direct links to them, two in particular. If they had operatives on covert missions anywhere in the world, as long as they had access to the BBC news, coded messages could be passed, Conon joked with the guys, "You're having a fucking laugh, surely not? No way was Carol Mckellaig passing on coded instructions on behalf of British Special Forces, No way?" Scouse smiled, "Why the fuck else would you specifically want to mention somewhere like Dingwall or Rogart or Inver or anywhere that has no real meaning unless it means something to someone? It isn't just so squaddies from these places who are abroad can give it a, hey hey that's where I'm from, no mate it's much deeper than that." They sat and watched the BBC weather and sure enough Carol Mckellaig appeared and after going through the motions of a good forecast and the press of a button, Dingwall, Rogart and Inver, places that Conon knew well all appeared on the screen, he turned to Scouse who just grinned at him and winked, "and she's fit as well mate." Conon mused that never again would he switch off the weather forecast and dismiss what the forecaster had to say.

Conon and Mack decided it was time for a stroll around Poole, time for Conon to buy some decent clothes and some other bits and pieces to keep him sane. They jumped in a taxi and headed towards town and were dropped off near to the town centre, it was bustling and after making their way around a few shops and buying a couple of pairs of jeans, some new desert wellies, some tee shirts and a smart casual outdoor jacket the two men decided on a couple of drinks before heading back to the base. They arrived at Corkers. "It used to be a wine bar when I was here last time Mack."

"It still is Conon." Said Mack, as they walked in through the door and by the look of things thought Conon, some of the women that were here the last time were still here too; he laughed and ordered a large glass of red wine, Merlot. Mack looked at the Highland man and said, "Why the hell not, make that two please." The barmaid smiled politely, she knew instinctively the two men were squaddies and more than likely Royal Marines. "Back in the day Mack I couldn't have asked for a glass of wine in here, a bottle of Sangria maybe but a glass of red wine, not a chance."

"Changed days Conon, modern times, I reckon we should arrange a night out, we haven't got much on tomorrow, well not that we know, so maybe tonight, what do you think?"

"Yeah sounds great." As Conon replied Mack was texting the others and arranging the night out, a small blow out would do them all the world of good. The two Marines finished off their wine and headed for the taxi rank and back to base for a shower and a good dinner before heading out on the town.

The four men ordered a taxi and decided that as Friday was going to be a kit day and pretty basic communications exercise they would have a night out, they spoke to Munro in his office who declined the offer of a few beers but if he managed to clear his desk of most of the burocratic nonsense he'd track them down and maybe have a few with them later, he only asked that they didn't get too drunk, Scouse grinned and in his guttural Liverpudlian speak said, "I'll keep an eye on them boss!" Munro replied.

"Yes Scouse, that's what worries me! Try and stay out of trouble."

"No problem Sir, we'll just have a few and be back in bed by midnight."

"Bugger off you cheeky Scouse git and have a good night."

Munro smiled as he listened to Scouse laughing as he walked along the corridor and headed for the exit.

The taxi pulled up at the main gate and the four men piled in, Scouse jumped in the front passenger seat and asked the driver to take them to Corkers wine bar, "Eh lads, that'll do for starters eh?" The other three mumbled in general agreement that anywhere that served cool beer would be a good start, ten minutes later the taxi pulled away and the four Marines entered the bar. To just about everyone that lived and socialised in the area they stuck out like sore thumbs, even though they weren't your run of the mill squaddies and they never caused trouble, there was something about four men who were obviously Royal Marines walking into any of the bars in Poole, the only thing most people who were even remotely interested in them wondered was, were they Special Boat Squadron, trainee drivers, landing craft crew or Marines on a selection course? The four men sat at a table and ordered a carafe of wine. Conon had been in the place over ten years ago and apart from an obvious lick of paint it was still pretty much the bar he remembered, Donnie nudged his elbow, "So you old fucker, thought you were going to sneak up on me today eh?" Scouse and Mack laughed, "Well you were getting a bit slow towards the end there Donnie and one thing I've never been short of is stamina!"

"Ah you'll fucking need it the next time coz I am going to bust your nuts big time old boy!"

"Just remember Donnie, many's a fine tune is played on an old fiddle!" The four men roared with laughter and Donnie, beaten by the quick wit of Conon for once shut his mouth and guzzled on his wine. As the evening progressed the four men enjoyed the atmosphere in the bar and decided that they would stay where they were and as the night wore on, quietly they sat at their table at the back of the bar keeping the volume down and trying not to draw any attention to themselves, they just sat regaling stories of battles fought and conquests won. Donnie who was the youngest sat in awe as Scouse told them about how he'd ended up deciding to go for the Shaky Boats as they were nicknamed, after he'd been volunteered to go on a weeklong exercise in Southern Helmand Province, the only thing was, he hadn't a clue he was working with a team of Special Boat Squadron Marines and two US Navy SEALS, Scouse was only there to provide radio and communication cover, the guy on the team who normally did that job had been injured playing football and there had been a big row about that but never the less, Scouse was delighted he'd been asked, "Highly recommended," he smirked as he grinned at the others. They had gone straight across the Pakistani border in a Chinook helicopter escorted by two Apache attack helicopters and after setting up surveillance on a house on the outskirts of a small town, the team were happy they'd located their target, Betullah Mehsud, they'd called it in and three of the team painted the house with lasers mounted on our rifles as the drone was vectored into their position, the drone could do the job by itself but with ground assistance there was far less chance of collateral damage. That swang it for me and I ended up volunteering as soon as I got back. Donnie apparently just always wanted to do it and after two tours in Afghanistan he got his wish, yes he'd had a few hairy moments but he reckoned the best was still to come for him, "What about you Conon?" asked Mack. "It's been a few years since you went through selection, how'd you end up where you got to?" Conon looked at the three men at the table, "My lawyer fucked me!" The four men all laughed again as Conon told them about the time he'd come home from a tour in West Belfast back in the eighties and whilst out there he didn't drink just trained and he was fitter than he'd ever been, anyway the first night home and he went out by himself got pissed and on his way up the High Street in Dingwall on his way to Cookies Chinese takeaway, he saw a pair of black shiny boots in front of him and when he looked up here was this Sergeant Copper in front of him, after deciding that all cops were bastards, quietly he added, he promptly got himself lifted and thrown in the back of the black mariah. Inside he'd realised the one big fault they

Yahweh

had was that you could see out but no one could see in and so he squatted on the floor like Linford Christie and he decided that if they didn't shut the gates at the back of the station he was gone!! History.... they didn't know who he was after all, so he'd get home grab his gear, get back to Arbroath, lie low for the last week of his Christmas leave and hopefully get flown out to Norway early for their winter training. So he told them about the gate not closing and about the merry goose chase he'd led the local coppers on for about three hours and about how he'd fallen asleep on his bed when he eventually got in and how his father had woken him up to let him know there was ten cops at the house to lift him. Scouse was wetting himself, Mack was listening and Donnie just sat with his gob open. Anyway the upshot of that was the Sergeant told Conon in his cell the next morning that two of his mates had come into the front counter demanding to see him and that one of the old cops, Jakey Mackay heard his name and said sorry lads he'll get out in the morning, turns out he'd told the Sergeant everything there was to know about me, he'd known me since I was a kid, so in the end I was running for fuck all. The Cop Sergeant then says to me you'll be right in the shit for this malarkey won't you? Yeah, I sure will, I told him, so he said well speak to your boss when you get back and tell him to call me and we'll sort out something between us, how does that sound? Fuck me I was delighted but shitting myself. First parade back at Arbroath, Company lines, the Sergeant Major gives it, "OKAY any one of you bastards been in trouble take one step forward now and when I stepped forward every fucker just started laughing, I was the youngest Marine on parade and he never expected it from me, he was raging, I thought he was going to drop me on the spot. Anyway he goes off muttering about killing me and my worst nightmares were coming and he phones the Copper. The Sergeant Major then calls me into his office and every fucker on the base heard him telling me he was going to make sure I suffered out in Norway. For two months I avoided him, don't ask me how I did it but I swear I avoided him for two months then one day I was sitting in the guard room and the guy I was on duty with says," Hey Conon, has Sticks caught up with you yet?" The Sergeant Majors name was Barker, I was reading a broad sheet newspaper that's all I remember and I put it on my lap, "No why?" I asked,

"Well he's on his way across here now." We both looked out of the window and sure enough there was Sticks marching through the snow heading for the guard room, before I could move the door was opening and all I could do was pull the paper up so it covered my face and I watched his boots stride passed me. "Morning lads," he boomed.

"Morning Sir," we replied and before he reached his office I saw the boots stop and turn back towards me, then as I looked down and saw the Sergeant Majors boots between my own, I felt the paper being pulled down and as I looked up I saw his pace stick on top of the paper forcing it down slowly and he just growls at me, "Thought you could hide all this time you little shit? Don't think I've forgotten about you!" I ended up in the Sergeant mess that Saturday night and cleaned everything there was to clean, plates, pots, roasting dishes, floors you name it, there was another guy there, Steve Watkins, he was a regular defaulter but a great laugh, mad as fuck. We ended up with about four bottles of wine, port, whisky and a platter full of sandwiches and I mind Sticks giving Watkins fuck and telling him there was no hope for him and to fuck off out of his sight, then when he'd gone he said he had high hopes for me and never to let him down again, promised him I wouldn't." "So did you go for the selection course after that Conon?" asked Mack. "No when I got home on leave I got into a scrap, they started it, two of them and the cops got me again, then the Sergeant Major got me again, only this time he drags me round to the HQ Sergeant Majors office, when he went into W.O.2 Shennon's office I was told to stand outside and wait until he called me, I didn't have a clue what the fuck was going on, I knew Shennon was Special Boats and that was it. So Sticks calls me into the office and he says, "Okay, you can go on a Special Boat Squadron acquaint course in September or you can go on a chefs course in October the choice is yours!" As my jaw hit the floor Sticks laughs at me and says, "Good lad, I think you'd make a shite chef for what it's worth!" The rest is history, here I am, had a great time, did a snipers course amongst others and got fucked over for basically saving about eight US Marines and I'm about to go on a suicide mission. Donnie could only sit and say, "Wow, that was some entry into the Squadron mate, I just hope the next part works out for you."

At midnight Mack very drunkenly announced that they should all speed march back to camp, stupidly they all agreed. The four men all began the jog back to camp and as drunk as they were not surprisingly they set a good pace. As they reached Hamworthy Park a car pulled up alongside them and a gorgeous brunette wound down her window and asked if they wanted a lift, a unified nuhhh rang out and then Donnie peeled off and said," Fuck you, you gay bastards, I'm in there!" The woman laughed as Donnie jumped into the cars passenger seat and Scouse shouted, "You'll be sorry in the morning Donnie." As the car did a turn into the park Conon, Scouse and Mack jogged on. They arrived back at the base soon afterwards and after a quick coffee in the NAAFI, they were showered and in bed by one A.M.

The routine for Friday morning was a relaxed one, the four men met up at breakfast and as they sat at the table Scouse was the first to ask Donnie about his trap from the night before, "Aye she was alright."

"What do you mean she was alright?" asked Scouse.

"Well, she pulled in and parked up, asked me if I was up for some fun, so of course I says yeah of course babe, the next thing I know she flicks a lever and I'm flat on my back with the seat down and she's got her hand straight down the front of my jeans, she unzips me and leans over and I swear it was the bestest BJ I've ever had, swallowed everything!" Scouse sat unable to put the spoon of porridge into his mouth.

"You lucky fucker!!"

"Not so fast mate, I then decided as I like to reciprocate the pleasures of the flesh with any lady friend I may introduce myself to, I thought well hell one good turn deserves another and as she lies back I slipped my hand up the inside of her left thigh and I start bulging again as I detect she is wearing stockings and suspenders!!"

"Go on, go on then," Scouse could hardly contain himself. "Well just as I'm thinking, condom or bare back, will I or wont I, I slipped my hand inside her knickers and she had a bigger cock than me!!!!!" The table erupted and every Marine in the galley turned and wondered just what Munro's team were finding so funny at that time of the morning, even Donnie was laughing. As the laughter subsided Conon leaned across the table and placed a hand on Donnie's arm,

"Just remember mate, always expect the unexpected." The table erupted with laughter again, the team were getting along just fine.

The four men stood ready for their Monday morning run, the PTI's were out on the course waiting, Munro stood with Professor Smith and Doctor Silva watching as Gunny Herman prepared the men for the run. The camp was buzzing, the jungle drums were beating about the return of a legend, Conon Bridge and he was spitting distance behind Donnie Dumpster on the endurance run last week and everyone knew how quick he was. Munro asked Smith how things were progressing, "Well Munro, Conon doesn't realise it but the implant has been kick started and the way he's been wired up basically means when the lactic acid kicks in he produces more adrenalin to counter act it, although if the truth is told we don't really know what will happen, he should in theory run faster and further the more he tries and he's a machine anyway so what we have, hopefully, is an old dog with every trick in the book and the ability to last longer than anyone else."

"I bloody well hope you're right Smith." Donnie was jumping about and prancing around like a cat on a hot tin roof, "Well Conon, feeling like an old fart today?" Conon stood and looked at the younger man and smiled at him, "What would you like to drink at the end of the run today Donnie, I'll make sure I have it waiting for you."

"Ha ha ha ha ha ha, a nice pint of cool lager from the NAAFI bar and I'll stand in the middle of the parade square bollock naked and drink it if you beat me old man!" Munro looked at the two doctors, "Is he going to beat him or not then?" Smith replied, "My money's not just on him beating Donnie, I think he'll probably manage a pint of lager himself before Donnie even gets back into the camp." Gunny Herman called the men forwards and boomed out some standard orders about fair play, helping others and enjoy the run gentlemen, "GO!!!" The four men trotted out through the main gate and disappeared from view, Munro, Smith and Silva climbed into an unmarked Range Rover and drove straight to the first check point, Herman was driving. As they arrived at the three mile point which was the start of the cross country section, they watched as all four men appeared through the trees at the end of the lane, Donnie was first then Mack then Scouse then Conon, hardly a bead of sweat between them. The four men ran passed the Range Rover and with some gentle words of encouragement from Gunny Herman they were off on the cross country section. All four were until they reached the dry tunnels, very evenly matched, the stones and boulders nearly blocked the first tunnel and it was a squeeze for all of them getting through the two sets of underground challenges, then they reached the pool crossing, Peter's Pool and as they ran up the embankment and out of the river crossing Donnie put his first real spurt on, he glanced over his shoulder and there expressionless behind him followed Conon. The two of them stretched away from Mack and Scouse. Donnie dug in harder, he didn't turn around again to see where Conon was, he could hear the older man's feet striking the ground right behind him, every step of the way. Conon felt great, fantastic, no matter how hard the little shit in front of him tried, he wasn't able to stretch away from Conon. At the end of the cross country section Donnie felt Conon on his shoulder and he could give no more, he glanced to his left, "Go on then, get the pints in," was all he could manage. Conon just seemed to drop down a gear and left the younger man in his wake, the PTi's about the remainder of the course encouraged Conon to give it everything, not that he needed any encouragement. He ran through the main gates and it seemed as if the camp was at a standstill, he ran straight to the NAFFI and asked for two pints of lager, he'd pay later, the woman behind the bar looked bemused but served him, he ran up to the parade square without spilling a drop and placed them both directly on the centre spot then he ran over to the office block where mainly WRENs and female admin staff worked. As soon as he entered the door he set off the fire alarm and ran back out to the parade square, he lifted his pint of lager and as he supped on the cool refreshment Donnie came around the corner, he knew he'd been well and truly beaten but he didn't expect to see Conon with two pints of lager and one almost finished and the alarm was sounding in the admin block, he stopped in front of

Conon who held out the pint, "I think the words were bollock naked in the middle of the parade square?"

"You fucker Bridge," Donnie looked and saw about thirty women all standing waiting to be counted, Donna was watching the two Marines it was just a fire drill after all.

None of them was expecting an impromptu strip tease by one of the Marines, Donnie stretched out for the pint, "Eh no, no, no, a deal's a deal Donnie." The younger man smiled and heard Scouse and Mack run onto the parade square closely followed by the training team in the Range Rover, "You fucker Bridge." Donnie laughed and began stripping, Munro intervened, "That's enough Donnie, Conon, well done astonishing run and you've made your point." Conon laughed and realised he wasn't even short of breath, whatever the good doctors had done, it didn't hurt a bit. Later in the day the four men sat in the ops room, nothing much going on apart from a tin pot type threatening to throw nuclear missiles at the United States from North Korea. Tomorrow was another day, they were heading for Brize Norton for parachute training and out to Canada two days later to utilise the huge wide open spaces, where no one would see them.

The team arrived at Brize Norton, they didn't turn any heads, the R.A.F. personnel were well used to all sorts coming and going, even though they were in two unmarked Range Rovers, Special Forces staff were just a normal occurrence to most of them. Munro cleared all four Marines and himself at the guard room, then they headed out to the training area where over the next few days they would do some ground work and then some static line work from a C130 Hercules and a Chinook before they progressed onto some H.A.L.O. jumps, high altitude, low opening. The next two days went completely without fault, all of them, Munro included were expert at jumping out of aircraft and the modern steerable chutes were superb to fly, even easy, if you knew what you were doing. Conon who hadn't jumped for a few years likened the experience to riding a bicycle, once you'd learned, you never forgot. On day three they found themselves at departures Brize Norton, the place resembled any other departure terminal with a similar bustling feel to it but there were Royal Air Force staff in place everywhere instead of the usual British Airways or Virgin or any other regional staff you would normally find at a busy airport. The five men sat waiting for flight R.A.F.101 Brize Norton to Gander, Newfoundland, it wasn't going to be the most exciting trip ever but by the time they were finished out there it would time for the big show. The five men boarded the Tri-Star aircraft at 0900 hours, flight departure was at 0930 and arrival at Gander was a shade over four and a half hours so plenty of time for sleep, they were all tired and they only woke up to eat the packed lunches the stewardess gave to them. They all finished everything and drank the paper mugs of surprisingly good coffee, Donnie gathered up the gash and took it to the back of the airliner where he tried to get the stewardesses mobile phone number, Conon looked over his shoulder and laughed, Scouse said, "He's a trier." Donnie appeared back five minutes later and announced she was meeting him on his return from where ever it was they were heading, he not surprisingly managed to look rather smug with himself.

The Tri-Star touched down and the hundred or so Welsh Guards disembarked, they were travelling onwards to Fort Wainwright, Alberta, so they were getting a break and a stretch of their legs, once the Guards were cleared from the aircraft the Marines disembarked and waited at an area away from the others to collect their kit, they then made their way out to a small set of buildings at the northern corner of the airfield known as the Ranch, the men got out of the vehicle and made their way into the building off Roe Avenue, it was used by the British Special forces and run by a local man who himself was once upon a time a member of the S.A.S. Andy Urquhart, he now worked as a Quarter Master for the British at the base. Andy welcomed everyone and showed them to the kit room, the flight suits were there and ready to go, the chutes were packed and checked, Munro was keen though for all of them to get some proper rest and although it wasn't even five p.m. he told Andy they'd go to the hotel, have a meal and a good rest and be out for a fresh start at 0800 hours the following morning. The team all appreciated the thought of freshening up, food and a warm bed, so after a brief meeting with Andy the team were taken to the hotel and within the hour all of them were in bed and fast asleep.

The following morning everyone enjoyed a hearty breakfast. Each of the guys had whatever they wanted and after a quick catch up of the international news on Sky TV they made their way to the airfield, all of them had slept well and they all felt refreshed and ready for anything Andy or Munro could throw at them. When they arrived they were met by Andy, he drove them straight to the building he worked from, the Ranch Hut, on route they passed amongst aircraft of varying shapes and sizes a Boeing 747 Jumbo jet, it was pure white from front to back and top to bottom, none of the Marines gave it a second look, it was just a cargo plane parked up waiting for its next long hauljob. Andy lead the Marines into the lecture room where they were invited to sit down, coffee was brewing in the corner and against one wall four sets of high altitude sky diving equipment were hanging waiting for the Marines, the suits were prototype flying suits, the jumper was dropped at high altitude and the suits were designed to give the user the ability, depending on the weather, to fly over thirty miles to their target, although unofficially the distances being covered by some of their counter parts in the Special Air Service were massively greater than thirty miles. After a morning of trying the suits on and lectures about rapid navigation techniques required for accurate landings and a look at some of the equipment that they would strap on to assist them, Andy invited the four men, Conon, Scouse, Mack and Donnie to jump on the bus outside, Munro jumped in the front with him. They headed for the white Jumbo. After climbing the steps at the front of the aircraft the four Marines wondered why they were in the giant aircraft which appeared on the outside to be no more than a cargo configured Boeing 747. Andy punched a several digit long pass code into the keypad, the door hissed and swang inwards, the Canadian man turned and winked at Munro and gestured with a nod of his head for the men to enter. Andy had a huge grin on his face which didn't escape Conon, the others including Munro stepped open mouthed into what at the forward end of the aircraft was a state of the art communications centre, everything was running on standby ready to go at a moment's notice, the air conditioning hummed and kept the interior of the aircraft and the equipment at an optimum running temperature. The men followed Andy who talked his way through the aircraft, explaining everything as he went, the Marines asked questions and all were answered. They reached the mid-section of the jet, again Andy entered a pin code into a keypad on the bulkhead and the door hissed and opened. They entered an armoury and stores section where every conceivable special ops toy was clamped to the racks before them. Even Conon was stunned at the array of weapons there was to choose from, there was every stick on bit and shiny thing you could imagine. The last section of the aircraft was no less secure than the first two, it was a departure lounge but one for paratroopers, surprisingly there was no static line equipment but there were tell-tale signs that they could all see. Conon looked out of the door they were standing beside and immediately noticed there was at least another ten meters to the aircraft, ten meters of what he wondered. As the four other Marines left and wandered down the steps after the short tour Conon turned around again and saw Andy stare at him with a grin on his face, "All in good time Conon, all in good time. This will be your way in, your way out will be slightly less obvious and definitely more dynamic, now let's go and try out the new jump suits." Conon walked with Andy towards the building off Roe Avenue, the others talked about just how far one of the suits on a good downhill slide with favourable winds would take them. Andy and Conon chatted about the next few days and Andy gave Conon a brief look into his own past, some of the things he'd done and some of the places he'd been, the majority of it all still classified, they followed the others back towards the Ranch and enjoyed the afternoon sun.

The men sat in the classroom and refreshed themselves with cool bottled water, some sandwiches were on the table for them to top up with and as usual the smell of fresh brewing coffee was permeating the air. The temperature outside was a balmy 18 degrees, it was a nice day. As they sat and talked about how they thought the new suits would work none of the Marines knew that Andy was holding back and so was Munro but within the next fifteen minutes the information and access they would be given on the base would surprise the four men.

Andy asked the men for their attention and asked them all to sit around the table in the centre of the room, Donnie was the only one standing up, he was guzzling water from a bowser and jumped when Andy spoke and threw himself at the remaining empty chair next to Munro, "Ok guys, sit tight and shut up. Everyone place your hands on the table." They all looked at each other with somewhat bemused expressions but they each placed their hands on the table, Andy produced what looked like a T.V. remote control and stepped towards the table and pressed a button, all five men, even Munro, who knew what was coming jumped slightly as the floor dropped beneath them and quietly the floor began to swallow them, "This, gentlemen, is where the fun begins." Andy chuckled as the floor lowered the men downwards and the ceiling began to close above them, the lighting automatically switched on and illuminated the shaft that they were slowly dropping down into. The lift, which they all by now realised they were on halted after a fifteen second ride downwards and after another press of a button on his remote control, Andy opened a door, a wall slid to the right in front of them. Beyond the door a short corridor lead into a fully functioning state of the art operations room, Andy stepped forward and beckoned for the Marines to follow him, they wandered forward with astonished expressions on their faces. Before them was a joint Canadian and British venture that was run by staff from all branches of each of the countries armed forces. There were monitors of all nature before the men. "The 747 above us gentlemen is crewed by these people down here, it's on permanent standby, there is a direct access chute from here to the aircraft and this has all been in the planning for some time." The whole place hummed with computers running and air conditioning working, the four Marines and Conon stood in awe of what they were seeing, there were men and women wearing all manner of uniforms working away taking no notice of any of the men now standing in their midst. The staff had all been chosen for their abilities but each of them had no family, no parents, no siblings, no husbands or wives, all dedicated to fight for the cause of good against evil. Andy was proud of what had been achieved and as Professor Smith appeared with Doctor Silva and Mr Black, Conon realised that the time for work to begin would soon be upon them, he looked at Andy and asked, "Why Canada, why have we ended up here, the Americans are surely ahead of us, that's what everybody knows yes?" Andy smiled.

"Conon, we have you, the yanks don't, thanks to Professor Smith. The reason we're here is so that you can be sent, with our help to find out what we've suspected for a long, long time. Out here there's thousands of square miles of nothing but wilderness and you know something about the mission we're here for just now but there are other unanswered questions and the British and Canadian Governments have decided that after the Americans have yet again baulked on another arms deal, to both our nations, the latest being the new JSF, Joint Strike Fighter project, they want to find the answers for themselves and that's where you especially come in Conon, the rest of the guys are your back up and support team, they're going to get you in the shit and hopefully out of it too, this is going to be the start of something hopefully long lasting gents. The Americans have been holding out on everyone for a very long time and anyway the real reason you guys are here is we trust the yanks less than we trust the Ruskies and just because the Cold War is over and we're all hugging on the outside, it don't mean it's safe to go to sleep just yet, that's why the British, the French and anyone else with a quiet submarine has been parked off the east coast of the United States spying on them for the last forty to fifty years, Jesus there have been more nuclear sub near misses off Atlantic City than anywhere else in the world, it's like a nuke sub parking lot and the Royal Navy have had a sub parked in Chesapeake Bay for at least the last thirty years!" Andy roared and laughed and announced how much it annoyed the Americans that even though they knew you guys were there, they could never find you. Conon couldn't help but wonder if the Royal Navy were ever there at all but someone had clearly sewn the seed.

Professor Smith spoke, "Gentlemen, shall we move to the conference room?" The men all followed the medical man and once in the conference room they were invited to sit and listen to what was to be a detailed operational brief for the mission they were all about to be sent on. Conon knew he was the lead man, the rest were about to find out they were his back up in what was probably going to become the scariest few hours of their lives.

Mr Black addressed the Marines, "Gentlemen about six months ago a Royal Navy submarine was parked off the east coast of the United States, she was on a routine reconnaissance and surveillance mission when they picked up a garbled message from someone who it appears was spying for the Americans on a small island in the East China sea, we have no idea who he is, the yanks have said nothing about him or his mission but it looks as if he's got himself captured and we have been wondering why the Americans haven't started any kind of diplomatic talks to recover their man and why the Chinese have remained so tight lipped about it." Munro interrupted Mr Black. "British Intelligence has been throwing everything at this one gents," and as he pointed to a large screen on the wall a map of the island, Luxi Dao appeared. "This place has got excellent access to the open ocean, it's got a very well-staffed research centre which the Chinese don't know we know about and a long straight road running up the middle of it which our satellites have proven is being used as an airstrip, bizarrely it runs straight into the side of a mountain, they've tried to disguise it as a simple tunnel but it's huge and nothing seems to go in and come out the other end after the minutes or so it would take to drive through it, oh and there is also a fairly large hydro dam system there as well, the general thoughts of our experts is that it's way too much for the surface constructions we can see on our satellite images for anything "normal" to be associated with it." Munro sat down and politely waved at Professor Smith giving him the floor.

"You may be wondering just exactly what my remit is in all this gentlemen, well the bottom line is my department at Porton Down has been tasked with trying to piece together the ingredients for the coating of the Russian sub that mysteriously disappeared off the Sound of Sleat about six months ago. We ended up stumbling over Luxi Dao, we have no real idea what's going on there but the Chinese are streaming in and out of the place with naval ships disguised as fishing boats and the Russians are pretty busy in and out of the main port there as well, it's almost as if there's a production line running the length of the island, the Chinese are piling stuff in one end and they and the Russians are shipping whatever is being manufactured there out the other end and curiously there appear to be submarine pens at the north east end of the island as well. We think there's mass manufacturing of chemicals going on but we really aren't one hundred percent sure. Our intelligence so far leads us to conclude that it's probably to do with the stealth coating we believe the Chinese have discovered and from the information we have there's probably chemical warfare agents being manufactured there as well." Munro spoke again.

"That's where we come in guys, the aircraft out there is how we get in, Conon, bottom line you're," Conon interrupted, "Expendable?"

"No, oh no you're not, you're here for all sorts of reasons, mainly you're one of if not the best we have at this kind of job."

The detailed plan about the flight out and the insertion was impressive. With luck they would be in, steal the information they wanted from the research centres mainframe computer by transfer onto portable hard drive which had been extensively modified by Smith's team to operate autonomously the second it was triggered, all Conon had to do was get in and out of Luxi Dao in fifteen minutes. For hours they poured over the plans, who would be positioned where and what kit they would carry, they had the benefit of a near three dimensional view with the modern surveillance equipment they had used to photograph the island and so by the time they started the mission each of the Marines would be able to run and move swiftly about the island, almost with his eyes shut.

So, Conon would do the dirty work and the others would be waiting to assist with the escape whilst Munro waited aboard the submarine offshore that would retrieve the team at least that was the plan. The team now had to get to know the system aboard the 747 that would deliver them onto Luxi Dao. Conon looked at Andy and asked him a question. "Is this where we find out about the mystery missing ten meters Andy?" Andy smiled.

"Yeah it sure is and I bet you'll be impressed too, let's go take a look."

Conon said nothing more but he guessed it was a dispatch area for paratroopers, it was clearly going to be state of the art if the rest of the aircraft was anything to go by, he couldn't wait to feast his eyes on what was within the ten meters they hadn't yet been given access to.

They all walked out to the 747 after they had been issued with inconspicuous looking boiler suits, just in case anyone was watching, the last thing they wanted was some sneaky spook from anywhere taking photos of five fit guys wandering about the monster jet wearing combats.

The hydraulic lift system that you would find at any airport was positioned over a disguised hatch on the ground which gave the Marines access to the underground operations centre and direct access to the aircraft, anyone watching would simply see several men coming and going from the container sized compartment and think they were loading the aircraft or carrying out repairs, it was simple and it was tried and tested. They made their way to the briefing room within the operations centre and began looking at photographs and plans of the island of Luxi Dao.

Unseen by the Royal Marines team, Mr Black who was a now ever constant shadow, had taken a call and quietly excused himself, the guys were so wrapped up in looking at base layouts, floor plans and the security systems at the

Luxi Dao research Centre they hardly noticed he'd left the room, they would be deep in planning mode for the rest of the day, the rest of the week probably and although his self-excusal wasn't acknowledged the others had all subconsciously seen him go, he may have been leaving the room for a number of reasons, he didn't have to put his hand up for permission so no one gave it another thought.

Black sat himself at the terminal and opened up the communications link to his boss back at S.O.E. headquarters, it really was an unknown, unseen, black ops security and espionage department, it was funded by money supplied by the government, veiled by the darkest cloak of subterfuge imaginable. The reason for the unit being sited underneath the BBC's broadcasting house was in essence desperately simple, in a modern age of Wi-Fi the competition just could not decipher so much information coming and going from one building, even so every last dot on any I or cross on any T was digitally encrypted, the SOE had the ability to work from anywhere as a standalone organisation but the myriad of tunnels, there since the second world war were perfect, they were blocked off from access from the building above but once upon a time Winston Churchill had walked through the very same corridors. S.O.E. Special Operations Executive, had existed since the Second World War; many believed after the war it had been disbanded but the cold war ensured the need to carry on with the work done during Britain's darkest times. The only difference now was that instead of their training taking place in areas such as Lochailort, Arisaig or Morar in the Highlands of Scotland, the bulk of the training was done abroad, in Australia, Canada, Antarctica and various other still reasonably quiet places all over the world where there were few prying eyes and those that were prying were being watched themselves.

The link went live and Mr Black saw his Commanding officer on the screen.

"Black, I hope you're well and everything's going too plan out there? I'll cut straight to the chase, our colleagues at Mi6 have been speaking to our colleagues at Langley, it appears that they have been informed through extremely quiet channels that the operative in detention at Luxi Dao is going to be executed in forty eight hours' time, the Russians are washing their hands of the situation, it appears they have discovered the operative is a double agent and they are quite happy for the execution to take place it sounds as if they are quite embarrassed and the Chinese will be doing them a big favour, it looks like the operative has been feeding the Americans information for years and has been caught spying within the research centre at Luxi Dao. The Chinese do not appear to know about the extent of the information that was being fed to the Americans and although the Russians will be getting rid of a problem quietly the Americans unfortunately want the operative back alive. We have also found out that the Russians have managed to persuade the Chinese to part with new chemical warfare technology in exchange for assistance with their space programme, however the Americans have also been getting in on the act and the operative has we now think been giving them highly detailed information on the Chinese chemical weapon formulas for their new chemical weapon and details of the manufacturing systems of the Chinese production line for the chemical production which this new stealth coating substance is a very useful by-product of, it's all quite unbelievable. After being inserted by the Russians at Luxi Dao as an advisor, the Chinese think the spy they've captured has only recently been involved in spying on them. In short the Americans have asked if we can assist with a rescue mission, they believe the operative may still be of high value when debriefed and they have placed the operative in the highest and most sensitive tier of their special operations wish list, they put the value of the information the operative has on what's going on at Luxi Dao as priceless."

"So what you're saying Sir is the guys have to be good to go in about twenty four hours at most and not the thirty or so days we thought they had?"

"Yes Black, in essence the Americans are claiming that they have no one that can do the job which we all know is a load of nonsense but clearly it's a huge risk, the bottom line is if anyone involved in it is captured then there country of origin has a huge diplomatic nightmare on their hands. The Chinese are opening up on the industrial front but they simply don't have the ability to feed their massive industrial and population explosion, a short while ago they had sixty percent of their working population out in the fields and now it's as low as thirty maybe lower due to the increased industrial activity in the country but they need their basic infrastructure expanded to keep pace with industry, the profits for anyone able to exploit the domestic markets there are massive, it's the new frontier, the auto industries, the oil, pharmaceutical, engineering, transport, you name them they want to get there feet in the door so to speak and if the Americans are caught in there with their pants down you can bet the Chinese will slam the door shut and the markets are just too big for them to risk it, hence the reason they've "asked us for assistance" and here's the carrot they're dangling. What they have promised us in return is of huge value, if we pull this off. They are going to provide the Royal Navy with two complete squadrons of F 35s and enough spares to keep them airworthy indefinitely for the new Queen Elizabeth class carriers. The operative is potentially worth billions to the Americans and us now and probably does hold huge amounts of highly sensitive information, just what though is the multi-million dollar question but the fact that the Americans are willing to pay such a high price for this rescue mission is sending out quite a message. Clearly it's not all just about the chemicals or the stealth technology. As you know the Americans have been holding back on signing over certain licences allowing B.A.E. systems to reproduce the F35's and they're worried that we are going to produce a version of the aircraft that will outshine theirs but they need our help and it looks like they're willing to pay a high price for this operative."

"Wow he must be some guy."

Black was aware of his boss laughing, it was almost inaudible but he was definitely laughing. "That's precisely what we thought initially Black but he's a she, Sonny Yvonyv, proven in Afghanistan and in Georgia, ruthless from what we know about her but went off the radar after almost being killed in Iraq, ironically by the Americans just over a year ago. It seems the Russians have got wind of the fact the Americans were planning a raid on the Chinese research centre and they've had Yvonyv put in to attempt to steal the formulas and all the information she could get but the silly bitch has gone and got herself captured in her attempts, we don't know how she's done it but it looks like she's well and truly fucked."

"Jesus, so there's a chance the Chinese are expecting someone to have a go at a rescue attempt, it gets better by the second, they are going to love this when I tell them."

"All the information for your brief is on its way, not that there's much deviation from the original plan only that we've had to bring everything forward in time considerably. Conon is ready according to what you've already told me and with help from his team they'll get her out before the Chinese or the Russians even know they're there. We don't believe the Russians are saying anything to the Chinese about this."

"I bloody well hope not Sir." Mr Black hung up and made his way back to the operations room, he was not looking forward to this briefing.

The Marines immersed themselves in plans of the research centre, they were spread out across the huge table in the middle of the briefing room, Munro was the first to lift his head but Donnie was the first to react. "Aye aye lads, news coming." By the time Black had finished the four Marines were sitting in stunned silence. Munro stood up and spoke. "Andy can you get the big bird running and ready to go, guys we need to do at least one trial run to make sure we are confident working the rigs and get familiar with the deployment system, get yourselves over to the changing rooms and get kitted up, Andy how long do

Yahweh

you need?" Andy walked over to a wall panel and pressed a button, the whole operations room looked like it was contorting, as the men watched Andy explained what was going on, "Gentlemen, the personnel you are watching are now making their way to predesigned positions and will be lifted into the aircraft which is parked directly above us, they will be transferred into the aircraft by a lift system that will conceal them at all times but outwardly it will appear as if we are loading cargo, they are being transferred to the aircraft now in prioritised requirement according to their individual roles aboard the jet, you guys will look like cargo handlers, let's do it." Mack spoke as the men watched the well-oiled team flow into place, "Thunderbirds are go or what?" Within ten minutes the Marines plus Andy and Mr Black were walking out to the 747. On-board they strapped in and the aircraft took off, according to the flight manifest they were twelve souls on board and empty heading for Heathrow U.K. In reality they were thirty two souls and laden to the teeth with the most modern hand held weapons systems available. The aircraft rose quickly to thirty five thousand feet and the four Marines quickly but professionally prepared themselves for their drop. Munro addressed them. "Behind the bulkhead you haven't even seen yet gentlemen is a unique deployment system, the hole for want of a better word at the rear of our Jumbos fuselage has been extensively modified, that's where we spit you out. The Marines observed the pods spaced out on trestles across the floor. "Obviously we can't slow down or we draw attention to ourselves. These gents are your flight pods, you get in with your kit attached as normal, we drop you and after a short fall the pod stabilises, three drogue chutes slow you down and the pod separates, that's you guys on the forward throw heading downhill as normal, the suits you're wearing aren't new technology, you'll all have used them before but the materials are state of the art. Basically everything is stealth built, radar reflective, the pods hit the water and begin to dissolve instantly and you guys glide for hopefully at least fifty miles."

Donnie spoke, "Fuck sake Andy, fifty miles?"

"Yeah and if you don't shut the fuck up and listen we'll be sixty out before you know it!" It was the first time they had seen Andy assert himself in any way. The Marines listened, "We're lucky guys, we can give you the wind you'll need for this one and it'll be dark by the time you land back at Gander. We'll be returning with an engine failure so that'll explain our return on the radio if any nosey bastards are listening." The four men geared up and were loaded two at a time onto the launch system, Mack and Conon first then Scouse and Donnie. By the time the pilot was calling Gander to report they were returning to the airport with an engine problem the four men were already out of the pods and gliding back towards the airstrip, they would be airborne for about thirty minutes, unheard of in sports skydiving.

As they dropped from the sky the four Marines all saw the lights of the airstrip ahead, the 747 was on the ground parked up and men from the office they rented on Roe Road were at work on the port inner engine doing nothing. Mack, Scouse and Donnie all landed on the grass strip outside the building no one had seen them, no one had seen Conon land almost sixty seconds earlier silently on the roof of the lecture room where Andy and Munro sat waiting whilst Mr Black watched on the CCTV system. Conon was lucky, the breeze had been near perfect and he'd landed on the roof with the force of a cotton ball, just now and again everything seemed to slot into place and everything worked perfectly, he lay in wait hoping the rest of the team wouldn't see him as they came into land, he must remember not to move, movement was a sure fire way of giving your position away. Luck was on his side and he watched as the rest of the team landed nearby. The Marines walked into the room to find Munro and Andy sitting with fresh coffee ready to warm them up, Munro spoke. "Where is he?" The three Marines all looked at each other and shrugged their shoulders, Donnie was the last to see Conon, arms in tight by his side and fucking off into the distance, as he put it. "Ok get out of your gear and let's not make a fuss but we need to find him." Andy and Munro went outside and began searching the immediate local area for Conon, within a minute the other three Marines were also outside and fanned out line abreast looking for the new team member, they were all thinking about the possibility that Conon may have injured himself, nobody dared to say anything though. Conon watched from the roof of the building as the five men passed beneath him, as soon as they were out of ear shot he dropped down from the roof silently and walked into the main room and poured himself a coffee. Fifteen minutes later the five searchers walked in and were greeted by Conon's smile, "Hey guys what's up? Landed on the roof, bang on target, and thought let's see if I can get passed you guys, it worked and I'm now thinking if I can get passed you lot then we could just pull it off in Luxi Dao, no?" Andy started to laugh, the rest all joined in. Mr

Black who had been watching everything on the CCTV system said nothing but was impressed.

The men were debriefed by Andy and Munro, the first practice run had gone well, extremely well but they all knew that was the only practice they would get and after a night's sleep they would be back at Roe Road in less than ten hours for more briefings and then it would be a flight of nearly twenty hours, Gander to Taipei under the guise of transporting goods for the electronics industry, the plans were still being worked out but the team were ready to go.

Out in the East China sea HMS Astute cruised at a depth of one hundred meters, her Commanding officer, Commander Walker, had twenty four hours earlier received an order to proceed to an area twenty miles west of Luxi Dao and await further instructions, the wheels that turned in the intelligence world were working overtime and although they weren't in Chinese territorial waters they were flirting with danger and that's what he and his crew had trained for. The executive officer was handed the signal and in turn handed it to the Captain, they were to move to a position four miles east of Luxi Dao, where they were going to have to retrieve a Special Bot Squadron operative, then at 0400 hours in twenty hours' time be prepared to retrieve a further four Special Boat Squadron personnel plus one, that could mean one of two things, they were rescuing someone or kidnapping someone. Walker didn't dwell on the possibilities or speculate out loud, he simply told the Executive Officer to make it so.

Yahweh

The 747 climbed to its cruising ceiling of forty thousand feet, heading for the west coast of Canada, it was 0600 hours, they would be over the drop zone at 0200 hours, their time and the four man team would have two hours to get in, get the info they needed, get Yvonyv and get out to the pickup point. They ran over the mission several times and checked and re-checked the gear. They could do no more, the four men were at the peak of fitness, Conon was ready and all of them had memorised their own particular part of the job, Conon was going in, through the front door, Donnie was covering the front, Scouse was co-ordinating everything on the communications side and backing up Donnie, Mack was laying booby traps for any potential pursuit on their exit route, he would actually be the last man out, priming the charges as the last man passed him along the escape route. The men tried to rest and relax as best they could.

Conon stood up and stretched, he looked at his watch, 0930 hours, they'd been airborne just over three hours, the gear had been checked and re-checked, he'd tried to sleep but unusually for him he couldn't switch off. Conon looked at the others, they were all asleep, he moved back through the aircraft until he found Munro, Andy and Black, they were sitting drinking coffee, Munro spoke, "Can't sleep Conon?"

"No, I'm closing my eyes but it's just not happening."

Munro reached inside his jacket and took out a small bottle of tablets, "Here Conon, pop one of these, it'll knock you out for at least four hours, I'll come and check on you then, make sure everything's ok." Conon reached out and took the small yellow jelly tablet from Munro, "Are we all ready for this Munro?"

"Yes, we are all ready for this Conon, you're ready for this and you won't fail, you're about to find out just how good you really are actually." Conon sat down and looked at the three men at the table.

"How far is this journey going to take us gentlemen?" Mr Black sat back and looked at Conon, then Munro then Andy, he returned his gaze to Conon and spoke. "In all honesty Conon we don't really know, we know the Chinese have taken a massive leap forward in the chemical warfare arena and the Russians have joined in thanks to the information passed onto them by Yvonyv. The huge dilemma we have is that we now know the Americans have thrown their hat into the ring and they are telling us, the partners in the "Old Alliance" nothing, they think we are unaware of the exchange of information going on, we also don't know how much they actually know so we really want to get Yvonyv to ourselves to speak to her before we hand her over to the Yanks. Conon laughed, "Talk to her, that's a nice way of putting it."

"Well you just worry about getting her out of the place and we'll take care of the rest, but just so you're ready........"
"Yeah always expect the unexpected, I doubt very much even if we get her and the information we're looking for out of this place that'll be the end of it." Conon stood up and threw the tablet into his mouth, "Would one of you gentlemen be kind enough to waken me in four hours' time?" Andy spoke and reminded Conon he'd look after him, the others were sound asleep, blissfully unaware of Conon's chat with the team leaders. Conon settled back into his bunk and switched the light off, his head sank back into the pillow and he listened to the whine from the engines, he drew the curtain back to give himself some privacy and sleep was almost instant, he drifted off, relaxed and comfortable.

At the table where Munro, Andy and Black sat, Munro asked Black to be more specific about just where they could end up. Black was not evasive but admitted they really had no idea and that if it was the worst case scenario then there was a possibility that they could all find themselves in deep trouble, "We could end up having to work our way into the Americans and that would be a complete nightmare."

"A nightmare? Are you able to tell us anymore?" asked Munro.

"No, not really gents, the truth is there's a lot hanging on just what Conon is able to extract from this mission but the bottom line is if the Yanks have been getting any info from Yvonyv at all then the people I work for and ultimately the government, will want to know how far behind we are and how much catch up we need to play. It'll be a bloody nightmare for us and for the likes of Conon who will probably end up having to go in where ever they're hiding whatever they have found out and steal it, and that'll be the easy part trust me."

Andy looked at Munro and smiled, "The systems that Conon may need for the next part of his mission, if it comes to that, are still being tested, the extraction system is old technology again but abandoned ironically by the Americans. They trialled a system that used a kind of hook set up on the front of an aircraft that captured a line sent up by a balloon that downed airmen would deploy. It was simplicity in itself and worked but the Vietnam War ended and the general concept was dumped and forgotten about. We are working on a very similar system using an old but highly modified Buccaneer airframe. There's a shit load of modifications to work on and then a lot of planning to get it all in place so we won't spook the Yanks but we'll get there and we'll be ready"

Munro was stunned that the Canadian was actually thinking so far ahead of the game and that he himself hadn't known anything about the extraction plan for the potential next phase, he hoped that Yvonyv would tell them that the Americans had nothing of value and that whatever information they found on Luxi Dao would buy the British time with the Chinese and Russians, if it was really needed though the Buccaneer would be sent to carry out an incredible rescue mission under the guise of an air display.

Four hours later Andy went to check on Conon, he was asleep and they were another hour away from crossing the west coast and heading out over the Pacific, he'd leave Conon for now and went to check on the launch system which would deliver Munro to the bowels of H.M.S. Astute in approximately six hours' time.

Yvonyv sat in the corner of her cell, beaten and dishevelled, her Chinese captors had done a really good job on her but she hadn't talked, there was no way even with drugs injected into her she would talk, she still hadn't talked and resolved to die before she would tell them what she had given to the Americans, they were going to kill her anyway, she knew it and they would have to, she just wouldn't talk. Yvonyv knew her time to die was close but what she didn't know was the Americans had thrown all their chips in by asking the British to rescue her, it was extremely high risk stakes, the Americans were gambling on the British rescuing Yvonyv and not getting any information from her themselves before they got her back, then they had some explaining to do.

Andy and Munro went over and over the launch system, Munro was still more than capable of looking after himself but this was probably going to be one of if not his last serious operational sortie before he was promoted and sent off to an administration job, more than likely advising some junior cabinet minister about how, when and where the men and women from the Special Boat

Squadron could and should be deployed, he didn't relish the thought. Andy and Munro sat at the table drinking coffee and talked about the probabilities of getting out of Luxi Dao unscathed and they both agreed that things would have to go immaculately well for the four man team to get out with Yvonyv and the information from the research centre, as long as Conon got to the mainframe then the gizmo the Porton Down team had devised should do the rest. Munro decided to try and get some sleep Andy went to the operations section to see that everything was going to plan and they were on schedule. Mr Black was hovering around, "It's all going to plan so far Andy."

Just off Luxi Dao in the East China Sea H.M.S. Astute sat silently waiting to move into her final position, they had the times and the position and no one else was about.

Exactly one mile away from H.M.S. Astute a surprise was waiting for the Royal Navy, the U.S.S. Saratoga, a completely secret and most stealthy of submarines lay in wait, they were listening to the Royal Navy who were totally unaware of their presence, Saratoga was an almost carbon copy of the Antaeus. The Americans had stolen a march on the British as far as the stealth technology was concerned, but then again they had stolen it from the Russians five years previously.

Munro was suited up and prepped for his drop, Andy helped him into the drop capsule and just as the container was about to be closed Conon appeared, "Good luck Munro, something tells me we're all going to need it!" Munro smiled and shook Conon's hand as Andy and Conon sealed the capsule shut. It was for all intents and purposes a high altitude launched torpedo carrying a human load. The system was primed and at the exact predetermined spot it was jettisoned from the rear of the 747. Munro felt the inertia from the launch, his stomach felt as though it was about to climb through his mouth but after a few seconds and the capsule had stabilised he settled down to the trip downwards towards the ocean below.

As the capsule stabilised Munro felt the first, then the second and then the third drogue chutes deploy and as he gave his oxygen mask and G.P.S. a last check, all was well as the pod separated and he rolled over and onto his front, there was almost nothing for him to fix his bearings on in the darkness so he concentrated on just falling face down for a few seconds before he assumed the normal free fall position and checked his altimeter, twenty thousand feet and falling, within five minutes he would be in the water and the divers from H.M.S. Astute would be nearby waiting for him, downwards he plunged, the air was warm and somewhere above him he was aware that the team would be getting geared up for their assault on Luxi Dao.

The four man SEALS dive team from the U.S.S. Saratoga sat on the surface on their battery powered seahorse mini subs. The mini subs were capable of forty knots but as the nature of the beast dictated, they were virtually invisible. The divers positioned themselves across a one hundred meter square grid, Munro should land smack in the middle but if he fell outside of the grid the splash detection sensors on board each craft would pinpoint his landing spot and they would grab him from right under the noses of the S.B.S. divers they knew were sitting ten meters below the surface but one mile out of position. Munro deployed his chute and drifted downwards towards the water, the four SEALS divers looked upwards and saw their quarry drop straight down and into the middle of the trap. Munro jettisoned his gear just above the surface, he bobbed up and began the wait for the S.B.S. divers, he heard a faint drone and then a small prick on the side of his neck, he didn't understand at first and thought it was a nervous tick, then he was aware that for a fleeting second he was obviously drifting into unconsciousness, whoever was taking him didn't want him dead just yet.

The S.B.S. team had heard Munro hit the water and they knew something was way wrong, it was definitely Munro that hit the water but he was almost a mile away from the drop point, for Sergeant Hunt it was a huge problem. Hunt signalled to the Astute what had gone wrong. Immediately Commander Walker smelled a rat and ordered complete silent running and went to the sonar room. Walker whispered to the sonar operator to keep an extra vigilant eye on all systems, someone was out there and he wanted to know who.

The sonar operator in charge, Chief Petty Officer Hunkins, listened with everything at his disposal and he fixed on the four objects which gave off a signature very similar to a pod of dolphins and then they disappeared, he immediately marked the position where all of a sudden there was nothing and enhanced the audio systems to pick up the faintest vibration in the water at the exact spot where there was nothing. "Got ya," he whispered to himself, Walker was standing right at his shoulder, "What is it Hunkins? I can't see a damned thing man!" Walker whispered.

"It's a black hole Sir, there's just so much nothing there, there's got to be something there that's for sure!"

"Follow it, don't let the bastard out of your sight!"

"Yes Sir."

The whispered commands were followed by hand signals from the Commander giving Hunkins complete control of the direction of the submarine, without question.

Munro was brought into the officers mess on board the Saratoga, he was told very quietly that he would be placed under twenty four hour guard and that if at any time he chose expose the position of his capturers he would immediately be sedated until he was delivered to his debriefers on their arrival at the U.S. Naval base at Pearl Harbour in two days' time. Munro wasn't stupid, he knew that if he gave the position of the vessel away he would be drugged and he needed to stay sharp and gather as much information about his capturers as possible, his debriefers were his route home, they just didn't realise it yet.

Mack, Donnie, Scouse and Conon were kitted up and ready to go, Mr Black gave them a final good luck pep talk and he and Andy checked over their kit and sent them on their way. As they descended and crossed the coastline of their intended target each man dropped several distraction devices, they all knew the route into and out of the target but hopefully the devices, all timed to go off at random intervals would confuse the inevitable pursuers. Twenty minutes later and within seconds of each other they landed on Luxi Dao, Scouse on the beach at a small cove near to the hydro dam, he immediately got to work on setting up secured comms, Donnie was next, he landed close to the top of the hill between the sports field and the hydro dam so he had a good over view of Conon coming and the escape route down to where Scouse waited for them all. Mack landed between Scouse and Donnie and laid several Claymores and flare traps that would kill or blind any potential pursuers in the darkness whether they were wearing night vision goggles or not. Conon landed on the running track of the sports field and was amazed that there was absolutely no one around, it was bizarre! He had gone for the high risk option against his handler's advice and it had paid off, no one was about, not one single person. He quickly gathered his gear and stowed his chute before sprinting across the running track and as he reached the doorway he inserted his electronic key into the card slot, in a mille second the alarm system had been overcome and fried by the high voltage blast of electric power, he saw a movement in his peripheral, on his right side, he instinctively turned and the night vision sensor on his helmet homed in on the figure twenty feet along the corridor, the shoulder mounted weapon spat a heavily silenced round at its target, all Conon had to do was look at it and the aiming system did the rest. The Chinese guard fell over without a sound. Conon entered the room with ease, the whole security system within the building had been disabled, he simply opened the door and walked in, there was no CCTV, such was the arrogance of the scientists within the complex they believed no one would even dare to try and enter the base. The lay out wasn't exactly as Professor Smith had described, there were subtle differences but the computer Conon needed to access was located quickly, he inserted the mass storage device via a USB port and watched as the box of tricks did its work, whether it worked or not was not his problem, he'd done his bit, now he just needed to get out and get to the beach via Yvonyv. He heard the first distraction device go off, it was about half a kilometre away near the main harbour, he looked at his watch, it had gone off too early and it really messed up his plans to rescue Yvonyv but he wouldn't give up it just wasn't an option. The five minute LED warning lights flickered subtly on the device as Conon sat tight and listened to the chaos building outside, come on, come on he muttered to himself, just then the lights all went to constant green, he simply pulled the box from the USB connection and stuffed it into a pouch inside his body armour.

Conon stepped outside the door of the lab and moved to the main door, he couldn't believe the body of the guard had not been discovered, the body lay where it had fallen seven minutes earlier, a pool of thick black blood had spread beneath the man's head, Conon moved closer to the door and watched for a second, the next distraction device detonated sending the local Commander responsible for the whole island into a frenzied rage, from his desk he told his adjutant to get his car ready and to bring him his gun, he would personally sort the mess out, whatever was going on. The adjutant did as he was told despite his belief that the fat fool would only cause more problems. Conon stepped out and ran to the next building for cover, Donnie watched from his vantage point, he couldn't believe the speed that Conon was moving at, the adrenalin had kicked in and despite his calm within, the drugs were working to give Conon all the advantages he needed. Donnie watched as the guards ran in the same general direction, towards the harbour, trucks drove down the main road and four helicopters also flew overhead towards the harbour. Only one figure appeared to be moving in the opposite direction, Conon. He arrived at the entrance to the building where they believed Yvonyv was being held, behind him he was aware of a jeep pulling up, a large fat man got out of the back seat, he had an automatic pistol in his hand and waved the man who opened the car door for him away, he shouted an order and the other man bowed and went to a side entrance of the building Conon was about to try and breach. The guards within opened the door when they saw the adjutant outside, he shouted at them to bring the woman to him, Conon waited out of sight, watching and within a few moments there she was, his target for phase two, Yvonyv, the fat man had done his job for him. She was dishevelled and clearly wasted but still apparently a handful, she struggled as her senses came back to her in the fresh air but she went almost limp as a jellyfish out of water when her guards dropped her at the fat man's feet. The fat man laughed and told Yvonyv that her efforts to keep her secrets were futile and that he was going to enjoy killing her, he lit a cigarette as all around him in the distance, distraction devices were going off almost every ten seconds. Yvonyv was on her knees with her hands tied behind her back, she looked up at the fat man whom she knew only as Mao and spat her best straight into his face, he wiped his face and she saw the rage grow in him instantly, then as Mao lifted his right hand and cocked the pistol with his left, the left side of Mao's head suddenly erupted, blood and brains splattered out of his skull. Donnie was watching over them, Conon felt another surge of adrenalin, and he suddenly believed that they were going to make it out of Luxi Dao. The guards were momentarily shocked but it was just enough for Yvonyv to launch herself to her right and into the bushes where she easily pulled her feet through her arms and started working on the plastic straps tying her hands together. Yvonyv looked up frantically trying to spot her guards but as she looked she saw a man in strange almost invisible like camouflage combats step out of the darkness ten meters away and shoot the adjutant and the two guards in the backs of their heads as they scrambled to find her. Conon strode towards her and spoke in perfect Russian, "You have only one chance to get out of here alive Yvonyv, come out and come with me now or you'll die, simple!" He waited for five seconds and just as he turned to start his run up the hill towards Donnie's position, she showed herself,

"Who are you?" she asked.

"Names Conon, that's all you get for now, no time to explain!" Conon pulled out his knife and cut Yvonyvs hands free, he grabbed her and started making his way out of the compound and to the position further up the hill, she followed without protest, she knew it was her only chance to escape.

Donnie watched as the two made their way to the perimeter fence and as he watched he saw two guards who were just too interested in the couple heading away from the chaos ongoing within the base but these guys were good, they used their cover well and he was able to see that they were not Chinese, probably Russian security advisors, Donnie laughed at the possibility that the two men were about be dismissed in the most definitive way. Donnie aimed at the first guy as Conon started cutting the fence wire, Conon pulled a Glock pistol from his side holster and gave it to Yvonyv who was instinctively watching Conon's back, she watched as the first of their pursuers was shot straight through the throat, rupturing his windpipe, neck and spinal cord, he fell and lay lifeless, suddenly she felt Conon's grip on the back of her shirt and he unceremoniously ripped her through the fence and dragged her to the ditch five yards away. "How many more are there?" Conon asked Yvonyv.

"There's one more!" Just as she spoke they heard the loud cracking snap of the high velocity round going over the top of their heads. Conon smiled, "Make that none, at the moment!"

The two of them got up knowing Donnie was a short distance away and he was watching over them and all that was going on about them.

At the beach Scouse lay in wait, the secure communications opened and it wasn't what he wanted to hear. "Scouse its Hunt here, looks like Munros been bagged, we're five minutes away!"

Scouse replied, "Roger, all received and understood, they're on their way, we'll be cutting it fine though! See you in five, out!" Scouse checked his watch and waited for the others to come.

Yvonyv and Conon reached Donnie who simply got to his feet and began running behind them, Yvonyv was in the middle, suddenly she felt safe but then there was an eruption of trees and ground before them, one of the four attack helicopters had found them, Mack saw the helicopter hovering about forty feet above the trees on the ridgeline about two hundred meters away, the team were close. Mack lifted the Stinger missile launcher onto his shoulder and fired, within three seconds the attack helicopter was blown to smithereens and the trio of escapees continued their run to the beach. As the three arrived at the beach Hunt and his team screamed across the water and onto the beach with their machines which looked like jet skis, they weren't. Scouse, Donnie and Mack stowed their gear quickly and donned the breathing equipment they would need shortly, Hunt pulled Yvonyv aside and told her she was with him, he placed the gear over her shoulder and told her she wouldn't be cold so she didn't need a suit and he pulled the craft around and pointed it out towards the sea, the others were already atop their mounts and waiting for Hunt who gave the signal and all five machines sped off at an unbelievable speed across the water and out of the bay, behind them the Chinese soldiers and a few Russian advisors still ran about trying to make sense of the chaos as the last of the distraction devices were exploding.

Ten minutes after starting their high speed escape Hunt slowed down to about five knots and as he looked around he was aware that the other four machines had pulled in line behind him and with the flick of a button he and Yvonyv began to sink beneath the waves, he felt her grip his waist just a tad tighter and he patted her reassuringly on the thigh and gave a thumbs up which she returned, he pushed forward on the control column and the vessel submerged. After a few seconds Yvonyv felt a shunt as a directional cable was fired out into the abyss, it was a homing device which began seeking out the tow that had been deployed from the trapping device on the deck of H.M.S. Astute. Two minutes later Hunt and Yvonyv were within the bowels of the leviathan, Hunt took her hand and lead her to a seat where he signalled for her to sit and strap in, Yvonyv did as she was instructed and she sat back and watched as the other four craft were retrieved and the main hatchway sealed. Yvonyv watched in awe as the nine men all stowed the craft and the water drained from the compartment. The main door opened as the men removed their breathing apparatus and the man in the doorway dressed in civvies asked Conon how it went, it was Black. Conon flicked a thumb at Yvonyv as he carried on getting out of his gear and he threw the small silver coloured box at the man and said, "Hopefully the information we need is in that, but that's your job to find that out now." The man left without another word and an officer entered as the men all waited to file out of the compartment. He spoke to Yvonyv, "Hello I'm Commander Walker I trust you're well? Anyway the ship's doctor will check you over and we'll just make sure, please don't speak to anyone, I assume you wouldn't anyway, oh and we'll get you some fresh clothes and a cabin and get you something to eat." Walker then turned to the rest of the men and said gents we have a slight problem, we think Munro has been captured by the Americans and is being taken to Pearl Harbour, we've had to break silent running to recover you guys but essentially we have received a signal from Northwood that basically tells us there's a delivery expected there, at Pearl Harbour, soon, we suspect it's Munro."

Hunt was next to speak, "Are we going after him Sir?"

"No we have people in place there so for now we just follow the submarine that he's on, the Yanks don't think we can but Hunkins on it and he's the best in the business, he's got us looking like a headless chicken for now as far as the Yanks are concerned but he assures me he's following ehhh yeah, nothing, I'll explain over a mug of tea gents, go get washed up and we'll do a hot debrief ASAP.

The Marines all showered and made their way to the galley on board the submarine. They were joined by the Medical Officer a short time later who escorted Yvonyv back from the sick bay, she was a bit beat up but otherwise in remarkably good shape, Conon was asked in the absence of Munro if he would take care of her and he gestured for her to sit beside him. All other crew members were asked to leave the galley, they all knew that the presence of Special Boat Squadron men on board was routine but the more experienced men amongst the crew knew there was something out of the ordinary about this group of individuals and the woman was clearly the victim of some sort of rescue mission, she'd probably been kidnapped months ago and the S.B.S. guys had gone in and rescued her. The crew were told not to rush just to leave the galley when they were finished. As the last man filed out, Hunt picked up the phone, he spoke to the Commander of the boat, seconds later Walker appeared and the galley was secured by armed guards at either end, he was accompanied by Mr Black.

"Okay gentlemen the long and the short of it, our part in this particular phase of any operation to recover sensitive information and Miss Yvonyv has been accomplished." Yvonyv spoke.

"You do realise that the Americans beat you to it? They were here about a week ago to attempt to steal the information they need to manufacture the antidote for the new nerve agent the Chinese have developed, they failed of course, typically gung ho and came in with attack helicopters and SEALS and never got passed the doorway, you guys are good though I'll give you that, four of you, now that's impressive." She smiled wryly. "The Americans were supposed to kill me, after my bosses in Russia realised I'd failed I was regarded as an embarrassment and they effectively gave the Americans the green light to go in and take what they could find, presumably for an exchange of information and on the understanding that I would be eliminated, all that and there would be no diplomatic row between the Americans and Russia. You'll find............."

"That's more than enough!" Yvonyv was cut short by Mr Black who invited her to leave the debrief and come with him, Conon was also asked to join them. Commander Walker carried on with the debrief with the other men.

Black walked along the corridor and into a small room he'd been given, Yvonyv and Conon followed him, Black closed the door. "Okay you two, time for a more formal introduction, Sonny Yvonyv, Conon Bridge, the two shook hands, Yvonyv hadn't noticed before but Conon was a very good looking and well chiselled man, she quickly averted her gaze but it hadn't gone unnoticed by Conon who sat down beside her. Black spoke again, "The Americans have definitely got Munro, they want to do a swap, they want their Chinese pilot back, and we're currently working on why............." Yvonyv broke in,

"He supposedly carries the antidote for the nerve agent, he's effectively immune so I suggest you hide him very far away or surround him with the best guards you have."

Conon sat and giggled as Black tried to conceal his surprise that Yvonyv was quite as in the know as she was, she looked at him, "Mr Black, I have ways of making men talk." Conon laughed as Black clearly tried to compose himself.

Mr Black spoke again, "The Chinese bizarrely stumbled upon a synthetic material when they were attempting to manufacture their antidote and one smart cookie discovered, again quite by chance that it had amazing stealth properties, they managed to mass produce it and sold it to the Russians for assistance with their space programme, some of Russia's best scientists are working alongside the Chinese at Luxi Dao and have been for a couple of years now. We believe some months ago a Russian submarine was compromised in British waters off the Scottish west coast and as you may or may not know Conon we are as interested in the stealth coating you found on the rope of the wreck as we are in the antidote but it seems Sonny may have given our boffins a short circuit to solving problem two, we're still working on the coating."

"So how come we know as much or as little as we seem to?" Conon asked.

"It was simple, the Chinese and the Russians were stablemates but didn't trust each other, the British and the Americans were long standing allies but trusted each other even less so everyone spied on each other and somehow the Americans have stolen the stealth technology from the Chinese we think, we're not certain about a lot of this, apart from Sonny being a double agent for the Russians and the Americans and we think at least one other is operating." Black was very vague about a lot of things and even his presence on the boat was a mystery to Conon. "So Black one thing's bothering me at the moment, if Munro was captured by the Americans, how did you manage to get yourself on board this sub as quickly as you seem to have done?" Conon could sense Black's unease and pressed him, "Well? An answer anytime soon would be good, people have risked their lives tonight to get information for our boffins, your boffins, it would nice to find out just a little bit more don't you think? And why have they taken Munro, is he a prisoner or a hostage?"

"I work as you know for an organisation that doesn't show up on any radar, anywhere. I have a background in telecommunications and early in my working life I started to do contract work for the Ministry of Defence, my, talents shall we say were spotted by M.O.D. talent spotters and here I am." Conon looked at Black with a raised eyebrow. "Okay, I was caught aged sixteen trying to break into M.O.D. computer files and some bright spark thought I should be nurtured rather than sent to prison, so you can see I had options. Earlier tonight we realised very quickly that it had gone completely wrong with Munro so we took the chance that I'd make it on board and here I am to try and help, there's nothing more sinister in it than that, the bosses at Northwood decided they wanted someone here that could start dialogue with Sonny as soon as possible or at least get her to shut up before anyone else got to her, sorry Sonny no offence."

"None taken." She replied.

"Why did they take Munro? Pass, it's a wild guess but I suspect they thought they may have been getting their hands on you but that's just a guess, no more than that.

Conon was interested in finding out what happened next. Black did his best to explain that it all really depended on where the Americans chose to take Munro and hold him, they knew he was probably holding highly sensitive information but he was also high value and the Americans would hopefully be happy to exchange him quietly for the Chinese pilot, they had a problem though, now the British knew how valuable the pilot was and so they waited for the Americans to open dialogue.

Munro was lead, blind folded and hands bound behind his back from the vessel, he sensed he was inside a cave or similar and transported by a hummer, he'd been in enough of them to know he was in one now, to a building about two miles away from where the submarine had berthed, he calculated that much without too much trouble, what he didn't realise was the submarine had berthed in a subterranean cavern specifically built by the Americans on the peninsula north west of the Marine base on Hawaii. After a very short distance the hummer was driven into a hanger and the doors closed before Munro was taken out of the vehicle and lead away to a room where he was seated and his blind fold was removed, he blinked several times, his eyes becoming accustomed to the light again. As he looked about he could see he was in a cell, a very well appointed cell but a cell. A man spoke and Munro turned to look, he was slapped across the face and told to face forward, he did exactly as he was told but he'd caught enough of a glimpse to see that his guard or guards were concealing their faces, he sensed there was at least three guards and the one he caught a glimpse of was wearing a black balaclava. He wondered why, then the guard spoke to him, "Sit where you are Major then we can cut the straps on your hands and you can get cleaned up and eat, we'll provide you with a meal, any requests?"

Munro thought for a second and asked for a salad and some water, he said nothing else as the guard cut his arms free and left the room, the door was locked behind him, Munro got up and surveyed his cell, a table and chair, a bed, on the bed there were clean clothes, a blue boiler suit, tee shirts, shorts and some socks. There was some National Geographic magazines on the table, some bottles of water and there was a shower and a toilet. Munro wondered how long would he be held here, he thought he was possibly somewhere near Japan or Hawaii, he had no real idea but knew the Americans had bases in both countries and guessed he must be somewhere near one of those regions, he had no idea what day it was or what time it was, there were no windows, no way of even guessing what time of day or night it was. Munro stripped off and showered, it felt good being clean and although he wasn't happy, he knew his men would be looking for him and the diplomats would be working in the background, quietly trying to persuade his captors that he should be released. The door opened as Munro dressed and the guard walked in with a tray and laid it on the table, he didn't speak but just turned and left, the other guard closed the door. Munro sat at the table and looked at his meal, the finest salad he had ever seen, he tucked in and resolved to keep his spirits up and stay positive, he just had to sit tight for now.

Hunkins last report to Commander Walker was that the vessel they were hopefully following was heading for Hawaii, the Commander had spoken with Mr Black who in turn had asked for a coded message to be sent to Northwood and to the Mi6 handlers he used at the S.O.E. command below B.B.C. headquarters. Northwood were happy to watch closely at what was going on in the Hawaiian island area and Mi6 had personnel in and around Honolulu that were now watching harder than normal for any out of the ordinary, non-routine activity. Within hours a spotter at the U.S. Marine base on Honolulu had spotted a heavily guarded building out near the firing ranges on the North east side of the island, he had been cutting grass and had supplied some superb photos. Not long afterwards Northwood had taken some satellite photos of aircraft on the military base nearby and an aircraft previously used by the U.S. for rendition flights had flagged up immediately. Several spooks had been ordered to watch the whole place, it was easy to watch for breaks in routine, especially when you were paid good money to work in the sun.

The Americans sent a low grade diplomat to the U.K. embassy in Toronto, Canada, he delivered a sealed attaché case to the front desk, it was to be delivered directly to the High Commissioner, Sir Howard Drake, he waited to be seen. He didn't have to wait long, a secretary appeared and asked him to follow her, he was taken directly to the High Commissioners office, the brass plate on the door read, "Sir Howard Drake OBE." The American was briefed to say nothing, Drake asked the American if he had any idea of the contents of the case, the American replied he had no idea at all and waited for the British Commissioner to speak. "I'll pass the contents on and no doubt we'll be in touch, thank you, you may leave." The American was ushered out by the secretary and escorted to the main door and left. By the time the American had left the building Drake was on a secure line to Admiral Currie at Northwood, England, the information Drake had been given was supposedly useful to Currie, a sealed envelope, typed on the outside was "Contents For The Attention of Admiral Currie, Northwood." The letter inside was typed on U.S. Consular headed letter paper, it simply read,

"Swap to be arranged, stand by for further instructions."

Yahweh

The Defence Secretary and several other high ranking officials were summoned to the Conference Room at Northwood, once they had all gathered Currie brought them all up to speed on what was going on, "Gentlemen, we have had boffins at Porton Down working on the composition of the rope recovered in the Sound of Sleat by the Special Boat Squadron about three months ago. I'm told we're very close to cracking it, to that end H.M.S. Ambush which has been in dry dock at Plymouth for about a month now, is being prepared for the first attempt at the new coating. The operation which was carried out by the Special Boat Squadron on Luxi Dao was a ninety nine percent success, however one of our men, Major Ben Munro is being held captive by our American friends, they think we don't know where he is but it's looking increasingly likely that he's being held at The U.S. Marine base on Honolulu. The Chinese Pilot is we now believe a carrier for the antidote to this new super nerve agent developed by the Chinese, he is currently on his way to our Antarctic Survey Base at Rothera, he'll be helping our Medical staff there and is being guarded by S.A.S. troopers. Our other team who rescued the Russian double Agent and stole the data from Luxi Dao are currently on Diego Garcia being tanned right under the noses of the American garrison on the base, they are being closely watched by our Mi6 aide. They are going to be returned to Canada soon for a few weeks where we will have them made ready for the next phase of the operation should our scientists and operatives in Antarctica fail to find out the solution to the nerve agent antidote. We appear on the face of it gentlemen to be making good headway, however, there is always a hurdle to be crossed in this case two." The men sitting around the conference table all sat silently and listened to Currie. "If we're right then the Americans have been working on this antidote in just about the most awkward bloody place in the world to get into and if our man does get in then he's going to have a bitch of a job getting out."

The Defence Secretary spoke, "Admiral Currie, the majority of us have some handle on what's been going on but I think I speak for most when I say, you're being a bit evasive, aren't you?"

"My apologies Mr Hammond, it seems according to our best sources, educated guesses, the Americans are working on this project in Area 51." There was a rumble of hushed conversation around the table between the partners sitting within the conference room. "Gentlemen, gentlemen." Currie brought the room back to order, "We have known for some time that the flights in and out of Area 51 on a weekly basis have been delivering scientists and guinea pigs and not engineers or test pilots or anything else of the sort it appears, we're putting a few pieces together and with our best intelligence it looks as if the Americans have now managed to replicate the antidote or are at worst not far off achieving it, our experts have an additional problem in that the data they stole is proving to be extremely difficult to decipher."

"I understand that the equipment required for the potential next phase is on schedule?" asked the Defence Secretary.

"Yes sir, the work on the aircraft is currently ongoing and the aircrews are currently in training, we're using remote locations in Scotland and if it's okay with you sir I'd prefer we said no more about that for now, in case it's not required."

"Absolutely fine Admiral Currie, are we done for now?"

"Yes sir."

"Okay, for some reason the Americans are moving very slowly on the diplomatic front, why they are dragging their feet quite as much over Major Munro when he is now in reality such a low grade player is baffling us, there are far more important issues we could be bargaining over but we're working on it. Fine, gentlemen watch this space, Admiral, I'll bring the P.M. up to speed within the hour." The room emptied and Currie sat contemplating just what would happen next.

Nearly six thousand miles away on Diego Garcia, Conon, Scouse, Donnie and Mack lay on the secluded beach lapping up the sun, they had been told not to get too drunk as they could be asked to move at a moment's notice, they knew they were heading back to Canada but for the next week it was R & R rest and recreation. The four guys lay sleeping and drinking beers on the beach, they were well away from the American garrison and were just another group attached to the Royal Marines detachment on the island. Donnie was the first to see Yvonyv coming, "Holeeeee fuck! Check this out. I gotta roll on my front guys!"

The others turned and watched the Russian blonde walk down the beach towards them, put simply, she had a stunning figure, Conon guessed, "34DD's guys."

"Nope, 36F's and how the fuck didn't we notice them before?" Mack said.

"You've all been busy playing with your guns you stupid fucks!" was Scouce's input.

She was wearing a leopard skin bikini and sunglasses, nothing else apart from a towel slung over her shoulder, she was carrying a bag and as she approached the Marines she shouted, "Hey anyone want to party, they let me out?"

Conon looked at the rest of the guys and said, "Anyone have any objections?"

Donnie replied, "Yeah why don't the rest of you fuck off?" They all started laughing. As Yvonyv got closer she stood beside Conon and dropped her bag and turned to place her towel on the sand, she was wearing a G-string bikini bottom, Conon flicked a glance at Donnie who grimaced silently as he saw Yvonyvs gorgeously formed bottom, the poor boy genuinely looked to be in severe pain but the others knew exactly what was going through his mind, they were all thinking the same after all. Sonny sat down and without missing a beat she asked if any of them minded her going topless, Donnie turned away as Conon smiled and said, "Of course not we're all adults." Yvonyv laughed and flicked a glance in Donnie's direction, she knew what she was doing.

"So Sonny, what have they been saying to you, they've been working with you for a while now?" Conon did his best to look at her face as she stripped her bikini top off but it was very hard not to notice that her breasts were simply fantastic.

"They've been asking lots and lots of questions and to be honest I can't really be arsed to go over it just now, we'll be going over most of it all again soon anyway I think." Sonny sat down on her towel and asked if anyone wanted a vodka and ice as she pulled a huge bottle of Smirnoff Vodka out of her bag and a cool box full of ice cubes. As the afternoon wore on the Marines and Yvonyv got drunk and enjoyed the sun and the warm waters of the Indian Ocean, they were all relaxed.

On Honolulu, Major Ben Munro was being spoken to by his American handlers, he had been poked prodded and had more blood tests taken than he'd ever heard of, Munro wondered why but he suspected the Americans had got wind of the work they were doing with Conon and they possibly believed the whole team was part of the test programme, he knew that was not so. The officer in charge had told Munro he was he was to be taken from his cell soon and would be flown to a secret location until a deal for his release could be brokered. Munro said nothing. Within the hour Munro was aboard the Lear jet and flown off the island headed for god knows where. The flight to Area 51 would take around six hours, armed guards sat either side of him.

On Diego Garcia the four Marines and Yvonyv staggered back to the accommodation, Donnie was as drunk as anyone had ever seen him and he was being held up by Mack. Scouse, Conon and Yvonyv were fairing little better but they were each standing on their own two feet. Yvonyv suggested they get freshened up and get some food. There was total agreement from the four drunk Marines and they went to their room whilst Yvonyv went to the block opposite. Inside the accommodation Mack dropped Donnie on his bed, he was asleep before he hit the pillow, Conon hadn't even seen Scouse get onto his bed but he was gone, out like a light bulb too, Mack and Conon headed for the showers. As soon as they were done Mack lay down on his bed, Conon asked him if he was hungry, there was no reply as he looked around, and all he saw were three very tired, very drunk Royal Marines.

Conon pulled on a clean tee shirt and shorts and the obligatory crocs, he threw some aftershave and deodorant on and went outside where Yvonyv was waiting. She looked stunning, her hair was still wet and her white tee shirt and shorts would get her into the galley, just and no more. Conon walked in front of her and opened the door explaining the others were lightweights, they went to the hotplate and filled their plates. After they'd eaten they headed for a bar on the base and drank on the decking outside, the breeze billowing in off the ocean was pleasant but still very warm and they chatted for ages about where they came from, how they'd ended up where they were and they carried on drinking until the small hours. About one in the morning Yvonyv asked if Conon was tired yet, "No, surprisingly not, I'm very drunk but not tired."

Yvonyv replied, "Hmmmm you have good stamina, I like that, I ehhh think we should go to my room and have some coffee?"

"Yeah sounds like a great idea."

As soon as she turned the key in the door Yvonyv stepped into her single room, it was cosy and had all the mod cons, en suite, double bed, fridge, air conditioning and T.V. Conon was invited to sit on the sofa whilst Yvonyv sorted out the coffee. "I'm very warm," was all that Yvonyv said as she poured the coffee, she walked over to the sofa and handed Conon his cup and placed her own on the table then she peeled her tee shirt off and slipped out of her shorts revealing a tiny white lace G-string, Conon felt the bulge in his shorts instantly as he tried to look cool and sip on his coffee. Yvonyv knelt down in front of him and pulled his zip down. He fondled her breasts, they were firm. They kissed and probed each other's throats with their tongues before Yvonyv pushed him back onto the sofa Conon lay on top of Sonny and kissed her gently and drifted off to sleep.

The next few days were sun, lager and sex, lots of it, all of it, but the fun wasn't to last long, Black appeared on the sixth day and whilst the Marines and Yvonyv enjoyed the afternoon sun he told them that in the morning they were shipping out. Yvonyv was to join them. They enjoyed the last of the sun that afternoon and then after dinner they all packed. Black spoke to them and told them that they should be ready to roll at 0700 hours in the morning and one of the Royal Marine transports would be there to pick them up and take them to the transport aircraft.

At 0730 hours the Royal Air Force HS 125 soared to its service ceiling and began the flight to Cyprus where it would have a short stop before carrying on to Brize Norton. The team would have a couple of days at Poole and from there they would ship out to Gander, Newfoundland where Andy Urquhart would be waiting with the brief and more importantly the new equipment needed for the next operation.

Black spoke to the team once the flight had settled onto its route, he explained to them that they knew the negotiations for Munro were stalling, the Americans believed the Chinese pilot was worth as much as Munro even though they now knew he wasn't and the truth was they had made a complete mess of the whole situation, they were now trying to bluff their way out and they weren't in any mood to lose face on the International stage either, their negotiators and intelligence believed they could, as they had done for many years keep the British appeased with the offer of free albeit dumbed down F35's and keep them out of the race for the antidote to the Chinese nerve agent. The British however had been taken in by false promises once too often. The Chinese had failed to dispose of Yvonyv, as a result the stakes were much higher. The Americans had stolen the stealth technology from the Russians, the Russians were trying to persuade the Chinese to part with the nerve agent antidote and the Chinese appeared to have both. Neither knew how much the British knew only the Americans had some idea due to their request to the British to assist with the supposed rescue of Yvonyv, how much of that was just a smoke screen they didn't know but one thing was certain, Munro was being taken to Area 51 and that meant real problems.

The British contingency plan was in place and if they pulled it off then it would be the ultimate invisible slap in the face for the Americans and it would probably set Anglo American relations back decades but it was a strategic risk the British Government were prepared to take, the Americans had fouled over the sale of F111s to the British many years before, resulting in the premature cancelation of the TSR2 project, they had offered much in the intervening years and again stalled on many deals, the new replacement for the Harrier, the list was endless and the dark workings of British power had decided that enough was enough, it was time for the British to flex some muscle and leapfrog their American allies, to regain the lead in some of the hottest technologies that were of any significance in the modern world, biological and stealth warfare.

The Buccaneer sat in the hanger at Boscombe Down with armed guards around it, it looked in its entirety completely identical to the S2B type flown by the R.A.F. which was retired from service in 1994, one airframe was kept in flying condition and serviced by staff at the secret establishment, this one was however a much modified airframe which when it left the base would give the outward impression that the R.A.F. were testing some avionics system for the new Typhoon or the F35 aircraft about to come into service soon. The Buccaneer had a rotating bombay and airbrakes at the rear which dramatically slowed the aircraft down, this particular aircraft had a refuelling nozzle in place that had been considerably strengthened and modified, not even the most observant aircraft enthusiast would spot any difference and the bomb bay looked completely unaltered from the outside but internally it had been converted to carry out a personnel recovery and was a fully functioning life support system that could be jettisoned, with the ability to self-propel if the need arose. The paint system used was highly experimental too, at the flick of a switch the paint on the aircraft was electrically charged and gave off a shimmering chameleon like appearance, it would seem as if the aircraft was trying to disappear and would confuse the hell out of anyone visually trying to pursue them.

The news from Porton Down was good and bad, the boffins working on the information from Luxi Dao were still struggling with the antidote but they had broken down the compound make-up of the rubber and had duplicated it. They now had a stable coating to apply to H.M.S. Ambush currently in dry dock at Plymouth for a refit.

Yahweh

At the Royal Naval dockyards, Plymouth, at dock 9 the Porton Down team were talking to the Naval engineers who were shortly about to commence the attempt to coat HMS Ambush in the new super stealth coating, they all knew it wasn't going to make her invisible but it was going to ensure that she gave off the signature of a coca cola can if it worked and if it did she would be sent on her mission immediately, Commander Crosswaight-Aires was part of the team being briefed and his crew were all soon to report for sea trials, standard procedure after a refit. The submarine would take approximately two weeks to get to her rendezvous and once there she would wait for further instructions. Olly, the Commander of the submarine was fully aware of what would be required of his crew. He had been on numerous missions with Special Forces men on board the various submarines he had served on before and as usual he had no idea what they were going to be getting into and this time it would be as usual extremely dangerous.

The coating work on H.M.S. Ambush took one week, there were no problems with the material application, which had been carried out by a specialist Royal Naval team and as the submarines crew arrived they were all single handidly taken aside and advised of the fact they had all signed the official secrets act and they were not to discuss any of the modifications to the vessel, the crew were all quietly joking though about being fucked going to sea in an experimental rubber duck. The submarine looked just as she did before they went on their annual leave, she was cleaner, almost brand new, as she should look after a refit and apart from a few new pieces of equipment fitted internally and computer software updates, outwardly HMS Ambush looked no different to when she had gone into dry dock. The crew were efficient and had her ready in good time dockside, they were ready to set sail for sea trials in record time and cast off at 0400 hours on the morning of Saturday the 11th of August. Within three hours they were in the English Channel and steaming for the open ocean. Everything was going quite routinely, almost normal, when Commander C&A asked the crew for deck hands to prepare for a recovery in five minutes, the experienced hands on-board knew something unusual was going on.

Twenty thousand feet above the four Royal Marines of the Special Boat Squadron leapt from the ramp of the C-130 Hercules and aimed for the area where the submarine should be, within ten minutes all four men had landed without getting a foot wet on the deck of HMS Ambush, they had secured their kit and although the crew would know exactly who they were they wouldn't be disturbed.

Commander C&A, as he was known to his crew gave the order to submerge and make a course for the mid-Atlantic, he had been briefed to make his way to an area off the west coast of the United States near San Francisco on the provision and understanding that the submarine would be as invisible as the Admiralty hoped she would be. Over the next few days HMS Ambush was hunted for by every asset the Royal Air Force had including the new Nimrod MR4 which was only flown in darkness so secret was its existence, not even the Americans knew the RAF were still flying the aircraft and they had not been scrapped as broadcast in 2010 and the Royal Air Force flew the five serviceable aircraft with handpicked crews.

Yahweh

The Royal Navy had sent more sonar buoys into the ocean than they'd wanted to but they hadn't found her, she was silent and nearly invisible and without doubt, if the RAF and the Royal Navy couldn't find her, no one else would be able to. Commander C&A was delighted and received confirmation of his orders to make his way to the west coast of America where he would receive further instructions on his ships next mission. It was all a bit cloak and dagger but he and his crew, all members of the silent service were used to those kinds of scenarios, this one was no different apart from the new coating on the submarine and the speed at which the whole exercise had taken place, the journey to the west coast of America would be routine for them, what happened after that would not.

At Boscombe Down the Buccaneer was ready to go, the American Air Force had for some time been requesting that the Royal Air Force send them a Buccaneer for an annual display at Travis Air Force Base, California. The request was never accepted, due to the operational commitments of the Buccaneers, however this year the timing was somewhat fortuitous. The Royal Air Force would send their last remaining airworthy Buccaneer via Gander in Newfoundland and would have the Empire Test Pilots red, white and blue liveried aircraft repainted in Gulf war colours she would be repainted as the "Sky Pirate" the Americans were delighted.

The crew were specially selected by the Royal Air Force, Ug Urquhart and Joe Slater, they were the last crew ever to fly the aircraft operationally and a backup crew of Group Captain Windy Gale and Squadron Leader Brearly would escort them in a Tornado as back-up in case of problems.

The Buccaneer lifted off from Boscombe Down at 0500 hours on the morning of Saturday the 18th of August accompanied by the Tornado GR4 and a VC10 tanker they would all be painted in Gulf War livery, they had a week to prepare for the assault on Area 51.

At Gander the Royal Marines team had started their preparations, Andy had a replica capsule for the bomb bay recovery system now in the Buccaneer on site and they had been practising launching the balloon recovery part of the escape system, it was simplicity in itself. At around midday local time whilst the team were having a break and enjoying a cup of coffee Andy came out of the office and looked east out over the rolling hills towards the ocean, "Ladies and gentlemen if you look out there you will very shortly see your new taxi service arrive." The Tornado appeared first and simply landed without any fuss, the whole airfield was quiet though and virtually no one was there to see the Buccaneer arrive, Ug dropped the aircraft from five thousand feet to twenty feet and as he guided the aircraft across the terrain and onto the lake for a southerly approach across the water, a huge vortex of vapour blew up behind the aircraft, the team all stood up to watch the display, this guy was crack pilot and nuts!!

Ug pushed the throttles to full open, the Buccaneer would handle flat out at any height, it was a dream to fly that way, and it was what she was designed to do, fly under the Russian radar systems during the cold war and drop nuclear weapons on the enemy before they even knew an aircraft had attacked them. Ug drifted the aircraft up over the end of the airfield and flew the Sky Pirate at full speed straight up the main runway, six feet above the tarmac, he overflew the base and slowed the aircraft down before coming back around onto the landing approach, Conon had seen the aircraft when he was serving in the Gulf and he felt like an old friend had arrived. They all watched as the two aircraft taxied to the hanger beside their offices and they were all delighted when Andy suggested that they go and meet the new members of the team. The main hanger doors were closed before the engines on each of the aircraft had been shut down, there was nothing unusual about the Tornado which had simply been sent as an escort but was flown by the standby crew, The Buccaneer however was a much modified beast and was painted with a highly reflective paint scheme which when charged with electricity gave the aircraft a strange shimmering appearance which confused anyone looking directly at it, the Royal Air Force had been experimenting with the system for a long time, since the 1950's when many of their aircraft had been turned out in their bare metal finish to allow the paintwork to be applied to any aircraft without notice. Within the hanger the ground crew busied themselves parking the aircraft and shutting them down, plugging in the computer systems that the ground crew used to monitor the on-board equipment. The crews unstrapped themselves from their ejection seats and carried out the last of the procedures to switch the aircraft systems off before climbing down the ladders to meet Conon, Mack, Scouse, Donnie and Andy, Munro and Mr Black stayed in the background as Ug shook hands with everyone and showed them around the Buccaneer. He took particular care to explain how the catch system worked to Conon, he'd been told this was the man he was going to have to snatch at high speed from right under the noses of the

Americans and if it all went to plan it would be a hell of a ride. Andy then showed the crews the pod devised for the lift, it was a highly modified Buccaneer bomb bay and it was crammed with survival equipment, manual and electronic. They all spent half an hour looking over the kit and then decided it was time to head to the hotel for some refreshments and to get better acquainted. The next morning they all attended at the hanger and were briefed on how the recovery system would work, they'd all had the brief before but it was the first time the team had assembled together, their first attempt would be with a life size dummy. The crew strapped into the Sea King support helicopter and left the base and headed north into the wilderness, about fifty miles north they landed and set up on Horse Island. They were far enough away to be out of sight but close enough to the base if they needed to work on any equipment modifications quickly. The times were checked and Andy harnessed up the life size dummy, they nick named it Humpty Dumpty. Ug and Slater were ten minutes out in the Buccaneer and heading straight for them, the drill was two hundred knots and two hundred feet, the aircraft was a pig to fly at that speed but they had to practice first, Andy began the process of launching the capture system. He pulled a toggle on what looked like a life jacket around the dummy's torso. The harness burst open as the compressed helium inflated a large balloon and a line of helicopter winch wire fed out until the balloon hovered two hundred feet above the ground. The balloon was picked up visually by Ug who spoke to Slater, "Here goes, let's see how easy this is going to be then." He aimed the Buccaneer straight at the balloon and just at the last second threw the aircraft onto its starboard side hooking the balloon line perfectly using the modified refuelling probe as a catcher, the aircraft pulled on the slack and the dummy simply rose elegantly into the air, the recovery systems then with ease pulled the dummy towards the bomb bay which rotated open and air deflectors caused a flow of air directing the dummy straight into the safety of the bay, it had all worked perfectly, better than any of them had dared hope, apart from Conon. The Marines and their support team all flew back to Gander where they met Ug and Slater, everyone was delighted with the first attempt. The next day they would go for an attempt at a live capture but it wouldn't be Conon, he was considered too valuable so Mack, who was very similar in build to him would go first as guinea pig. On day two of the trials, Conon helped Andy on the rig that he would wear for his escape only today they were trussing Mack up, the gear looked easy enough and was a modified parachute harness. Once he had landed and made his way to his target, Munro, they would break him out of his prison and with luck on their side the Buccaneer would be loitering somewhere out in the Nevada desert, hopefully evading the low level radar systems and inevitable fighters that would be launched to blast them out of the sky, the Americans would not be happy about their innermost sanctum being invaded. The three men stood and signalled for the Buccaneer to make its pass, Conon and Andy stood a safe distance away and watched the modified bomber come around onto the approach, Slater hit what they had now called their cloaking device then the Buccaneer slowed down as if she'd hit a brick wall as soon as the air brakes were deployed and Mack watched as the thirty tonne cold war designed bomber almost disappeared as it approached, "Holy Fuck, this is the scariest thing I've ever done!"

Was the last Conon and Andy heard him say as he was surprisingly gracefully plucked from the ground and smothered up into the bowels of the Buccaneer, screaming and wailing as if he was on the Pepsi Max challenge at the Blackpool Pleasure Beach. Within seconds the bomb bay had rotated closed and Ug had propelled the aircraft at full throttles and flown the bomber at low level out of the training area, flat out with its cargo, the system to camouflage the jet worked like a dream, all the team saw was a shimmering mess in the sky but it was impossible to make out it was a thirty tonne bomber. The team raced back to Gander. On their arrival Mack was sitting in the briefing room grinning like a Cheshire cat. "Bit nippy on the bollocks Conon but what a ride!" Everyone laughed at the Highland man's report on how the system worked. The rest of the day was filled out with practising, practising and more practising. The team had a lot of work to do preparing Conon for where he had to get himself once he'd been dropped and landed in the base, it was the most audacious plan any of them had ever heard of but it was just about their only option, it could very well be a one way ticket.

The work being done in the Antarctic at Rothera base was completely negative, despite the numerous and in depth attempts they had at duplicating the viral antidote being carried by the Chinese pilot, nothing worked. The scientific team were now beginning to doubt whether or not he was actually carrying anything other than a brief to throw them off the trail as long as possible. The scientists and researchers were struggling to determine just who if anyone was infected and maybe turning the pilot over to the Americans in exchange for Munro might not be

Yahweh

such a bad option after all. The wheels within Mr Blacks underworld were turning, they had been working quietly in the background all along and they were beginning to realise that the Chinese pilot wasn't what he was being cracked up to be, he was a red herring in fact, and now as a result of his interrogations they had found that deep within the inner circles of The British Government, someone was feeding information to their age old adversarial enemy; Russia. Behind the scenes Blacks colleagues had been working tirelessly with G.C.H.Q. who in turn had found out that a mole had been working within the Ministry of Defence, someone high ranking, they had told the Russians about the UKs ongoing spying operations against the United States, they had told them that the French and most European countries with a submarine had been spying off the American coast and how they, the Americans had stolen the information about the stealth coating for the submarines, that the Chinese had discovered the nerve agent as a result of a by-product from the coating and a meeting with the Secretary of State for Defence was hastily arranged, Mr Hammond wasn't going to like it but his secretary was feeding information to a low grade Russian official at their U.K. embassy, S.O.E. spooks had flushed him out and identified him as Brigsinov, he didn't know it but he was in the open, now they had to determine how to handle him and quickly.

At the meeting Mr Hammond met with the head of S.O.E. Known only as "FQ." Hammond knew exactly who he was but no one else outside of the Prime Minister and a very select few in a very small circle of professional colleagues knew the man's identity that was the way it had to be. The meeting was swift, they had to quickly find a way of getting the exchange between the Americans and the British sorted out. The Americans wanted the Chinese pilot because they believed he carried the antidote and the Brits wanted Munro back for no other reason other than he was British. S.O.E. would arrange it. There was one question though, if the Americans were so convinced some one was carrying the antidote, who was it? S.O.E. would find out. Nothing was signed, nothing was recorded, and the meeting ended. FQ was told only to resolve any problems and to use whatever means he had at his disposal, in truth the Secretary for Defence had no idea what resources FQ had at his disposal.

At area 51 Munro sat within his cell planning his escape, he knew the wheels would be in motion to effect his release but he had no idea just exactly what was being done. He was surprised by many things he'd heard or not heard over the past few days, he knew his cell was above ground level and that was a major bonus, he'd heard next to no aircraft activity so he suspected he was being held captive in a very remote spot. His guards kept to the same routine, routine was good because people became complacent but it was bad for him because well-disciplined men ran like machines under such conditions. The door of the cell was opened every morning by an unarmed guard, presumably so Munro couldn't over power them and arm himself but there was always a way of escaping if one was being held captive. He planned at least to get out of his cell and as far away from his prison as possible and to send word to his colleagues of his whereabouts, for now he slept and when he wasn't sleeping he was training, doing press ups, sit ups, squat thrusts any manner of exercises to keep himself fit and keep his brain from going numb.

Mr Black was contacted by FQ and ordered back to the United Kingdom, he was to escort Yvonyv, it was explained to him that she was to act as the go between and liaise with the Russians, she would be watched and safe at all times but it appeared that diplomatic developments were now moving rapidly to effect the exchange. The Americans were getting the Chinese pilot, he was already being flown out of Rothera, Antarctica and was on route to Toronto, Canada where the order for Munro to be handed over would be signalled. The Russian, Brigsinov would be contacted and simply asked to jump ship, defect or he would be eliminated, it kept things simple, and after all he would be needed to testify against the Defence Secretary's aide for passing on classified information. S.O.E. set up the meetings with some ease, the Chinese pilot was handed over and the Russian Brigsinov capitulated as soon as he saw Yvonyv sitting at the table in the café where he had been told his next meeting would take place, he knew in an instant the game was up, he could return to Russia if he managed to get to the airport and on board the aircraft but life back in his homeland would never be that same, he chose the easy option and left quietly with Yvonyv and her accomplice, Mr Black. In Toronto the Chinese pilot also knew his part in the charade was over but for the good of his country he was happy to sacrifice himself to the Americans, he would be quietly repatriated in a few years' time and live the life of a National hero, his imprisonment was a small price to pay. The whole deal with the Americans for the F35s was very much on the back burner, there was now a huge lack of trust behind the scenes, the perceived underhandedness of the British was countered by the lack of communication from the Americans, no one was trusting any one at this time and how much longer would the state of play continue? Signals had been sent to HMS Ambush to proceed with plan "B," they were to carry out a routine spying mission in the North East Pacific. They were to stand down from any further actions in respect of their previous orders, the British still wanted to see how stealthy she really was and would find out that much if nothing else. Conon and his team were somewhat relieved to discover that the rescue mission was no longer required and that Munro was coming home, they would proceed to San Francisco and collect him themselves at Travis Air Force Base, unfortunately though no one had told Munro.

At Area 51 the cell door opened, Munro lay feigning sickness on his bed. Initially the guard wasn't taken in but when he saw the vomit on the floor beneath Munro's head he lunged forward to check on the prisoners' welfare dropping the tray unceremoniously. As the guard leaned forward Munro sent his elbow crunching into his nose knocking him unconscious instantly, the second and third guards rounded the door but Munro was up and ready, he sent his right boot straight into the groin of the second guard, he fell convulsing on the floor as the third one was met square on with a head butt from Munro that broke his nose and sent him crumpling to the floor. Munro quickly searched the three unconscious guards, he found swipe cards, a set of keys, two nine millimetre Beretta pistols, six clips of ammunition and two radios, a Gerber multi tool, a head torch, a respirator and a mobile phone, he threw everything in a small pack one of the guards had. He quickly tied the three guards up and closed the door making sure there was no way they could move to help each other, it wouldn't be long though before they were missed. He had no idea he was almost about to be released, no one had told him, this just was not supposed to be happening. Munro made his way along the long corridor, he moved forward with one of the Berretta pistols at arm's length, as he looked in one room he found a bank of computers all humming away seemingly abandoned, four external hard drives lay on one of the desks, he grabbed them and followed the fire escape signs which gave him the easiest and quickest way out of the building, it was simple and within three minutes he was outside and no one had seen him. Parked outside was a grey painted Hum Vee, no one was about or near the machine, he quickly checked his bearings it was a fine clear day, it was already warm and Munro guessed it was about eight A.M. He climbed into the truck and turned the start switch the beast fired into life, as he drove away from the building he checked the door and glove boxes, he found maps, a set of binoculars and switched on the main set radio within the vehicle. It didn't take him long to realise where he was. Without knowing it Munro was about cause a lot more problems.

The Hum Vee sped off along the dirt track away from the building that had been Munro's prison, he looked in the mirror and saw that it was a hardened shelter sitting on its own with no security fence or out buildings although looking around and seeing nothing but mountains all around him and the track stretching off into the distance Munro guessed that any one getting out of the place would probably be dead before they reached safety unless they knew what they were doing or exactly where they were going. Munro drove on and headed for the high ground, he had to get as much distance between himself and his prison before the guards were missed, he also knew the radios would be fitted with GPS, he had to let his friends know he was safe and discard the radios. Within the hour Munro was cresting a ridge and stopped to survey the landscape before him, as he looked out across the vast open expanse that was Area 51 he knew exactly where he was, the radio suddenly crackled into life, "Alpha one-one, status check, report, over." Munro knew it was the guard's controllers checking their welfare, they were probably overdue and that meant he was running out of time, the clock was ticking. The radio message was repeated and then the airwaves went silent. Munro had no idea which direction he should go in, then about four miles to the west he had his answer.

In the distance Munro could see the dust being thrown up into the air, he had to act fast and as he drove down the track towards the desert he threw the radios from the Hum Vee, next he set about tearing the main set from the mounting it was on, it might buy him just a little time, he hoped the mobile phone would work. Munro stopped and couldn't believe the there was a full signal, quickly he dialled the line that took him directly to the operations room at Royal Marines Poole, he passed a simple and straight to the point message to the WREN radio and signals desk operator on duty, she didn't get a word in and all she got from Munro was a coded message telling the Commanding officer that it was a message from Major Munro, he was on the run within Area 51 having escaped from the Americans and that he needed to be rescued. The messages were passed and the Americans were contacted at the highest levels, Munro was on the run but he didn't need to be but what the Americans knew was that Munro was on the run in the most secretive place on earth and they didn't want him there, under those circumstances, they couldn't risk him finding anything out.

Munro disposed of the phone, he knew the Americans would quickly trace it and the only possible likelihood of a rescue from this place was one of two possibilities, one, he would yomp all the way to safety, highly unlikely as he knew the whole desert was covered with vibration sensors and cameras covered the place almost entirely, in fact they were quite possibly watching him now. The other option open to him was he could go to ground and use evasion tactics until the team sent in the Buccaneer to extract him that was what he hoped they would do. The patrol of guards were steadily approaching his position at speed and he realised he had to get away from the immediate area and hide, in this place it would take every piece of skill and trick in the book that he had to avoid capture. Munro pulled the interior mirror from the cab and stuck it inside his shirt, he abandoned the Hum Vee and ran towards the nearby hills, in ten minutes he would be in good cover and then it was a cat and mouse game. As he reached the first set of rocks he looked up and saw a small series of caves, they were under an overhanging rock face so he would be missed by any overhead surveillance and he was armed so he could if needs be repel a small assault, if only for a short time. As Munro got closer to his hide out he watched the other two Hum Vee approach, the closer he got to the caves he realised they were perfectly formed and uniformly spaced, they were man made, he wondered now what lay within. As Munro climbed up to the first cave the smell of oil grew stronger. As he clambered inside the cave and cover, the surface of his hide felt strangely slimy, which it shouldn't be in this place, there was no obvious signs of water nearby which very soon he would need but it was when he smelled his hands he realised he was smelling oil and the air was unmistakably gooey with the viscosity of oil. Munro waited until his eyes became accustomed to the light before he moved any further inside the cavern. After what was probably about twenty minutes he could see his way and he moved slowly to the back of the cave, the stench of oil was almost overpowering and he tried to make sense of it but felt his senses churn and then he passed out.

At Gander the team were quickly assembled and told that Munro was on the run having escaped, all but Conon and Andy laughed. The rest thought it was hilarious that Munro had escaped when he didn't actually have to but Conon and Andy were very quick to ask the question why had he felt it necessary to escape and more importantly if he hadn't actually killed anyone, why weren't the Americans simply putting assets in place to tell him he was a free man, it was all very strange.

The Americans had moved quickly to let the British know that Munro had broken free from his place of captivity and they were taking steps to resolve the situation, however within the hour and practically whilst Munro had been communicating his message to Poole they had reported that due to a most unforeseen and tragic chain of events Munro had been killed by an overzealous security guard who had not been made privy to the fact that Munro was to be released, he had simply caught Munro out in the open and did what he had been trained and paid to do, shoot trespassers. A meeting with the P.M. the Defence

Secretary and FQ the head of S.O.E. was hastily arranged, FQ brought the P.M. up to speed and simply asked him to sanction the flight of the Buccaneer, it was good to go and due to appear at an air show on the west coast of America as cover for what the British had assumed would be a covert rescue mission. Then FQ dropped the bombshell, the P.M. had heard the stories and rumours like many others but it still didn't prepare him for what he was about to be told. "Mr Cameron for the last forty years or so the United States Government has been going to incredible lengths to stop all monitoring of its facility at Area 51, we were fooled like everyone else for a long time into believing they were carrying out testing of highly sensitive aeronautical projects which they were to an extent, then a lateral thinker came along, a guy who came through Oxford and went to work at GCHQ, he started snooping around off projects, which was neither encouraged nor discouraged and asked why were the Americans buying, drilling, extracting and generally accumulating more oil reserves than they were actually using, far more. The statisticians could manipulate figures as much as possible but when it came to a deal where the Saudis wanted the best fighter in the world at the time and they bought the English Electric Lightening the Americans were furious, it cost their defence industry billions at the time but not only because they lost valuable defence contracts, the British Government at the time tied the Saudis into lucrative defence and oil exploration contracts for decades. Basically the Americans know the world oil reserves will run out one day but the world economy isn't run by money its run by oil and whoever has the oil has all the chips. In short Mr Cameron the Americans have more oil reserves under their sovereign territory than any other country on earth as a direct result of how much they've bought, stolen and drilled for. And it's all stored at Area 51, not alien space ships or skunk aircraft which have been used as a cover story for the rest of the world for the last forty odd years. We think Munro may actually have discovered evidence of what's out there but we need to get him back and find out for definite."

Mr Cameron asked questions, "The Americans helped us open up the North Sea, why?"

"So they could plunder our reserves, the best quality crude in the world but it was about that time the Saudis wanted the Lightening and being Arabs they'd deal with anyone and pay anything to get it, we had our own oil but they guaranteed to supplement our supplies until the North Sea was fully up and running and as I already said they tied themselves into lucrative arms deals for decades. The maths was simple but it infuriated the Americans who have been trying to deal under the table with the Saudis ever since, the Bush dynasty is a prime example of how they have gone about their business."

"No wonder Middle Eastern policies are so fucked up. So who is the genius that worked all this out or am I not permitted to know?"

"Oh you know him Mr Cameron, his name is Black, Mr Black."

The P.M. didn't need to hear anymore, most of it was way beyond what he needed to know he simply told FQ to bring Munro home.

Yahweh

The Sky Pirate painted Buccaneer sat on the runway at Gander, the VC10 tanker also painted in Gulf War livery was to escort the Buccaneer under the guise of escorting the plane simply as a tanker and support aircraft but on board the full team of Royal Marines, swimmer canoeists and Andy also sat, primed ready to carry out the rescue should the plan to drop Conon and rescue Munro fail. The VC10 took off two hours before the Buccaneer, Mr Black and Yvonyv had made it on board just in time, Conon was pleased she'd made it, Black brought everyone up to speed with the latest details on how the handover of Munro had gone spectacularly wrong and how even now they couldn't be sure that Munro was actually alive but they would proceed on the basis that he was, it was good enough for the team, they all liked Munro. Two hours later Ug slammed the throttles on the Buccaneer forward and both he and Slater were pushed back into their ejector seats as Sky Pirate accelerated down the runway, he knew it was probably the last time Sky Pirate would ever fly but what a flight it would be, the thirty tonne bomber roared down the runway and gracefully drifted up into the sky, they were on their way.

Munro woke up, to his left he could see daylight so he figured he hadn't been unconscious for long, the smell was sulphurous and he had probably moved too far into the cavern too quickly and was overcome by the fumes. He sat up and gathered his senses; he pulled the head torch from the small pack and flicked it on, he pulled the respirator from the pack an pulled it over his face, then shining the beam of torchlight around he discovered he was in a huge cavern, he slowly stood up and walked to the back of the space. The floor dropped away from him and he stopped, as he shone the torch downwards he couldn't see anything just blackness. He looked around for a stone and threw one over the edge into the abyss. Two seconds later he heard the strangely baffled sound of the stone hit the liquid below. Still shining the torch downwards he could see that the liquid whatever it was, it was definitely not water. Munro very quickly realised it must be oil of some kind but he knew nothing of any crude or naturally occurring oil in that part of the American desert, Texas and one or two other places yes but Nevada, it was baffling. Little did he know at that time he had just unearthed one of the United States of Americas greatest kept secrets.

Yahweh

At 1100 hours local time the Royal Air Force VC10 landed at Travis Air Force Base, California, the Buccaneer was one hour behind and cruising at fifteen thousand feet, Ug and Slater were twenty miles north of the infamous Area 51 and right on the edge of the areas no fly zone, the Americans had, due to fuel limits sanctioned the Buccaneer to skirt along the periphery of the test area, it was very naïve of them but not unexpected. Ug flew the aircraft and Slater sat in the back operating the cameras and watching the scenery go by and just then Salters eye was caught by a glint from below, way out to the east, when she looked again it was definitely a signal, a reflector of some kind, she alerted Ug up front and pin pointed exactly where she'd seen the flashes blinking, whoever it was, was signalling Morse code to them, Slater suddenly exclaimed, M-U-N-R-O! He's spelling MUNRO. Ug could do nothing too obvious but wagged the wingtips of the bomber, hopefully it would be enough for Munro to know they'd seen him. Fifteen thousand feet below and twelve miles away Munro had sat watching and had seen the VC10 pass an hour earlier but no one had seen his signals, he knew the Buccaneer was due to show up for a display at Travis Air Force base and he waited patiently then through the binoculars he'd seen the unmistakable shape of the Buccaneer and hoped they'd see his signal, he saw the aircraft wag it's wings and smiled, he would be rescued soon. Ug told Slater to call it in on the secure network. Immediately the team aboard the VC10 got to work and waited for the Buccaneer to land, the memory stick was transferred straight to the computer on board the VC10 which had more than enough hardware on-board to carry out the necessary download, within minutes they had a close up shot of Munro standing signalling and they had his exact position, in one hour the Buccaneer would take off for a rehearsal and the rescue mission would commence.

Out in the Pacific, aboard HMS Ambush the signal was taken to Commander Crosswaight-Aires, he was simply instructed to take his ship to a position approximately one hundred miles west of San Francisco, then to have the Special Boat Squadron team readied and briefed and wait for the pick-up, it was probably the most audacious mission he had ever heard off and he hoped for everyone's sake that the guy they were hopefully rescuing was worth it, he made his way to the bridge.

Munro had spent the last twenty four hours running, evading his pursuers, he'd employed every trick in the book, they had sent dogs after him, he'd had to kill three so far but they'd stopped coming, not because the Americans were going soft in any way but probably because they'd realised he would continue to kill them, they weren't any form of deterrent. He just had to wait until the Buccaneer showed up again and with it hopefully Conon, there was no other way a rescue from this place could be made, none that he could imagine under the circumstances that could possibly be performed, Conon would probably parachute in and they would both be recovered by the Buccaneer, it was the only way.

At Travis Air Force base the team quickly cobbled together two harnesses, they would simply attach those together using caribinas. It was time for the Buccaneers supposed first rehearsal flight and Conon was loaded into the Buccaneer away from prying eyes, then once aboard Ug and Slater taxied the jet out to the end of the runway and waited for the air traffic controller to give them permission to take off. Conon found the capsule was strangely comfortable and communications with the crew as one would expect were excellent. At sixteen hundred hours local time Ug was given clearance from the tower and the ancient bomber designed during the cold war era slowly lumbered down the runway, at about one hundred and fifty knots she began to rise into the air and as she gathered speed Ug muttered into his mouth piece, "Please let this go well." The American air controllers just thought he was possibly a touch nervous at the thought of throwing the old bomber around and hoping he was going to give the crowd a flawless performance, nothing could have been further from the truth as the Buccaneer disappeared out of sight.

As soon as the Buccaneer had gathered speed the engines were pushed to full throttle and Ug dropped the jet down to ground level and began the torturous flight towards Area 51, Slater armed their cloaking system, the shimmering paint job. The air control operators were going frantic trying to contact the crew but they were ignoring all radio messages, it was going to be a one way flight for the Sky Pirate. As a precaution four F16s were scrambled from Nellis Air Force Base, the Americans were watching and listening to everything going on, they suspected and even anticipated the Brits would try something but this was way beyond what they had expected, the lumbering old bomber would be no match for their nimble fighters though, it would be a turkey shoot, the four pilots didn't account for the ability of Ug Urquhart and Slater though.

The Buccaneer screamed through the valleys and hugged the hills as Ug flew onwards towards the test area, in just under ten minutes he was going to have to show the Buccaneers soft under belly to whoever was waiting and both he and Slater knew they would be waiting. Slater spoke to Ug, "They are about four miles ahead of us and closing, fast, four F16s and they are actively seeking us so keep us down here as long as possible Ug."

"Your wish is my command Miss Slater, just hang on tight."

Ug kept the bomber as low as he had ever flown and at mind numbing speed the jet screamed towards Area 51. "Okay we're one minute away from our drop point," Slater informed Ug, he pulled hard back on the stick and spoke to Conon riding below in the bomb bay capsule. "Sorry about the rough ride Conon but we're just about to spit you out. Hope it all goes to plan brother and good luck."

"It's okay Ug, I'm quite enjoying it actually but some fresh air would be enjoyable." The three of them laughed at Conon's relaxed frame of mind, then every alarm in the jet went off as two AIM120 Slammer heat seeking missiles locked onto the Buccaneer as she climbed through three thousand feet, Slater went to work and launched flares and deployed all the countermeasures she could then she told Conon to get ready, hopefully Munro was down there somewhere and watching what was going on, he was.

The flares took care of the first missile but the second kept coming and as the bomb bay rolled open and Conon was launched into the air, Ug got confirmation from Conon the release was good and he slammed the stick forwards and the jet screamed back towards the ground as the second missile sailed passed the tail end of the Buccaneer now plummeting towards the desert floor. The F16 pilots couldn't believe they'd missed the old bomber but they'd been warned it would be no push over despite their spunky young arrogance. Ug continued to push the Buccaneer in a vertical dive towards the ground, the Americans were stunned by the performance of the thirty tonne jet, none of them had ever seen one fly before, they had only ever seen footage of the bombers at the Red Flag exercises in the Nevada desert where the Buccaneers were thrown about in the sand dunes and virtually disappeared whilst being filmed. Their surprise was short lived as the bomber levelled out and disappeared into the valley below, they were all experienced enough to know that they needed the only advantage they had left at their disposal, height and they levelled out at six thousand feet looking for the needle in the haystack. Ug pushed the jet so low, almost in an instant it vanished from their radars, all he had to do now was avoid the aggressors and wait for the signal from Conon.

Conon watched as the Buccaneer dived towards the ground followed initially by the four F16s, he wasn't surprised when it disappeared into the valley below and the four American jets then pulled back and climbed to regroup having lost the element of surprise, the American jets fanned out at about six thousand feet, the four pilots probably hoping to get a visual fix on the bomber soon, the new paint job would make that just a little bit more difficult than usual though. Conon drifted downwards and as he scanned the ground below he saw what he was looking for, Munro sent six flashes straight at him, he also saw several soldiers closing in on Munro and they weren't being friendly. Conon aimed for the spot and sent the coded message to the jet and others listening, "X-ray." It simply meant that he'd made contact with someone on the ground, hopefully it was Munro. Conon hit the deck and within seconds he was looking straight into the face of Munro. The two men shook hands, it was a very British thing to do, then Conon said, "Put this on and let's get the fuck out of here." He handed Munro the harness which he donned with ease and Conon sent the one word signal to the Buccaneer, "Yankee." It meant he'd found Munro and they were ready for the pick-up, at the same time Slater pin pointed their exact location. Ug pushed the stick hard over to the left and the massive jet turned around and flew down the valley towards the point he was directed to by Slater. As Ug pushed the jet down through the narrow valley he was being bombarded by Salters constant updates on where the F16s were, he listened to and absorbed all the information but ignored her and looked ahead for the balloon, there it was a mile ahead and at one hundred feet, he hit the air brakes and the jet almost stopped dead in the air, from six hundred knots to one hundred and fifty in a very short distance, Ug and Slater were held in place by the straps securing them to their ejector seats. The lead F16 screamed in behind the Buccaneer and the pilot was so taken by surprise in his attempts to avoid running up the back side of the bomber, he slammed the stick instinctively to his left being left handed and rammed the jet straight into the rock face, Conon and Munro watched as the hillside erupted and hoped to god that Ug hadn't been distracted by the American aircraft slamming into the hillside. The Royal

Air Force pilot ignored everything around his aircraft, Slater would take care of the counter measures and he would take care of the flying, he slammed the controls to the right and as quickly back to the left and switched the air brakes to close and he saw he'd captured the balloon. As the Buccaneer gathered speed again he heard the code word from Conon, "Zulu." They were on board they had recovered Munro and all they had to do was get out of Area 51, every anti-aircraft system between here and anywhere was now looking for them though and Ug had thought the next part out for himself. He pushed the jet to its limits and flew as low as he dared and straight towards the most populated areas he could find on his route out towards the eastern Pacific. The remaining F16s and now four F15s from Nellis were scouring the skies for them but as Ug pushed the jet towards San Francisco he knew that if he made it to the city limits there was no way the Americans would ever attempt to blow them out of the sky, every mobile phone in California would have it online within minutes. The alarms in the old jet were going off constantly, Slater was doing a sterling job fending the aggressors off, using every counter measure she had at the jets disposal and despite Ug believing in his own mind he was ignoring her, so well-honed were they as a crew he knew he was reacting instinctively to every command she gave. The Buccaneer crossed over the city limits of San Francisco at one hundred feet and ahead Ug spotted the Golden Gate Bridge, last salvage afforded by the land and built up area beneath them was running out fast but once passed the iconic landmark he knew that the F15s and F16s at sea level just wouldn't be able to keep up with them. He pushed the old girl down onto the waterfront and the crowds turned and watched in awe as they thought they were being given an impromptu air display. Ug was hitting six hundred knots as he pushed the jet down to ten feet above the water, the Americans had now backed right off, there was no way they were going to wreck any aircraft or be seen to openly destroy a Royal Air Force Buccaneer, someone would see everything. Ug flew the Buccaneer flat out and straight under the Golden Gate Bridge. The Americans headed for the high ground, this chase was not going to be won at sea level but they were working frantically trying to come up with options, why was this guy heading for the open ocean, their anti-submarine and ocean patrol vessels were telling them there was nothing out there for the Buccaneer to aim at but still the ancient bomber sped on disappearing into the blast of vapour it threw up.

The two Special Boat Squadron divers readied themselves and launched their speed jets from the hull of HMS Ambush, the Buccaneer was twelve minutes away. They surfaced and looked east, they saw the jet approaching and they also saw the F15, call sign Buckaroo, behind her, the American pilot was no novice, he was a veteran of both Gulf wars and had flown several tours over Bosnia and Afghanistan and more importantly he was not scared and ready to carry out his orders to the letter. In the Buccaneer Conon and Munro were readied for the launch, they called into Slater who pressed the arming buttons on the escape capsule and from ten she counted down, four, three, two, one, launch. Conon and Munro dropped from the Buccaneer like a torpedo but the water vapour cloud being thrown up by the jet was so big the American missed the pod being dropped as he fired his missile. Ug pulled the Buccaneer up and as Slater called in they had another missile heading straight for them, he told her to, "HANG ON." Two seconds later the missile slammed into the port exhaust on the Buccaneer and the order to eject was given by Ug, Slater was gone, closely followed by Ug. The American pilot watched as the two parachutes drifted downwards and the Buccaneer landed on the ocean, he was surprised the bomber didn't break up and remained virtually intact. Buckaroo rose to two thousand feet and called in the rescue co-ordinates, he circled and left the area, his colleagues were stood down, the British pilot had been embarrassed, the diplomacy and arguments between the British and American governments was not his concern, his mission was over.

Conon steered the capsule towards HMS Ambush, there was very little for him to do, he punched in three numbers and the capsule went onto auto pilot, above them Slater then Ug in quick succession hit the water, as they looked up they were astonished to see the American jet circle them and then roar off towards the mainland without any real contact, the S.B.S. divers approached them just below the surface and without any fuss they gave them their breathing apparatus and masks. Within a minute the two aircrew were being propelled downwards into the abyss, darkness was approaching rapidly and the Americans would never have seen them being rescued, when they arrived they would search the area given by the American pilot who had shot down the Buccaneer but they would find nothing. HMS Ambush sat one hundred feet below them, the capture systems were in place and the two craft were remotely guided on board. Ug and Slater were stripped out of their flying suits and given dry gear as the bulk head door opened, it was Munro who met them.

"Thank you so much for your help, it looks like we've got some really juicy stuff on the Yanks so hopefully it'll be a good debrief." Ug and Slater shook his hand. Conon looked at Ug and said, "Shame the old birds gone, she did us proud." He was sure he saw a tear in the pilot's eye as he left and headed for the galley.

Six thousand feet below the Sky Pirate rested on the bottom, she had done herself proud, no one would be troubled enough to recover her and the Royal Navy would monitor her for the foreseeable future or until it was safe to carry out their own recovery.

On the bridge of H.M.S. Ambush, Commander Crosswaight-Aires asked the signaller to send a one word message to Northwood, "YAWEH."

Above the American helicopter sent out by the Naval rescue squadron based at Travis found no trace of survivors, they dropped several sonar buoys but there was nothing, no survivors, no ships, no submarines, nothing.

Below them the Russian vessel Antaeus had watched and listened into every move that the Americans and the British had made, her crew were impressed with the Royal Air Force pilot, he was obviously a very brave man. Silently they sat suspended in the water at five hundred meters listening in on their old adversaries.

H.M.S. Ambush heard every single signal, they had even detected the signal given off by Antaeus as she slowly followed them, and it was identical to the signal H.M.S. Astute had recorded off Luxi Dao when Munro had been captured by the Americans. The result of the mission was sent to Admiral Currie, he was delighted and asked for his car to be brought to the front of the building, he had a meeting with the Secretary for Defence to attend. They had recovered Munro and made some pretty astounding discoveries and flushed out a Russian mole in the process. There work though was not done. They knew the Russians were still out there but as long as they were the British knew they had the contacts and the ability to steal anything the Russians could produce, it served their interests to have someone else doing all the donkey work and they would reap the rewards of someone else's hard work and investment.

HMS Ambush arrived back in Plymouth with her cargo of Royal Marines on board, waiting at the dockside were, Admiral Currie and the Secretary for Defence, Mr Hammond with a small entourage, in the back ground Professor Smith and Doctor Silva stood looking as inconspicuous as possible. Munro was congratulated and handed over the hard drives to the Admiral, who in turn handed them to Professor Smith, little did they know at the time but the four hard drives contained some of the most explosive information ever to be seized by the British and what was more the Americans knew the information had been stolen and there wasn't a damned thing they could do about it. Conon and Munro were whisked away for full medicals and to be debriefed, they were at the Medical Centre at Professor Smith's laboratory within the hour and plugged in. Munro understood why Conon was being checked over but not him, "Major Munro, you weren't made aware but you too were part of this project, about two years ago you went into hospital for a minor procedure on your left shoulder, at that time you were fitted with a small sensor which effectively told us where you were and if needed would give you a sort of turbo boost, similar to Conon, we knew what was going on most of the time, the Americans just didn't know which buttons to push." Conon and Munro were cleared and given a full bill of health there were no issues regarding either men and now they knew Munro would never get lost and Conon hopefully would never get caught. As the two men sat back in the Operations room at Poole watching the Television screens, news of a problem with the new F35s being bought from the Americans had emerged, the Americans were reluctant to share some of the more sensitive software for the aircrafts operating systems and the British were stalling on paying out any money until it had been resolved. Elsewhere reports were appearing on American West coast news channels of a UFO that had been pursued across the Nevada desert by American jets before the strange craft had plunged into the sea, the Americans were denying they had shot anything down but two F15 pilots were being shown on screen being interviewed live by reporters, "Turn it up, turn it up," Conon shouted, Donnie did the needful. Clearly the Americans had had time to work out a cover story.

"Can you describe what happened out there gentlemen?" the reporter asked.

The younger pilot went to speak then turned to his superior officer a Major, "Just say what you saw son."

"Sir I'm not sure?"

"Just say what you saw."

The younger pilot looked at the camera and spoke, "Well we were sent out to search for an unidentified aircraft and when we arrived on scene I saw what looked like two men on the ground, they were being fired at by ground forces and then a ship of some kind appeared and almost stopped dead in the sky, it picked up the two guys, I don't know who or what they were and then it was gone, we tried to keep up with it but it was too low and way too fast. I don't know if it was a space ship or not, it sounds stupid." The older pilot spoke.

"Thank you ladies and gentlemen that'll be all for now."

One reporter shouted amongst the melee scrambling for information, "Sir did the aircraft fly under the Golden Gate? Was it you that shot it down? When did this happen? How many days ago?" The two pilots walked away, they had fed the beast with information now it would be sensationalised by the press and then buried; job done.

Analysis of the hard drives stolen by Munro revealed some highly classified and hitherto unknown material. The team couldn't believe how serendipitous the find was, a truly remarkable theft of highly classified information. The find detailed some of the most secret workings of the American military, interesting pieces amongst the many thousands of documents was a report on how at the end of the Second World War the Nazis had secreted tonnes of gold in Norway and not Switzerland as previously thought, it was all information gleaned from the likes of Doctor Werner von Braun and his associates. Never before had they actually been able to trace any large quantities of the treasures stolen by the Nazis but here was hard evidence that they had shipped large amounts to Norway whose sea ports remained open all year round, so allowing the material to be shipped out, probably to South America, only it was still locked away in a massive underground series of tunnels the Germans had built on the Ose Pass near Bjerkvik, close to Narvik. The work previously suspected being done by the Americans in the submersible stealth world was there and there was confirmation of the existence of the U.S.S. Saratoga. Several subterranean bases being operated by the Americans were pinpointed and the work the Chinese were doing on stealth technology was coming off the computer in reams. Other information found was going to take months to catalogue but the big one was the oil find and details of just how much there was stashed under the desert floor, it would give Britain real leverage, it was a huge bargaining chip. Whatever the powers that be chose to do with the information it was now out of their hands but Smith and Silva knew they had a team well and truly ready to rise to any challenge.

12399428R00153

Printed in Great Britain
by Amazon.co.uk, Ltd.,
Marston Gate.